BAD TIMES
at
HORSESHOE STATION

By

R. Bruce Sundrud

For Nolan:
The adventure never ends.

Chapter One

Cydney, darling of the vidstreams, lay sobbing on the deck with her doll clutched to her chest. Victor ignored the girl and watched the approaching casino through the porthole. The pilot cursed as he struggled to match orbital speeds.

The *Nairobi* shuddered, as she had been doing repeatedly since she was holed by a meteoroid that shouldn't have been in their orbit. The engineer patted the wall as though trying to reassure the ship. "She's tearing herself apart," he said to the pilot. "If you don't get us to port soon, we'll fireball and take Ruby's Casino with us."

"Shut up." The pilot tapped his keyboard and grimaced. "She's doing what she can. If I can get her rotated against the airlock, you better get across fast."

Cydney screamed and kicked her feet on the deck, demanding attention. The small white poodle licking her face wasn't helping to calm her hysterics.

Victor had been on a walking tour of the *Nairobi* when the ship had been holed, a VIP tour marred by the bored comments of Cydney. The vibration they had felt seemed a minor thing, but then automatic doors slid shut and brief cries of desperation came over the intercom as the passenger quarters lost life support. As far as Victor could tell, his uncle was among the victims and so was Cydney's mother.

The pilot, neatly dressed in black with gold piping and buttons, had performed a miracle in getting the crippled ship parallel to Ruby's Casino. He was trying for a second miracle in getting the ship to dock. "I'm down to maneuvering thrusters only, and I don't...." He twisted a dial and glared at a readout. "...don't know how much fuel I have left. We're bleeding like a stuck camel."

"Camels don't bleed easily, mate," said Ricardo, a darkly tanned man in a safari outfit whose forced grin was accented by a thin mustache.

"Goat, then. Shut up."

The *Nairobi*'s itinerary called for it to go into orbit and to shuttle the passengers directly down to the surface of the planet, down to Horseshoe Station where stood a model frontier town and a corral with horses. Ricardo was to guide them on an expedition to hunt red apes and other alien game. Victor's uncle had paid handsomely for their vacation, and Cydney's mother was spending money from her daughter's vidstreams career.

Now, besides Victor, the only ones left alive on the dying ship were the pilot, an engineer in a stained jumpsuit, Cydney in hysterics, and Ricardo. And the white poodle.

"What would you do if the airlock were aft instead of up here?" Ricardo asked.

"I'd get in the suit, go aft, and let you all die," said the pilot, interrupting his constant cursing. "There's only one suit up here, and it fits me. I'll need it anyway, when we dock."

"Why?"

Victor felt the *Nairobi* rotate. The orbiting casino was so close that its shape could no longer be seen, only the girders and plates that surrounded the circular airlock.

"Because I need to stop whatever's happening below decks. Fuel's leaking and getting mixed with oxidizer somewhere. If either tank ruptures...." The pilot growled at the engineer. "Could you make that girl shut up? I'm about to throw her out the airlock!" He reached overhead and flipped a switch.

4

A woman's voice crackled over the speaker. "...NOT dock, we are NOT prepared for guests, we are NOT open yet, you must go directly down to the planet. Can you hear me? Back off, do NOT dock, we are NOT...."

The pilot grimaced and cut off the voice. "Nice to be wanted. Good thing airlocks can be operated from the outside." He glanced at an overhead monitor and adjusted his cap, the perfect model of a luxury liner crewman. "Almost there. Get ready to move fast. You'll be light because we're near the center of the station's spin, and I don't know how long I can keep us connected."

Ricardo inched over to the door of the airlock and grabbed a stanchion. The engineer, a round-faced man with thinning hair, pulled the vacuum suit out of its locker and readied it for the pilot.

Victor heard a thump, followed by grinding noises. The *Nairobi* had latched on to the casino's dock. "No time to equalize," said the pilot. Their ears popped as the door to the airlock slid open and a gust of air rushed in.

Ricardo leaped through the door. The pilot dropped his cap and began pulling on the vacuum suit with the help of the engineer. Victor realized that it was up to him to get Cydney off the ship. There had been a handler with her, a patient man with a fixed smile, but she had sent him back to her room to get a hair band or something and the man was probably dead by now.

Victor had never picked up a young girl having a fit. Should he try to make her stand or should he drag her out by the arms? There was no time for niceties, so he settled for scooping her up like a bride on the threshold. She weighed almost nothing, but she rewarded his rescue by screaming and biting his arm.

He grimly maneuvered through the airlock as the poodle, literally bouncing off the walls, seemed determined to make him trip.

No sooner had he stepped onto the deck of the casino than the door began to shut again. The engineer dove through just

5

as it closed, and metal shrieked as the *Nairobi* tore loose from the airlock.

"He's not going to make it." The engineer pushed himself up off the floor. "Something just went off back by the engines." He looked overhead as though expecting the *Nairobi* to smash through the station at any moment. "He didn't have his helmet on."

"No?" said Ricardo. "Ah, the poor bloke."

Victor set Cydney on her feet, and she kicked him in the shin. "Ow! Stop that!" he yelled, and she threw herself on the floor and took to hysterics again.

"Down," said the engineer, pointing to a wide elevator. "We're not safe here." Victor grabbed Cydney's wrists and dragged her into the elevator, which smoothly descended a couple of floors.

Their bodies now a comfortable weight again, they emerged into a carpeted foyer, with passageways left and right. Dark wood paneling covered the walls, the grain opulent with red highlights under the indirect lighting. Brass decorated everything, railings, lights, even the frames of two large bulletin boards, which had nothing on them except one scrawled sheet of paper with names and room numbers.

Between the bulletin boards the words RUBY'S CASINO were embossed in gold, and beneath it a thick window revealed the curve of the blue planet below.

"Here we go, mates," said Ricardo. "A stay at a stellar-class resort. I wish everyone was alive to see it."

Cydney got up on her knees, hugging her doll and frantic poodle with one hand while wiping her eyes with the other. She reminded Victor of Alice in Wonderland, if Alice had brown curls and dressed in garish colors and striped leggings. He had seen Cydney on the vidstreams, singing and dancing in saccharine productions, insufferably cute but popular enough to have made millions. Now her wavy brown hair was tangled and her eyes and nose were red.

She stuck out her lower lip at Victor. "I want my mom! Right now!" she demanded, her clogged nose making her voice thick.

He didn't know if he should be blunt with her or do what adults do, pretend everything's going to be okay when it wasn't. He chose honesty. "I don't think she made it."

"Make them bring the ship back!"

"I don't think the ship's ever coming back."

"I didn't want to come on this stupid tour! I want to go back to my room!"

"Listen, little one," said Ricardo, "your room is probably in a million..."

They were interrupted by the arrival of an angry woman who drove her electric cart as though it were an assault vehicle. She looked to be in her thirties, her dark hair tied tight behind her head and her face like a storm cloud before the lightning strikes. Two men ran behind her, one tall with thick glasses, the other short and sweating. They both carried hunting rifles.

The woman stopped the cart and leaned her arms on the wheel, flanked by the two men. "Get your carcasses off my station," she growled.

Ricardo straightened his neatly pressed safari shirt. "Unfortunately, Ruby, we can't do that. Our ship is gone."

She straightened up as though she had just seen a snake. "Ricky? You've got your nerve, coming here!"

"Sorry, Ruby. Not my choice. Our ship had a bit of a..."

A bright flash flared in through the circular window. The engineer drew in his breath and held up his hand, demanding silence. After a moment they heard muffled thumps, and a bell began ringing insistently in the distance. "Sorry," he said, "but I think your airlock's damaged, and the *Nairobi*..." He shook his head.

Ricardo pulled his hat off and cursed silently, looking at his boots.

"What just happened?" asked Ruby.

"I was telling you," said Ricardo, "we got holed. Took a piece of meteorite, I guess, tore the ship open, shimmied the engines. The pilot got us to here, but that was all."

Ruby leaned back in her seat, her expression unreadable. "So the Chancel Corporation loses one of their ships? And you wind up here." She cleared her throat. "There are no meteoroids in this orbit. How could you get holed?"

Ricardo shrugged and put back on his hat. "I don't know, but it happened. Softball size, probably. Big one would have split us; small one wouldn't have caused so much damage."

"But we've got sweeper satellites," said the man in glasses. "This orbit is clean."

"Well, then," said Ricardo, his eyes narrowing and his smile thin, "our ship is tip top, you only imagined you saw an explosion, and that's the supper bell ringing."

Cydney broke in with a loud whine. "I want my mom!"

"What's your name, young lady?" asked the woman on the cart.

Cydney stood up, her lip stuck out again. "What's yours?"

"I run this station, girl, and you are an unwanted guest, now answer me! Your name?"

"I don't want to be here! I want to go to my room!"

Victor coughed. "Her name is Cydney."

"Sidney? A boy's name?"

Cydney rolled her eyes. "That's Cydney with a C, not an S, and a Y, not an I and I want to go to my room NOW!" The poodle cowering behind her heels jumped back as she stomped her foot.

Ruby's eyes drifted off of Cydney as though she had ceased to exist. "Ricardo, Cydney...." She looked expectantly at the engineer.

"Prescott. Gary Prescott."

She nodded. "Gary." She looked directly at Victor. "And you are?"

"Victor. Benningham."

She raised an eyebrow. "Your father is Craig Benningham?"

"That's my uncle. He was on the ship. He's....." He couldn't finish the sentence.

I can't believe he's dead.

Only an hour ago, maybe two, his uncle had waved goodbye absent-mindedly as Victor walked out of the suite to join the tour. It was just a walk around the ship, showing the engines and the kitchens, the navigation stations and the bridge, ending in the grand stage where they were going to see a rehearsal of this evening's musical, probably the only reason that Cydney had agreed to go.

They never made it to the bridge.

"I'm sorry to hear about your uncle," said Ruby.

Cydney screamed. "Stop it! Stop talking! Take me to my room!"

"Young lady," said Ruby with firm politeness, "what is your problem?"

"Her mother was on the ship," said Victor.

"Oh. I wasn't thinking." She lost some of her stiffness. "I am so sorry. I'm not used to children." She turned to the sweaty man beside her. "Ramon, could you take this young lady to, ah, to the quarters next to mine and get her...." She looked lost for words. "...get her something, a sweet roll and a soda, maybe?"

Cydney held her doll against her chest and looked at Ramon, her eyes wide, her chin trembling. She looked like a balloon deflating.

She's used to getting her own way. But no one can bring back her mom, or her room, or her things. She's never had to deal with anything like this before.

And I know exactly how that feels.

She grabbed Victor's hand. "No! Don't let him take me away! Please? Please?" She buried her face against his ribs. Victor looked at Ruby and raised his eyebrows.

Ruby held up a hand, stopping Ramon. "Never mind. Looks like she chose herself a guardian. Cydney, you stay with Victor and do what he says. Okay?"

Cydney mumbled something. Victor felt the small poodle dance nervously on his shoes.

"Now listen," Ruby continued, her eyes sweeping all of them. "My name is Ruby Tierney. I'm the captain, judge, and jury of this private facility. What I say goes. I can marry you and I can bury you. I can have you thrown out of the airlock without a trial or a spacesuit if you give me cause. You came here in a Chancel Corporation ship without invitation, and they've been giving Belle Enterprises, which owns this casino, nothing but trouble. And *you*," she pointed to Ricardo with an accusing finger, "you may run safaris down on Horseshoe and impress the tourists, but you've never been to Australia in your life so don't give me that fake Aussie accent."

Ricardo rubbed his shirt and looked sideways at Victor. "Raised in Chicago." He shrugged. "Listen, Ruby, the tourists eat it up. I'm a fair dinkum, mate. But, hey, a buck's a buck. I'll stow it."

"Thank you." Ruby rubbed her forehead with her fingers in thought. "Your ship got hit by a meteoroid. But the sweeper should have kept this orbit clean. Oscar," she said to the tall man in glasses, "you need to check out the sweepers."

He nodded, pulling a flat device from his pocket and tapping it. "I'll get on it."

She looked at the four of them and spoke as though meeting a new class of recruits. "We're not open yet. The construction crew just left. No shops are open, no shows are running, no gambling tables are operating. There is no kitchen crew. In two weeks we will have a cleaning crew here to set up, and two months from now the grand opening is scheduled." She laughed without humor. "There's no linen on the beds, no towels in the bathrooms. If we were open I would charge you, but we don't even have cashiers."

"I don't mind working," said Gary.

Ricardo nodded. "I can cook meals, Ruby, especially from the barbie. Excuse me. Barbeque." He smiled, but Ruby didn't.

Victor said nothing. At sixteen standard years he had no useful skills, just a broad background from private tutoring after being kicked from school to prison to school. With sudden concern he slipped his hand into his pocket and felt the packet of pills he always carried with him. His supply of pills had been destroyed with the *Nairobi*. He had only three left.

Three more days of being normal.

Chapter Two

Ruby showed them to the guest wing and told them to take their pick of rooms, but they that would have to take care of the rooms themselves; it would be weeks before the next ship would arrive with the crew for Ruby's Casino.

Victor, reluctantly accepting the role of guardian, chose a grand suite with separate bedrooms and baths for him and Cydney. The faucets were dazzlingly gold-plated and the lighting over the shower came from a chandelier. The shower looked intimidating with handles and rows of nozzles up and down the sides. Cydney, much calmer after getting away from the adults, looked at him like he was from the country and explained how the shower worked. She was used to such opulence.

Victor carried linen and towels from the storeroom, and while Cydney locked herself in her bathroom and showered forever, he put sheets on their beds and spread out the bolsters. Oscar knocked on the door and delivered a crate and floor pads for the poodle. "Don't let that dog run loose," he said. He adjusted his glasses and went on his way.

Victor sat on the overstuffed chair and flipped through the channels on the vidscreen. Some channels had place holders for when the casino went live. Libraries of entertainment were available, some classic, some racy, some the latest action vids. There was even a children's collection, including episodes of Cydney and the Pirates. He heard the blow dryer cut out in Cydney's bathroom, so he switched to a documentary on the Horseshoe planet.

The narrator was describing some unique plants discovered on the planet when Cydney came back in a floppy white robe and threw herself on the couch, her hair frizzy, her doll under one arm. "Don't look at me! There's no soap, there's no shampoo, there's no rinse! I look horrible!" She pulled open the front of her doll and began tapping buttons inside.

"What are you doing?"

"Calling Mom." She frowned at it. "No signal. I can't call anywhere."

Victor clicked off the vidscreen. "Cydney, your mother didn't survive."

She looked up suddenly, her eyes wide, and then her face shifted to pain. "Yeah, I know, it's just...." A tear breached her eyelid and began sliding down her cheek. "...I just said goodbye to her, sort of, this morning, and I ought to be able to just, you know, hit her number and..." She waved her hands helplessly, curled up and sobbed.

I don't know what to do to comfort her. My mother died, and some friends of mine, and now my uncle, and I still don't know what to do.

He felt guilty over not feeling as bad about losing his uncle as Cydney did about losing her mother, but one effect the pills had was to stop him from feeling much of anything. Except guilt.

Should he pat her on the back, or just let her cry it out? He settled for scooting over and resting his hand on her shoulder as he clicked back to the planet documentary.

A woman in jeans and a western plaid shirt displayed a bat-like creature that ate holes in fruit and laid eggs inside. A man in a safari outfit replaced her; he pointed to a mounted specimen covered with red fur.

It had two eyes, dark, without pupils. The mouth was open and the lips were spread to show serrated upper and lower ridge plates where earth apes would have had teeth. The arms, raised in a threatening pose, seemed to have too many joints and ended in too few fingers. The magnificently colored fur surrounding the head stuck out, making the creature look larger

12

than it was. "The great red ape is the dominant species on Horseshoe Planet, mates. Certainly, it's the fiercest. It was a bloke like this here male that killed a friend of mine."

Ricardo!

Victor leaned forward, trying to listen over the diminishing sobs from Cydney.

"The smaller females aren't aggressive like the males," Ricardo continued. "When we spy a troop, we'll move in and point out the male, but you're not likely to mistake him because of his size. We stay beside our guests at all times when we're on safari..." He hefted a hunting rifle. "...and we've never had a guest get hurt. We'll help you get a trophy fur of a great red ape that you can display with pride on your home planet!"

Cydney got up and blew her nose. As she sat back down, he clicked off the vidscreen again. After an awkward silence, he said, "I'm sorry."

She pushed her frizzy hair back and shrugged.

He shifted uneasily. "Your doll is your phone?"

"She's not a doll and she's not a phone." She sniffed. "She's Peggity Polybot. She's my PDB."

"A polybot? I read about those, but nobody can buy them yet."

"No, *you* can't buy 'em yet. My agent got me one because...." She stopped and glanced around the room. "'Cause if I get kidnapped, she's got a 'crypted chip and they can find her, and if I get hurt, she can fix me."

Victor was impressed. The science streams had buzz about the polybot technology, but he had not heard of a commercial model. "How did your agent get it?"

She shrugged. "He knows people. He spent money."

"Can you watch vidstreams on it?"

She shook her head. "She's a PDB, not a PD. She keeps me safe. 'Sposed to, anyway." She closed it and clutched it to her neck, her eyes shiny again.

She's going to take a long time to get through this. When Dad died, I kept getting over it and then over it again. Maybe

13

I'm still not done getting over it. And now Uncle Craig is dead and I don't feel anything.

"Let's go scrounge up some soap," he said. "Even if there's no passengers or crew, they've got to have some supplies, maybe some stuff in the stores. We'll find food for your dog."

"Don't be silly." She put her hand on the dog's back and reached under his belly. She pushed, and the dog stiffened and fell over. "He's just a robodog."

"You're kidding. Really?" He knelt beside the dog and looked at its eyes and stroked the fur. "It sure fooled me."

"I don't like him."

"You don't?"

"My agent got him so I'd have something cute for press meetings, but he's set too hyper and no good as a watch dog. I should have left him with ...." She winced and shrugged.

He stood up. "Anyway, do you want to go see what we can find?"

"I guess so." She pulled Peggity's arms longer, snapped the hands together to make a strap, looped it over her head and slid off the couch. "Don't tell anyone he's just a robodog. My agent wants people to think he's real." She went into her bedroom and changed back into her Alice outfit.

The hallway was carpeted, with different colored lines low on the walls. "Follow the red line, you get to the gambling area," said Victor. "Green goes to dining, yellow to shopping, blue to kids' area...."

"How do you know all that?"

"I read while you were showering. There's a sign inside the door."

"Look. The floor goes up."

"That's where the spin comes in, you know, to give us weight. When we get there, it'll seem flat and this part here will look like it curves up."

"I know, I know. Don't teach."

"Sorry."

After passing endless doors, they entered an area designed for children. Victor wanted to look into the arcade rooms, but

14

Cydney pulled him ahead, following the yellow line which led to tiny shops with open doors. The reason the doors were wide open became obvious when Cydney tried to leave a shop wearing a hat. A beeping escalated into sirens and flashes until she put the hat back on the rack.

"Autovend," she muttered, opening Peggity.

"What?"

She pushed the opened polybot against a meter on the side of the rack, and then slid the hat's tag through it. "There. Autovend. So they don't need so many people. I just bought this!" She put the wide-brimmed sequined yellow hat on her head and twirled. "Go ahead! Buy anything you want! My treat!"

"Why is this place stocked? I thought the regular crew wasn't here yet."

Cydney shrugged. "I don't know." She soon had several bags of what Victor thought were awful choices, when they spied a shop specializing in outdoor wear. "Cool!" Cydney yelled, and soon danced out of a dressing room in white safari clothing. "Look at this! And..." She struck a pose. "No sales lady going 'I can't believe I'm waiting on Cydney!'" She pinched her own cheek. "Oh, Cydney, aren't you the cutest thing?" She poked her finger at her mouth as if she was gagging herself, and then pointed to Victor. "And look at you!"

He shrugged. He had found a less flashy version of rugged wear, a tan outfit complete with a tied-brim cloth hat and a shirt and pants with many pockets. The durable leather boots came with waffle soles.

He also wanted a souvenir. It looked like he wasn't going to the Horseshoe Planet, but he wanted something. The shop had racks of post cards with shots of the jungle, the model pioneer town named Horseshoe Station, and people playing the casino slots. Some were silly, some were rude. He picked up one showing a red ape, but he bypassed t-shirts, caps, and magnets with RUBY'S CASINO on them.

High behind the counter he found something he liked: a multi-purpose knife with several blades and accessories. The

15

pearl sides had RUBY'S CASINO inlaid in gold. When he saw the price tag, he whistled.

"What?" asked Cydney.

"Nothing," he said, putting back the knife. "Way too expensive."

"Don't be silly. I'm Cydney, remember? If you want it, get it."

"You're sure?" He picked up the knife again. He loved the weight of it. It was a souvenir, but a solid one.

She shrugged. "Get two. Get 'em all. It really doesn't matter."

He ran the tag through the reader, and slipped it into his pocket.

Cydney paid for their outfits with her polybot, and then tied a broad bandana over her head like a pirate's kerchief hat. Looking into a mirror, she tapped a few steps. "We're Cydney and the Pirates, we sail the seven seas...." she sang to herself. She stopped abruptly and sat down on a stool, looking solemn. "I don't think I can do it any more without Mom." Her eyes grew shiny and she looked at him as though lost.

Victor sat on a bench opposite her. "That's hard. My mom died a few years ago, and my dad a while before that."

"My agent got me the money, but it was Mom that helped me be Cydney. She yelled at me sometimes, but...." She looked at her new boots and shrugged, and then she covered her face with her hands and started crying again. After a few minutes the sobs weakened, but she remained huddled. Victor tried to think of something to talk about, to distract her.

"Cydney, how old are you?"

She studied him with wet eyes. Leaning towards him, she whispered, "Twelve."

"But on the vidstreams, you look like eight or something."

"I was, when I started. But I'm still small for my age, and the animators, because you know Cydney and the Pirates is all animated but me, they make me act like I'm still eight. My agent's going to try to get one more year for me. But without Mom, maybe I'm done already." Her eyes looked weary. "Then I'll be normal again. I guess."

16

"Is Cydney your real name?"

"It is now."

"What did it used to be?"

She stood up and wiped her nose. "I'm hungry. Let's follow the green line."

*

The green line led to an empty dining hall, but they ran into Oscar, who looked down at them through his thick glasses and then took them to the worker's dining area in the other wing of the satellite. The table was plain and functional and the floor was washable composite. Dinner was sealed trays from a walk-in freezer. Ruby, Oscar, and Ricardo were already eating. Cydney chose a chicken dinner, and Victor pulled out a meat pie and heated their trays in a flash oven.

"I've got a chef coming that should make this place one of the top ten," Ruby said to Ricardo around a mouthful of noodles. "We even have a greenhouse set up for fresh herbs."

Victor took a few bites of his meat pie. He could not tell if it was beef or Septimus swamp beast. Probably beef, because swamp beast would taste better.

Ricardo wiped the corner of his mouth with a white cloth napkin. "Pity we won't be here to try him out."

"Yes. A pity." Ruby sipped her coffee and looked at the far wall. "If word gets out that a ship was lost here, I don't know. We could lose clients."

"Nah, we won't," said Oscar, wiping his glasses on his shirt. "Titanic sunk, but people still went on cruises."

Cydney pushed her half-eaten tray to one side and made a face. "This tastes awful."

Oscar grunted, pulled Cydney's tray in front of him, and started eating it. "I can get the airlock fixed tomorrow," he said. "Gasket's torn and I'll have to machine a new hinge plate, but it shouldn't be a problem."

"Can't we call down to the station and have them send up a shuttle?" Victor asked.

Oscar shook his head. "No. First of all they don't want to talk to us, and second, cruise ships bring their own shuttles. As far as I know, Horseshoe Station doesn't have a shuttle to send up."

"Did you check the sweeper satellites?"

He stuffed a forkful of potato product into his mouth. "That's next."

Ruby put down her cup and frowned. "I wanted that done right away."

"You didn't say that."

"Yes, I did."

"No, you didn't. You said 'check the sweepers.' And I'm going to, next, but we'd be in big trouble without a docking airlock. As it is I'm going to have to crawl over from the other side and I hate going outside."

"I want those sweepers checked out right away."

He nodded, turned, and tossed his empty trays into a disposal chute. "I'm only one man. That Gary guy that came from the *Nairobi* is just a design engineer, not a repairman. I'm going to have to show him everything. All he wants to do is eat and sleep."

"Isn't there anything good to eat?" whined Cydney.

Ruby took a breath before answering. "If you go deeper in the freezer, you'll find some frozen sweet rolls. Why don't you get some to take with you?"

Cydney made a face, slid off her chair, and went into the freezer.

Ruby glanced at Victor. "How's she doing?" she said quietly. "She looks terrible."

"She cried a lot," he said. "She'll probably cry some more."

"I was never the mothering sort, but it would be easier if she weren't so damned insufferable. Listen, if it gets too bad, there are some chocolate bars high up in an unmarked box. Let them thaw first."

Victor nodded. "I have a question. Why are the shops stocked when there's no one here?"

18

"There were people here. The construction and the finishing crew. They were buying things at the shops up until they left. And when the operating crew arrives, they'll use the shops also. That's why I had the stores stocked. It's not like people can go anywhere else if they need something."

Cydney returned with a plastic sack of frozen sweet rolls and Ricardo got to his feet. "It's been toppers and everything," Ricardo said, "but Victor, Cydney, how about we go look at the gun shops? See what they have in the armory?"

Ruby frowned. "Ricky, these children are underage, they shouldn't be playing with guns, and I don't want any inventory shrinkage if you take my meaning."

"Everything will be paid for. Our young lady's not the only one with a balance chip." Ricardo patted his front pocket. "And don't worry about the youngsters; I've taken many their age hunting."

Cydney looked at Ricardo with sad eight-year-old eyes. "Can you take me to my room first? I don't want to see any guns and I really miss my doggie."

"Sure, little Missy, anything you want. I can carry your packages for you, if you like."

She grabbed Victor's hand, and as they walked out of the dining room she looked up at Victor and smiled secretively. She didn't miss her robodog, but Victor could understand her wanting to skip the guns.

*

"You're wincing. Relax through it. Don't force it."

Victor raised the pistol and aimed at the target projected on the bullet-absorbing wall. Half breath. Slow squeeze. Keep the eyes open.

BAM!

The pistol bucked with the recoil, and he let his forearm drop back into position.

Beside him, Ricardo nodded. "Better. Once more. Own the gun, don't let it own you. Put that bullet in the center."

BAM!

19

Victor dropped the clip from the gun and opened the chamber. Then he laid the gun down and pressed the button that enlarged the target display. Ricardo raised his eyebrows. "Say, good score, mate. You sure you've never shot pistol before?"

"Not a real one. Just, you know, arcades."

"Okay, I'll grant simulators can help with aim. These hunting pistols are a different breed though. Heavy. You did good."

"Why not use the modern stuff? You know, high voltage guns, drop them in their tracks if you hit them anywhere."

Ricardo laughed as he put the pistol into a holster and hung it on the rack. "Romance."

"What do you mean, romance?"

"Not hearts and flowers romance. I mean adventure, I mean the frontier, the American west, Argentina, the savanna of Africa, the high plains of Olympia Prime. There are no bragging rights with electronic weapons. These," he hefted a hunting rifle and pushed a clip into it, "these are the guns that make the blood sing." He restarted the target projector, shrank the target, and fired six shots dead center, rapid fire. "There," he said, his eyes glowing. "That's what I mean."

He took out the clip and passed the rifle to Victor, who hefted it. "Solid. Can I get one of these?"

Ricardo took the rifle back and placed it on the wall. "You're a bit young to carry one of these around, and unless it's your birthday, I'm not buying."

Victor patted his pockets, already knowing he had nothing to buy with. He had his med ID, pocket change, and his remaining pills. And a beautiful knife. "No, it's not my birthday." Ricardo seemed in good spirits, so Victor risked a question. "You and Ruby knew each other before?"

"You might say that." They walked out of the armory and got several strides down the hallway before he added, "Yes, we knew each other. Almost got married, actually."

"You're kidding."

"Truth. Oh, we were totally hooked on each other, smitten, you might say. Like a bonfire. But it didn't work out."

Victor didn't say anything. He had found that if you stayed silent long enough, adults would keep on talking.

"Trouble was," said Ricardo, "well, *she* says the trouble was, I was too interested in roaming and she wanted to settle down. I say she was too interested in...." He rubbed his thumb and fingers together. "... 'ka-ching!' and she wasn't happy about my..." He mimicked holding a rifle. "... 'ka-pow.'" He shrugged. "I got involved in Chancel Corporation, running safaris, and she helped found Belle Enterprises. We didn't part friends."

"That's too bad."

"Yes, life's funny that way. Now my cruise ship's a bunch of debris and here I am stranded on her station. We don't even know how to talk to each other, now. Ah, look here, the arcade room."

They had arrived at the play area, with some rooms for children, some for teens, and some for adults who never got tired of playing. "Care to give the Wild West a try?" asked Ricardo.

Victor would have preferred going to his suite and reading, but he could tell that Ricardo wanted to do something to cheer him up. Victor smiled and nodded; most of the time when adults tried to cheer him up it was a burden, but he tried to be polite.

"Ruby went with top quality," said Ricardo as he placed his chip on the reader and powered it up. "This one has all the whistles, bells, and drums to boot."

They took gun belts off the wall, which they buckled low on their waists. Ricardo began tapping the keyboard to set up the simulation. "I'll be Ricardo the Desperado. Long name, but unique. You can be Victor the...."

"No."

"What?"

"I'd rather watch you play."

Ricardo turned to him, hands on his hips. "Have you played this before?"

He nodded. "Yes, but..."

"Come on, it's my credits. Humor me." He turned back to the keyboard. "Victor the...."

"No. Not Victor."

"No?" Victor raised an eyebrow. "It's a good name. It means winner, I'm sure you know."

"I don't like Victor."

"Okay." Ricardo started typing. "We'll call you Vic."

"No," he said, sharper than he meant to.

"What's wrong with Vic?"

"It's not a good name in....in school. They'll call you Vicky, or Vicks, or something like that."

"I see." He looked at Victor plainly, the sort of look that said he understood the hidden context. "How about your last name? Bennington?"

"Benningham." Victor kicked the floor idly as though kicking a stone. "Don't like that either, actually."

Ricardo looked as though he was going to ask a question, but instead smiled heartily and said, "How about Ben? Is Ben okay?"

Victor shrugged. "Sure."

"Ben. Ben the Kid." Ricardo tapped the backspace. "No, Benny the Kid. Rolls off the tongue better. You good with Benny the Kid, mate?"

"Yeah, sure." He tried to smile for Ricardo's sake. Counselors had already had long discussions with him about his attitude towards his name, telling him it wasn't the name itself that was the problem. It didn't matter. He still didn't like the name Victor Benningham. Benny the Kid was better. Anything was better, that wasn't tainted.

I hope Cydney or whatever her name is, is okay alone. I shouldn't stay here too long.

"Don your caps. I'll go first," said Ricardo. They put their caps on their heads and slipped the wraparound visors over their eyes. Ricardo pressed START.

Acoustic guitar music riffed, and the lighting changed. A western town appeared, complete with false fronts, watering troughs, and an old miner sitting on a rocking chair. A breeze rolled the tumbleweeds, and the smell of fresh sage wafted over them. At the end of the dirt road a pair of saloon doors opened, and a man with a mustache as wide as his black sombrero emerged onto the street, silver spurs jingling with each slow step.

"Ricardo the Desperado, it's time for a showdown," the man said with a sneer, his rough hands poised over his six-shooters. "Are you ready, podnuh?"

Ricardo grinned. "I was born ready, podnuh!"

Chapter Three

Ricardo shot the bad guy dead center.

A beep sounded, and a score of zero flashed against the clouds overhead. The figure in the sombrero fell backwards and vanished.

"Zero points?" said Ricardo.

"You've got it on QuickDraw," said Victor, lifting his visor and peering at the game's monitor. "You can't draw until they do."

"Oh, of course. I knew that." He rolled his shoulders and shook his fingers. "Let's try this again."

A different character walked out onto the street, this one with blue eyes and a red bandana around his neck. "So it's come to this, has it?" the red bandana gunslinger said. "Are you ready?"

Ricardo flexed his knees, his hands poised. "Ready when you are." The wind picked up, whistling through the false front of the wooden saloon. The tempo of the music quickened and the miner in the rocking chair dived for cover.

The red bandana man reached for his gun. Ricardo whipped his guns out and shot three shots rapid-fire. "Argh! Yuh got me!" cried the gunslinger. He toppled backwards and faded away. A score of 250 flashed overhead.

"Got him!" said Ricardo.

"They get faster."

"Shame it's got the kid filter locked on. I like to see the blood where I shoot."

24

Victor didn't answer. He had seen enough fights with real blood. He'd rather just have the bad guys fade away.

One by one, three more men emerged from the saloon doors to challenge Ricardo the Desperado, each yielding a higher score. The last one was a steely-eyed character with calf-skin gloves and a tailored shirt. "You ready, punk?" was all he asked. He spat on the ground, cracked his knuckles, flexed his arms, and drew without warning.

Ricardo got off one shot before his guns went dead. The score flashed 1450, GAME OVER, and declared his ranking as "VIGILANTE." Funeral music played as a horse-drawn hearse trundled off towards the sunset. The steely-eyed man chuckled, touched his hat, and pushed back into the saloon.

"Good job," said Victor.

"I could do better. Your turn."

"Nah." He shook his head. "I just wanted to see it. I ought to get back."

"No, really. Take your turn."

"I'd rather not."

They looked at each other while a harmonica joined the guitar in the background and the miner came out and sat in his rocking chair. "I'd like to see you give it try," said Ricardo.

Victor sighed, shrugged, and took his place. He cursed himself for not thinking ahead.

The Black Sombrero man stepped out onto the street. "Benny the Kid, it's time for a showdown! Are you ready, podnuh?"

Victor put his hands just above the handles of his guns, and tried to relax and concentrate.

Black Sombrero shot him before he got his guns out of the holster.

"Bad luck," said Ricardo, restarting the game. "Give her another go, mate."

Black Sombrero stepped out on the street. "Benny the Kid, it's time for a showdown! Are you ready, podnuh?" Victor tried to estimate how long it took the Black Sombrero to draw the last time, and then pulled his guns. He fired, the bad guy toppled over backwards, but his score was zero.

25

Ricardo smiled and started the game again. "Like you said, you've got to wait 'til he reaches for it. Third time's the charm."

Third time was not the charm.

Fourth time was not the charm.

Fifth and sixth times were not the charm either.

It wasn't until Ricardo let the game continue instead of resetting it that it lowered its difficulty setting for Benny the Kid. A man in ragged coveralls and a straw hat moseyed out of the saloon, went "Yup, yup, here we go," and elaborately reached for his gun. Victor shot him four times and would have shot him again if he hadn't faded out.

Sadly, any character near the skill of Black Sombrero meant death for him. Even the Drunken Norwegian got off a couple of shots before toppling over.

In the end, it was a Chinese Cook that last killed Benny the Kid. The score flashed 35, GAME OVER, and the rating SNAKE-OIL PEDDLER. Victor pulled off his cap in frustration.

Ricardo took Victor's guns and put them back on the rack. "I don't understand, and I don't mean to be nosy, but I know you know how to shoot. You've done this before. Are you sick or something?"

"Yea, something. I'm on medication, and slows me down a little."

"Oh. I'm sorry. It's not anything contagious, is it?"

"No, it's nothing. The pills help me, but I just can't respond quick."

"What're they for, if you don't mind me asking?"

Victor picked up his bag of new clothes. "Saint Jude called it Hyper-D."

"What's that? Like ADHD? I thought they cured that."

He shook his head. "Opposite. I'm the first case they identified, but now that they know about it, they've found a couple others."

"What's the difference?"

"My brain starts thinking too fast; I move too fast, everything else seems to slow down for me."

26

"It sounds the same as ADHD."

"No, it isn't. I can concentrate too much in a situation; when I'm into it I think faster and move faster than other people. It's gotten me in trouble. A neurologist found a medication that slows me down, but it really grounds me, so I can't do things like this." He waved at the Wild West game.

Ricardo clasped Victor on the shoulder and smiled too broadly. "You're doing fine, as far as anyone can tell. I'm proud to know you."

You don't know me. And if you did, you wouldn't be as proud as you say you are.

But that was the way adults were, falsely encouraging and optimistic.

Ricardo chattered on as they walked, falling into tour guide mode. "Listen, Benny the Kid, this really wasn't the way it was in the Wild West, you know. If you really had a bad guy after you, you hid behind a barrel and shot him." He made a gun with his hand and shot someone with his finger. "Or you came up from behind and knocked him out with a piece of lumber. Trust me; they did not walk down the middle of the street like the old western vidstreams, trying to see who could outdraw the other. How silly would that be?"

"Didn't they?"

"Nah. Didn't happen, except by accident, and then they ran away from each other while firing blindly. Only true part about that simulation we played was the bystanders ducking for cover. Oh, it's great entertainment, great stories, but in those days, rifles were best for killing your enemy. Pistols were for rattlesnakes and for shooting your horse if you fell off and got your boot twisted in the stirrup and was being dragged all over the landscape. Nobody ever stood in the middle of the street waiting for the other guy to draw."

"Shucks, now I'm all disillusioned," said Victor with a half smile. Ricardo meant well, but Victor remembered how Ricardo had leaped out of the airlock and left him behind with Cydney. Ricardo could not be counted on.

*

27

Victor watched more of the documentary on the Horseshoe Planet before going to bed. The safaris rode out on horseback at dawn to hunt the fierce red apes, followed by a crawler with supplies. Victor had never ridden a horse, but he had backpacked into the New Zealand mountains, camped in the wilderness and swam in the frigid rivers.

He showered in the luxurious bathroom and got into his old clothes to sleep. He should have bought pajamas when he and Cydney were in the stores, but it hadn't occurred to him.

The room was comfortable and the bed even more so. The pill let him sleep easily, so easily that he was completely disoriented when he heard shrieks and someone clambered onto his bed and grabbed him. He turned on the nightstand lamp to find Cydney's face buried in his ribs. "What's wrong? What happened?"

She waved an arm. "There's awful things in my room!" She started to cry and buried her face again.

He patted her back, his mind thick. "What awful things?"

"I don't know, it was just all eyes and voices and grabbing things."

"Stay here," he said, and started to slide out of the bed.

"No, no, don't go, don't leave me!" Her fingernails dug into his arm.

"Ow! Okay, okay. Don't you want me to go check?"

She didn't answer, just held on and hyperventilated.

He waited until her breathing slowed and she was down to sniffles. "Now listen," he said, "I'm going to go look in your room. You stay here. I'll turn on all the lights, okay?"

She nodded, clutching his pillow when he got up. He turned on the lights and looked carefully into Cydney's room.

He found nothing, as he expected, just jumbled boxes of things she had purchased and the remains of the bag of sweet rolls. Cydney was obviously not trained to keep her room neat.

"You had a nightmare," he said as he returned. "There's nothing there."

"Are you sure? I'm scared."

"Nothing. Just junk is all. Bits of sweet roll."

"Can I sleep here?"

"No. Go sleep in your own bed."

She pulled the pillow tighter against her and whimpered, her eyes white with fear. She was not manipulating this time, she was genuinely afraid. It was only nightmares, but she had just lost her mother, and who knew what kind of life she had led as a child star?

He relented. "Okay. You can sleep on that side of the bed. Just stay there and be quiet."

"Okay. I will. Thank you." She scooted to the far edge and squeezed herself under the sheets. "I'm sorry."

He turned out the lights and lay down, punching his pillow until it was comfortable.

Cydney sniffed a few more times, and then asked tremulously, "Victor?"

"Yes?" The blackness of sleep was sliding over him again, and he hated being pulled back from it.

"Um, please, would you be my boyfriend?"

He snorted. "No! Don't be stupid, you're way too young to have a boyfriend! Go back to your room."

"No, please! I'm sorry. Please don't be mad!"

He exhaled and tried to relax, tried to let the day slide away from him. He knew she meant nothing by her request; she had lost her mother and was grasping for an anchor. He was just the wrong person to be that anchor, especially for a girl who looked and acted like an eight-year-old brat. Morning on the station would come all too soon. He exhaled and tried to relax, to let himself drift back into sleep.

"Victor?"

"Now what?"

"Um....would you, maybe, would you be my big brother?"

Oh, for Pete's sake.

He didn't want to nursemaid a rude self-centered child.

On the other hand, she was scared and she had no one, not even a tutor or a nanny. And she had been open with him when they were alone, mostly; she only put on her act when others were around. He knew what it was like to be alone, with no one to rely on or confide in. She needed a connection to another living being.

"Yeah, fine. I can be your big brother."

A stifled sob. "Thank you."

"Now go to sleep."

"Okay."

*

The large screen showed an angled view of a coastline, the shore misty from the crashing waves. Victor increased the magnification, trying to see something besides the round-leaved trees.

Cydney pointed. "What's that icky thing?"

"Looks like a plate crab," said Ricardo, his booted feet up on the railing, his thin mustache freshly trimmed. "Legs all around the edges. Plankton feeder. Not bad eating, but only a ring of muscle inside. Too much work to cook, in my opinion, but the tourists are impressed."

Victor thumbed the control that aimed the casino's telescope, looking further into the jungle. "Think we can see any red apes from here?"

"Not this close to the shore. They like the low hills best. More vines, taller trees, we call them tangle trees. More prey for them to hunt."

"Think we can find Horseshoe Station?"

"Maybe. Zoom out a bit."

Victor rolled back the view until most of the planet was visible on the screen.

Ricardo put his boots on the floor and sat up. "Okay, mates. Who can tell me why this is called the Horseshoe Planet?"

Victor started to speak, but Cydney blurted out, "'Cause it looks like a horseshoe?"

"Not the planet, of course," said Ricardo, adjusting his hat, "but that northern continent has the appearance of a horseshoe, if you're generous. A geologist told me that ages ago it was a solid continent that separated, two tectonic plates drifting apart,

30

except at the bottom there where that volcano sits, and so it formed that shape. A million years from now, it'll be two continents."

Cydney rolled her eyes. "He's teaching again."

"People usually tip me for it, young lady," said Ricardo. "Be grateful."

Victor moved the view to the western part of the continent. "So where's the station?"

"We're moving away; it's at the horizon. You need to wait a while before our orbit brings us back over it again."

"If you're done playing with my telescope," said a frosty voice behind them, "I'd like to check up on Oscar."

"Hey, Ruby," said Ricardo, getting to his feet and doffing his hat. "Come in and make yourself at home."

Victor let go of the controls and moved so that Ruby could take his place. She sat without comment and pulled out a keypad. Taking a scrap of paper from her pocket, she typed in some numbers with one finger.

The planet on the viewscreen rolled away as the telescope changed direction, and the blocky shuttle Oscar was piloting appeared on the screen with a backdrop of non-twinkling stars. Victor guessed that the number Ruby typed in was a transponder frequency that let the telescope find the shuttle.

The shuttle appeared to be motionless, but he knew that was an illusion. Oscar was dropping back to check on the sweeper satellite, a tricky bit of orbital navigation.

Ruby tapped some more keys. "Oscar, can you hear me?"

The speaker rasped. "I'm not getting paid enough for this."

"Stick to the point. Are you getting anywhere with the sweeper?"

"Nothing. I've rebooted it over and over by remote. Keeps getting hung up partway."

Ricardo leaned over Ruby's shoulder. "Maybe we could point this telescope at the sweeper, see if we see anything?"

Ruby pursed her lips and grumbled. She looked through several online folders before she found a number to enter into the telescope.

31

The field of stars shifted, the screen magnified, and the sweeper satellite became visible.

It was a bulky structure, with solar panels and laser arrays extended. The entire structure was slowly circling around a central point like a dog on a chain.

"That's not right," said Ricardo.

Ruby leaned forward. "You're darn right that's not right. How long has it been doing that? It looks like one of the lithium drives is spinning it. Oscar?"

"Yes?"

"I've got the sweeper on the 'scope, and it looks like it's got a drive pushing it in circles. Can you shut that drive off?"

"Not from here. I'm going to have to get next to that...." He muttered an angry epithet, "....and wrestle it down. I'll let you know in an hour or so what I find."

"Got that." Ruby leaned back and chewed on a cuticle, watching the sweeper making lazy circles in space.

Ricardo sat beside her. "Why is that drive doing that?"

"I don't know," she answered, without looking at him. "The sweeper wouldn't have gotten hit if it was functioning; it protects itself. If I didn't know better, I'd say someone left that drive on the last time they serviced it, which would be just before the last crew left." She glared at Ricardo. "I need to review the members of the last crew. I bet someone was in the pay of Chancel Corporation."

"Oh, now, Ruby, no one would do something like that. Endanger the lives of people? You can't be serious."

"You don't know the people you're working for, Ricky. The higher you go in Chancel Corporation, the more corrupt they get. This sabotage has not been a simple matter of business competition."

"Still, I can't believe they would deliberately damage a piece of safety equipment." He brushed some lint off his sleeve. "Don't you have anyone else that could diagnose that sweeper?"

"No. There's just Ramon and Oscar. And that engineer named Gary that came with you, but Oscar says he's useless. That's it until the crew ship comes in."

32

"I want to look at the oceans again," said Cydney.

"Here," said Ruby as she left the seat, "look at whatever you want."

"Ms. Tierney," asked Victor, "why don't Belle Enterprises and Chancel Corporation get along?"

"He should answer that." Ruby looked pointedly at Ricardo.

"Not me." Ricardo raised his hands in surrender.

Ruby folded her arms. "From the time this planet was discovered, Chancel looked at Horseshoe as something to exploit and run roughshod over. They've monopolized it and stifled any competition, which is why we decided to build up here in orbit. Those so-called safaris are nothing more than excuses for rich people to shoot animals they haven't taken the time to understand. Belle Enterprises wanted to make money through sight-seeing, ecological vacations, activities that wouldn't harm the biology."

"Boring stuff, in other words," said Ricardo. He winked at Victor. "She doesn't like the guns and the danger."

Ruby's voice hardened. "No, what I don't like is killing things we don't understand. You haven't studied the food web; you don't know what part these creatures play, and you don't know how much damage you're doing. By the time we get some interplanetary laws to protect this planet, who knows what will be lost forever?"

"Oh, come on now, Ruby. These are common beasts, not rare, and we don't hurt the females. The young are already on the way. We're just harvesting the bull males. Besides, it's a chance for men and women to live the way we used to before we got over-civilized, to get out in the wilds and to fend for ourselves."

"Is that why you have a crawler with wine and gourmet cuisine following as you fend for yourselves?"

"These are high-class people; they demand their luxuries."

"While they fend for themselves."

"The money's good. Isn't that what matters?"

Victor could see that the words were getting through, but not the meaning. It was too painful to watch, even though on

33

the surface it seemed a simple discussion. He sat down beside Cydney and helped her with the telescope controls.

They were focused on some slow-moving grassland creatures that looked vaguely like rhinos when a call came in from Oscar.

"Ruby, we've got bigger problems than I thought."

Ruby turned away from Ricardo. "Speak to me."

"This sweeper's been down a long time. Some big stuff has drifted into this orbit, and it's moving fast. There's some, wait a minute, some....."

Oscar fell silent, and the four of them stared at the speaker, wondering what was happening.

Victor's stomach tightened.

Then Oscar broke the silence. "Ruby, get everyone into the rescue pods, now. Hurry! My sensors just picked up some large stuff coming your way fast and there's no way I can get this sweeper fixed in time. I'm so sorry, Ruby, I didn't go when you asked, I'm sorry, and now oh my lord, look at those...I can't....Ruby, get out of there! Get....!" A burst of static, and the speaker fell silent.

Ruby put her hands over her mouth, her eyes wide with unbelief. Then she turned to them and shouted. "The escape pods are beyond the workers' kitchen, that way! You heard him! Run!"

Ricardo leaped out the door of the observatory and disappeared. Victor grabbed Cydney's hand and pulled her up from the chair. "Let's go."

"What's wrong?" asked Cydney, holding back. "What's happening?"

"Asteroids are in our orbit and we need to get to the lifeboats! Move!"

She let him pull her along, and they ran behind Ruby. They passed the shops and the passenger dining area, still closed. They ran past the casino area, dark except for a few work lights.

They ran into Ricardo as they passed the shooting gallery. He had the pistol belt over his shoulder and a rifle in his hands.

With the butt of the rifle, he smashed a glass case that held ammunition.

"What are you doing?" screamed Ruby. "Looting?"

"Planning ahead!" He reached in and grabbed some boxes.

Victor kept running, pulling Cydney along. She wasn't resisting but he was not going to take any chances.

They were ahead of Ruby and Ricardo now. They ran past the arcades, through the worker's quarters, and past the workers' kitchen. Ahead, where he had never been, Victor saw the doors that led to the rescue pods.

The first pod door was open but as they approached, it closed. Through the thick glass, Victor saw Gary the engineer, pressing buttons in the rescue pod. Secondary doors closed, and Victor felt the shudder as the pod pushed out into space.

Ruby stopped behind him. "What just happened?"

Victor looked up at her. "Gary took a rescue pod."

"He what? All by himself? How *dare* he!" She tossed a sailor's curse in the direction of the vanished pod and ran ahead to the next one. The door was firmly closed, and she began tapping frantically on the keypad next to it, trying to get it to open.

"Hurry," said Ricardo, "before whatever hit Oscar hits us."

"I'm trying to remember the code!"

Victor stepped back, looking over the doors. They were automated, designed to open in case of emergency. Unfortunately, the ship did not know there was an emergency so the doors remained closed, probably protecting the rescue pods from inebriated passengers.

An idea hit him. "Stay here," he said to Cydney, and ran back to the dining area.

"What are you going to do?" Cydney yelled as she followed him.

He ignored her and searched along the walls. As he suspected, there was a handle on the wall by the flash oven marked FIRE. He shattered the safety glass that covered it and yanked down the handle.

Bells rang and water sprayed down from the ceiling. He grabbed Cydney's hand and ran back to the pod doors.

The doors were open now, all of them. Ruby and Ricardo were already in the second pod, and Victor pulled Cydney inside.

The rescue pod had padded seats designed to handle a couple dozen people in a double circle. Ricardo shoved the rifle, gun belt, and ammunition into a mesh bag between some outer seats; Ruby hurried down to the center where the controls were located.

Victor pushed Cydney to a center seat, but before he could sit down, she shouted. "My doggie!"

Victor looked back at the pod entrance, but Ricardo held up his hand. "Stay put!" The doors closed and the pod launched. Victor and Ricardo toppled to the floor. "Listen, mate," said Ricardo as they got to their feet, "you don't go back into a burning building after a pet! Never!"

"Strap in," shouted Ruby. "We're going to be weightless in...."

The thrust ended and Victor floated helplessly off the floor.

Chapter Four

A recorded voice, calm, cheerful, and feminine echoed in the rescue pod. "Welcome to Bell Enterprises Rescue Pod Number Two. Please strap yourselves in immediately. This is an emergency situation."

Victor grabbed the back of a seat and dragged himself towards the center. The recording sounded like a vidstream supermodel describing a chocolate dessert.

He had been in weightlessness before but was never comfortable with it. To him the worst part was not the nausea but the bagginess of his clothes and the way his legs stuck out in all directions.

Ricardo windmilled his arms helplessly until he bumped against the low ceiling. He attempted to grab something, but only succeeded in bouncing himself back down. He clambered into the first seat he contacted and pulled the harness over himself.

Victor slipped in beside Cydney, who looked at him with unreadable eyes. Then she covered her face and started crying.

Ruby cast an annoyed glance at Cydney before bringing up a view of her casino on the viewscreen. "Look!" she said, pointing. "Another pod just launched! Ramon must have gotten out. That's everyone."

Cydney cried out, "Except my doggie!" and wept dramatically and loudly. Victor ignored her histrionics. He knew that Cydney didn't care in the slightest about the robodog. As usual, Cydney was acting for her public.

He watched the viewscreen. He had to admit that the outside view of the facility was lovely. Incoming tourists would have been dazzled by the colored array of lights that graced the slowly rotating casino, especially against the backdrop of space. He wished they had been approaching for a fun vacation rather than fleeing in a rescue pod. "Do you see any meteorites?"

"They're not technically meteorites until they hit the ground," said Ruby. "They're meteoroids, if they're small. I think Oscar ran into meteoroids like the one that hit your ship." She expanded the view. "Although what drifted in from the asteroid ring might be bigger."

"We're sitting ducks out here, you know," said Ricardo from the outer circle of seats. "We should start the landing sequence."

"I'm not going to start this pod down unless I have to." Ruby wrung her hands nervously. "Maybe this will pass us by, maybe we can dock again."

"You don't know how to fix that sweeper and neither do I. Even if we can go back, we'll be helpless."

"The next ship will bring another engineer. He can fix it."

"Be reasonable! You said that was a month away, but right now there's stuff flying all over this orbit."

Ruby gripped the sides of the control table until her knuckles were white. She had no answer.

The debate suddenly became moot. A large gray object passed beyond the casino, and then another one underneath, looking like a diseased potato.

The third one hit.

The lights on the casino flickered out and it split into two unequal pieces, the smaller one spinning away, scattering debris. Ruby cried out as though she had been stabbed.

Victor grabbed her hand. "Let's go, before we get hit."

She nodded, unable to speak. Her hand hovered over the red button in the center, and she glanced up at the viewscreen one more time. More objects swept past, smaller but just as deadly.

She pressed the button.

"Rescue Pod Number Two is now initiating planetary landing," said the cheerful female voice. "Please remain seated and keep your arms tucked under the harness. If you have any loose objects, for your safety and the safety of those around you, please tuck them into the elastic mesh between the seats."

Cydney broke off her crying and looked at him with worried eyes. "What's happening?"

"We're going to land on the planet." As though his words had triggered them, the pod engines started up and he felt pressure pushing him back into the seat. The pod rotated and began reducing their orbital velocity. He hoped they would drop down fast enough to avoid the meteoroids rolling through their orbit.

He turned to Ruby, who had her eyes closed and her jaw clenched. "Where are we going to land?"

"I don't know." She opened her eyes and patted her seat's armrests nervously. "I never thought I'd have to use one of these pods. It will put us down on land, not water, but it could be anywhere. It's all automated, and we never had them tuned yet, they're all on factory settings. We weren't open yet."

Ricardo spoke up. "I'm sorry, Ruby. I truly am. That was a beautiful casino, and it would have been a sure hit. It's a damn shame."

She nodded, her eyes filled with pain.

The viewscreen showed nothing but a shifting star field. Victor pulled a plastic information sheet from a mesh pocket and looked at the sketch of the rescue pod. A trio of drives provided the propulsion, and three parachutes on the rim would help soften the landing. On the side opposite the entrance door was sketched a tiny bathroom.

On the back of the plastic information sheet was a drawing of several people sitting under a tree and eating, with the rescue pod sitting neatly in a field behind them. The text said that the pod carried food for a week, but that rescue would arrive within 24 hours.

When the pod began to shake from contact with the atmosphere, Victor's stomach relaxed. They were finally below the danger area from the meteoroids. Now it was just a matter of surviving the descent, and for that, they were in the hands of the designers of the rescue pod. There was nothing they could do.

Cydney grabbed his hand. "Are we going to be okay?"

He smiled reassuringly. "We're going to be just fine."

I lied to her. I'm turning into a grownup.

*

The viewscreen showed the stars fading out and the sky lightening as they entered the atmosphere. A red glow appeared as the skin heated. Eventually they saw wisps of high clouds, and then the woman's voice came back on, cheerful and confident. "The parachutes are about to be released to slow our descent. Please lean your head back and rest comfortably as there will be some shaking in the cabin as they deploy."

Cydney cried out as the cabin suddenly jerked and the pod rocked violently. They sagged into their seats as though a fat person had just sat on them.

It was only a moment, though, and then the ride smoothed and the engines quieted down. "We will now be maneuvering to a safe landing location," said the happy voice. "Please remain in your seats and keep your harnesses securely strapped. I will tell you when we are about to land."

"I hope she's picking us out a good spot, right next to the Station," said Ricardo.

"She'll land where she lands," said Ruby. "I don't particularly care, as long as we survive."

The engines roared and Victor could feel the pod shifting. The viewscreen showed puffy clouds racing by.

"We are about to land," said the calm voice. "Please remain seated until we have come to a complete stop. There may be some unexpected movement as we make contact."

Ricardo grumbled. "As we tumble down some cliffs."

As if answering, the recording said, "Please brace yourself. We are landing now."

40

To Victor it felt as though someone on the outside began slamming the pod with sledgehammers. He was jerked right and left, spun around, and rolled head over heels. Cydney screamed and Ricardo cursed.

The silence when they finally stopped felt deafening. Hot metal ticked as it cooled, and Victor pulled his hands from the armrests he had gripped in panic.

The pod was tilted sideways. Only their harnesses kept them in their seats.

"We have now landed," said the voice triumphantly. "Belle Enterprises and Rescue Pod Number Two are pleased to have brought you safely down to the planet. We advise you to remain inside until the exit light turns green, showing that the outside of the pod has cooled. You may now undo your harness and walk about the pod.

"Rescue will arrive within 24 hours, so if you go outside please stay within sight of the pod. Also, please be sure to take all belongings with you when you leave and thank you from Belle Enterprises! Have a good day!"

"Careful, mates," said Ricardo. "We're not level."

"Tell me something I don't know," snapped Ruby. "If you fall, Ricky, you're going to fall on me!" She was on the down side, looking up at them.

Victor reached for his harness buckle. "I think I can climb down, if I just...."

The pod rocked.

Everyone froze, but the pod settled back to its original position and sat still.

"What was that?" asked Ricardo.

"I'm scared," said Cydney, grabbing Victor's arm.

Ruby unsnapped her harness. "We're unstable, is what that was."

"Well, don't unbuckle, then," said Ricardo. "If we start rolling you'll break your neck. Or you'll break my neck."

She paused, holding the harness in mid-air. "I don't know. We might be better off getting out quick."

"Can you look outside with the viewscreen?" asked Victor.

Ruby looked over the controls and shook her head. "The only things working now are the lights and the homing beacon."

The pod rocked slightly.

Ruby removed her harness. "I can't just sit here. I've got to do something, anything." She swung around in her seat and climbed down to the outer wall, now acting as a floor.

Victor saw the exit light change color. "It's okay to go outside. The exit's green." He unbuckled his harness and climbed down, using the pillar of the central control table as a step and sliding down the same chairs that Ruby used.

"Help me!" cried Cydney, and Victor grimly climbed back up and helped her down.

Ricardo slid and half-fell to their level. He rubbed the back of his neck and looked up. "Are we going to have to climb up to get out that door?"

"That's the bathroom door," said Victor.

"Then the exit door is...."

Ruby stomped her foot. "We're standing on it."

Ricardo leaned over, his hands on his knees. "How does this open? This sign on the door says, 'When the exit light is green, enter the code...'" He read the code that was taped on the keypad, and tapped it in. "'...then pull this handle, slide this lever....'" He knelt down and pulled the handle marked PULL. He slid a lever marked PUSH, and then exhaled. "There's a little bit of a problem."

"I can see that."

Cydney clung to Victor's arm and looked anxious. "What's the matter?"

"The pod's lying on the exit door," said Victor. "We can't get out."

"But we've got food and, and didn't the lady say that help would be here in 24 hours?"

"Food?" asked Ricardo. He walked up the slope and pulled open a cabinet.

Empty.

He opened the one above that, and then climbed down and tried the ones he could reach on the other side.

42

All empty.

"So where's the food?" Ricardo looked at the other storage bins too far above to reach.

Ruby stared at the blocked exit door with tired eyes. "I told you. We weren't open yet."

"You didn't stock food in the rescue pods?"

"We! Weren't! Open! Yet! We were still under construction! There was some food...." She took a breath. "There was some food in the pod that Gary took. Pod Number One was stocked, and it could have held all of us."

"Well, that's just great." Ricardo put his hands in his pockets and leaned back against the tilted floor.

"It's not my fault, Ricky! I had the pods ready and I had food in the one we should have taken. Don't blame me."

Cydney whispered, "Why do grownups always fight?"

Victor shrugged, and spoke up. "Excuse me. Does it matter that there's no food, if rescue is coming within 24 hours?"

Ruby arched her eyebrows at Ricardo. "Do you want to answer that?"

He pulled his hands out of his pockets. "Sorry, mate. Horseshoe Station doesn't monitor for rescue pods, especially not on Belle Enterprises' frequency, and there aren't any other colonies on this planet. We're broadcasting but nobody's listening."

Victor looked from Ricardo to Ruby. "So what's supposed to happen next?"

"There is no 'next.'" Ruby wrung her hands in frustration. "This wasn't supposed to happen. I mean, yes, the pod did what it was supposed to do. It got us down. We're alive and we're on the planet."

"And trapped," said Ricardo.

"And I can't help it if the only other people on the planet aren't willing to launch a rescue!" Ruby snapped.

"We're not trapped," said Victor firmly. "This pod is round, and we just felt it rock. It rocked that way," he pointed to his right, "so if we all climb up that side, the next time it rocks, it might move more and free up the door."

43

"We don't know why it rocked," said Ruby.

"That doesn't matter; he's got a point," said Ricardo. "We'll never push that door out with the pod lying on it, and we can't pull it in, and unless you've got a cutting laser, we're not going out through the walls."

Victor could see Ruby trying to come up with some reason to disagree with Ricardo, but she couldn't. She nodded, and they climbed up as far as they could on the wall and struggled into seats on that side. "We could be on the edge of a cliff, you know," she said once they were still. "We could roll off and fall half a mile. We ought to strap ourselves in again."

They snapped their harnesses tight and waited. Cydney gripped Victor's hand.

Painful minutes passed until the pod rocked, and to their disappointment, settled back. Then it rocked again, further. It paused, tantalizingly, and then continued to roll.

They had not been on the edge of a cliff, but wherever they were, the pod made several revolutions before stopping again, shaking them about and eliciting more screams from Cydney. This time it stopped in a more horizontal, almost-level attitude.

They unsnapped their harnesses, Ruby entered the code into the keypad by the door again, and Ricardo kicked the door open.

Victor expected sunshine. Instead, there was a dim twilight. Ricardo started to step out, and then caught the frame. "The first step's a lulu, mates." He turned, knelt down, and lowered himself out the door.

Victor exited next, and Ricardo helped him down.

The outside of the pod still radiated an uncomfortable heat, and Victor stepped back from the pod and stumbled on the uneven ground. He steadied himself and looked around.

It was his first time on Horseshoe Planet, and he drew in a deep breath, smelling the cool moist air with the faint tang of alien life. Wherever they had managed to land, the sun had already gone below the horizon. In the gathering dusk, he could see that they were on a broad brush-covered foothill. A fitful breeze came down from the hills above them, and when it gusted, one of their landing parachutes filled with air and tugged at the pod.

"That's the problem," said Ricardo, as he helped Ruby and Cydney down from the pod.

Ruby grimaced, trying to straighten her tied-back hair. "That parachute should have detached."

Ricardo tugged on the lines and tried to collapse the parachute, but the wind gusted harder and kept the parachute spread. The pod rocked, threatening to roll further.

Victor patted his pockets until he found the souvenir knife, and he opened the largest blade. He asked Ricardo to hold the line taut. The blade was factory sharp, and after some sawing, the line parted. They cut a second line, and the parachute flapped loosely, a danger no longer.

"Where are we?" asked Cydney, but no one had an answer.

Below them they could make out the edge of a forest, above them part of a mountain range. When Victor looked straight up, he could see a star. "Wherever we are, we're not going anywhere tonight."

Ricardo straightened his shirt. "Well, then. Survival mode. We need food, water, clothing, and shelter. We will not starve overnight, so food's not critical. We can't look for water in the dark, but we'll survive that too."

"I'm thirsty," said Cydney.

Ricardo ignored her. "What we're wearing will have to do, because it's all we have. As for shelter..." He reached up patted the pod, now a dark mass in the fading light. "She's stable now, even though she's tilted. We had best spend the night inside. The seats are padded, and we'll be warm."

We're on the planet and not in space, so he's taking charge. Ruby might not like that.

"Why did we all get out if we just have to get back in?" asked Cydney.

Ruby reached up and felt the lower edge of the doorway. "I remember that there's supposed to be a ladder or something."

Ricardo helped Victor climb back into the pod. By the side of the door he found a panel marked LADDER that they had overlooked. The rope ladder had solid steps, and once he unrolled it, Cydney, Ruby and Ricardo easily climbed back in.

It seemed to take forever to settle down for the night. Ruby dimmed the lights; Ricardo found some aluminized rescue blankets, crinkly but warm. Victor read the endless instructions alongside the toilet. There was no water inside, and because of the tilt, the facility was useless except as a source of paper.

They reclined the seats until reasonably comfortable. Victor felt sleep coming on him; he could have slept soundly on the floor if he had to.

The door had to remain open for the sake of air, but the blankets kept the chill away. He listened to the sounds of the night as he began to drift. Something made a ratcheting noise like a socket wrench; something else made a soft pinging. Far in the distance, something huge roared.

It was a new world, a strange world, but he did okay in the wilds. Whatever tomorrow would bring, he would be able to handle it easier than walking into a new school or institution. Or prison…

Cydney tapped his arm. "Victor?"

"Yes?"

"I have to go to the bathroom."

Chapter Five

A faint rustling sound woke him.

He opened his eyes, pulling himself up from the dark of sleep. In the filtered light of dawn, he could see across the double ring of seats to the empty cabinets beyond. He swallowed. His mouth was dry and his stomach empty. Cydney slept in the chair next to him, her mouth open, her face relaxed, her wavy brown hair tangled.

He stretched his neck and looked towards the open portal, wondering what had made the rustling noise. He could see the light seeping into the ship, and the brush in the field beyond. Something moved in the portal, but he couldn't make sense of it. He rolled over, wiped his hand over his face, and looked again.

Reaching into the ship was a long, blue-gray tentacle, probing tentatively. It had concentric rings and moved like a snake.

Ricardo was already on his feet. "Don't move," he whispered.

"What is that?"

"Big trouble. That's what we call a Gray Reaper. Stay where you are. Let me deal with it."

He heard a gasp behind him. Ruby sat up, her hand over her mouth, her eyes wide with fear. The tentacle swept across the floor, swinging towards the sleeping Cydney.

"Keep the girls inside," Ricardo yelled, and leaped onto the snake-like limb.

From outside the portal came a loud squeal and the tentacle curled around Ricardo's waist. He gripped it like a wrestler and tried to pin it down, but it dragged him inexorably towards the exit.

"What should I do?" yelled Victor, getting to his feet.

"Stay put! I've got this...." His sentence ended in a yelp as the tentacle hauled him out the portal.

Ruby and Victor collided with each other getting to the portal, but Victor turned around to get the hunting rifle. He prayed that it was loaded as he rushed back to the entrance and climbed down the rope ladder.

Shouts, bellows, and dust marked where Ricardo fought a writhing mass of tentacles. The reaper easily outweighed the man, and one of its foot-thick tentacles was wrapped around Ricardo's waist. The tentacles centered on a dark oval body with a ring of blinking eyes. The Reaper bellowed repeatedly, though Victor could not tell where the mouth was. The tentacles thrashed about too swiftly for him to count.

Victor expected the Reaper to rip off Ricardo's head at any moment. Ricardo kicked at the beast, shouting and swearing, but steadily and surely it was dragging him further away.

Victor fumbled with the rifle, cursing himself for not studying it before. He did not know how to cock it or how to take off the safety; he couldn't even tell if it was loaded.

Fortunately, the rifle's readiness didn't matter. With a cry, Ricardo peeled the tentacle from around his waist and threw himself to the ground. The Gray Reaper squealed and rolled away through the brush, kicking up dirt right and left.

Ruby cried out, "Ricky! Are you hurt?" as she ran to him. Victor shouldered the useless gun and watched the reaper disappear over a ridge in a flurry of tentacles.

Ricardo lay face down, his shoulders convulsing. Ruby rolled him over and put her hands on his cheeks, looking for injuries.

Wait a minute. Ricardo's not acting right....

Victor's eyes narrowed.

48

Ricardo wasn't choking. He was laughing, louder and louder, his head back and his mouth open. Ruby looked at him perplexed. "What?"

Ricardo pushed himself up on his elbows and wiped his eyes. "That gets 'em every time! Whoooeee!"

Cydney yelled from the portal. "What was that awful thing?"

"A Gray Reaper," shouted Ricardo, sitting up. "Just a scavenger."

"But it was killing you," said Ruby. "It pulled you out of the pod and...and...."

"No, no, no." Ricardo grinned widely and dusted off his shirt. "It was just looking for food, whatever it could find. Small things, dead things. I had to hang on to it just so it wouldn't run away." He hooted. "You should have seen the look on your faces."

Ruby punched Ricardo's shoulder hard enough that he fell sideways. "You beast!" she shouted. "You worthless *pig*! I thought you were being killed!"

"Ow! Hey, it's all part of your first visit to the planet! It's an initiation. I do this with all the tourists. Scares the pants off of them."

Victor slid the rifle off his shoulder. "I almost fired at you."

"You couldn't. The clip's in my pocket."

Victor wasn't amused. "I might have had the pistols. I know how to use those."

Ricardo rubbed the back of his neck, chagrined that no one was finding his joke amusing. "You're smart enough; you wouldn't have fired carelessly."

"To protect Ruby and Cydney? If it meant killing you while killing that thing, I would have." Victor looked at Ricardo with a level gaze.

"Yes, well, it certainly didn't come to that, did it?"

"No, it didn't." Victor tossed the rifle to Ricardo and climbed back up the rope ladder.

Cydney grabbed Victor's arm. "I don't understand."

"Ricardo was just pretending that thing out there was dangerous. He was playing a joke."

"Oh. It sounded like he was dying."

Victor shook his head. "His idea of fun."

"I'm hungry. And I'm really, really thirsty."

"We'll go for water now. Get your things."

She wrapped her doll's arms around her neck and stuck her hands out to show that they were empty. "I don't have any things except Peggity. I was wearing my outdoor stuff when we had to run, but my other new clothes got left behind."

Victor buckled the gun belt around his waist, and then tucked ammunition into his cargo pockets. "I'm sorry about your robodog, Cydney."

"It was just another toy. Thanks for thinking about it."

"Ricardo was right, though. It could have killed all of us if I'd gone back inside. You saw what happened to the casino." He put on his hat, wishing he had his New Zealand backpack filled with cook gear and spices and clean underwear. "Let's go see what their plans are."

When he descended the rope ladder, Ruby, still in the gray pants and white work shirt she had been wearing when they had to abandon the casino, said to Victor, "You shouldn't be carrying guns around."

"I know how to use them."

"They're dangerous. Ricardo should carry them."

"Ricardo has the rifle."

Ricardo interrupted. "Let him be, Ruby. I checked him out at the firing range. And in this wilderness, having him armed will keep us all safer."

"I don't like it." She folded her arms. "We had alarm chips put in those weapons so they wouldn't be taken from the range. I knew it would cause trouble if guests wandered off with them."

Ricardo changed the subject by waving his arm at the forest. "We need to decide which way to go."

"We should stay here." Ruby looked up at the rescue pod towering over them. "People have lost their lives by leaving their crashed airplanes or transports."

"That was only when there was a chance of rescue. No one is going to know that the casino was lost until your supply ship comes next month, and even then, they probably won't have a planetary shuttle with them. The *Nairobi* had one, but it was a pleasure ship and we were planning on going down to the planet."

"Won't they come looking for us?" asked Cydney.

"As I said, no one monitors for distress signals here. Do you have a communicator with you?"

Cydney frowned. "Sort of, but it isn't getting a network. I can't call anybody."

Ruby looked despondent. "We weren't ready to.... This pod wasn't equipped with one."

"How about the pod that Gary took? Did it have one?"

"I don't know." She spread her hands. "Look, Ricky, what was important to me was getting the gambling equipment installed, getting the lights for the performers running, getting the whole thing put together. We didn't think about disasters that weren't supposed to happen, or about trying to contact people like Chancel that wouldn't be happy to hear from us."

Ricardo brushed the side of his thin mustache with his fingertip. "The *Titanic* wasn't supposed to have disasters either."

Cydney rolled her eyes. "Can't we just go?"

"The trouble is," said Ricardo, "that I have no idea which direction to go to get to the station, or how far it is. It could be just over the mountain or on the other side of the planet."

Ruby turned in a circle, surveying the mountain above them and the forest below. "You don't recognize this place?"

Ricardo snorted. "I've never been more than a hundred kilometers from Horseshoe Station, and this is a huge planet, practically Earth-size. It's like being raised in Miami and suddenly being dropped off in Tibet. Except you don't know it's Tibet, and there's no one to ask."

"Excuse me," said Victor. "How did you find your way back when you were on safari?"

"Homing beacon," said Ricardo. "Horseshoe Station keeps a constant signal going. It reassures the guests."

51

"Cydney, can your polybot find a homing signal?"

Cydney frowned and pulled open Peggity. "Maybe. I was only looking to see if I could make a call."

Ricardo peered at the opened doll. "What is that? I thought it was just a rag doll."

"It can do different things," said Cydney.

Ruby looked over Cydney's shoulder as she tapped the buttons. After many frowns and much tapping, Cydney said, "Okay. I found something. There's a strong signal coming from....." She turned around in a circle, and then turned back, slowly. "...from that way." She pointed, and then lifted her head.

She was pointing at their own rescue pod.

Ricardo lifted his hat, ran his fingers through his hair, and laughed. "Well, that's good. We won't lose our rescue pod. Any other signals?"

Cydney glared at him and turned her back. She resumed tapping at her polybot.

Victor stepped aside and looked at the new world, now highlighted by the morning sun. The forest below them consisted of tall, sturdy trees, but the gray-green circular leaves trembled like aspen. The shrubs the pod had landed on had narrow green leaves that smelled faintly of sour lemon. Creatures like butterflies with huge gossamer wings chased each other lazily, landing briefly on the shrubs.

Something in a shrub slurped, and a butterfly disappeared.

The mountains looked bare, but here and there stretched a patch of sprawling green. The clouds were the same clouds as those that graced the skies of Earth or Septimus. In some ways, the planet felt so alien because some parts felt so familiar.

"There," said Cydney.

Victor broke out of his reverie. "What?"

"There's a signal almost the same as the rescue pod, but weaker, over that way." She pointed towards the southwest, and then moved her finger further west. "And one even weaker that way."

"Probably Gary and Ramon's rescue pods," said Ruby.

52

"But THAT way," said Cydney, pointing northwest "is the weakest signal, but it's real different than the others."

The direction she was pointing was beyond the forest.

"Then we go northwest," said Ricardo. "That would be Horseshoe Station and a ride off the planet."

Ruby shook her head. "I'd say southwest."

"Why?"

"Even if Gary left without us, he's got supplies in his pod. And I'm going to give him a piece of my mind." Her face fell. "And of course, we left without Ramon. We owe it to him to try to find him. If we survive."

Ricardo smiled. "Of course, we'll survive. After all, you've got me."

"Can't we just go?" asked Cydney. "I want some water right now!"

"Of course, young missy." Ricardo bowed his head. "We'll go, and we'll go southwest first, towards other rescue pods. Have we got everything? There will be no coming back."

Victor started to say yes, but paused. He had learned not to trust himself. Without saying anything, he clambered back up the rope ladder and went through the pod once more, opening every drawer he could reach.

On the pillar that held the controls, behind a long thin panel, he found a light but solid pair of slip-joint pliers and a screwdriver with an interchangeable flat head and Phillips head. He puzzled over finding these particular two tools in an empty ship, but gratefully slipped them into a cargo pocket in his pants. After one long look about the pod that had saved their lives, he slipped out the door.

It was time to leave.

*

The sun was overhead before they found a trickle of water that coursed its way down the hillside. Ricardo held Cydney back while he looked upstream.

Satisfied, he said, "It looks okay. Drink slowly; it's probably icy cold."

Cydney stuck her mouth in the water and sucked it in until she gasped for air and belched. Victor waited until Ruby and Ricardo had drunk their fill before walking upstream and scooping up handfuls of water, watching the surroundings as he sipped.

The shrubs in this area stretched taller than Ricardo, but were not proper trees. They sprang from the ground as a thicket of branches, spreading out like a fan to catch the light. In between was a mix of bare gravel and tough mat-like plants.

He felt in his pocket for his last pill and hesitated. Should he take it? He did okay in the wilderness; it was just in civilization that he didn't work right. Perhaps he should save it for when, or if, they managed to rescue themselves.

He opened his hand and let it be.

Ruby complained that she only had on deck shoes. Cydney demanded food, and Ricardo pointed out that they should all be grateful that it was summer on the northern hemisphere -- they had no coats or gloves, just the thin aluminum rescue blankets. If they had landed on the southern continent where it was hard winter, they would have had to stay with the pod until they starved or died of old age.

Victor stepped away from the tiny stream and examined the shrubs. The yellow-green leaves looked tough and stringy. Some of the branches had seedpods hanging from the tips. At least, they looked like seedpods; the tip narrowed into a wicked-looking thorn. He pulled one off and carefully split it open with his thumb, finding four bean-like seeds nestled inside. "Ricardo?"

"Yes?"

"Can we eat these?" He held up the pod with the seeds showing.

"Ah....as far as I know."

"As far as you know?" Ruby raised her eyebrows. "Don't you know?"

"Well, not about these. The plants around Horseshoe Station I know, but they don't have these plants there."

Victor popped a seed into his mouth and chewed slowly, waiting for the taste.

"What are you doing!" Ruby looked him like a mother who found her idiot child dancing on a roof.

Victor shrugged and put another in his mouth. They were bland but not distasteful. It reminded him of raw potato. "I'm seeing what they're like."

"But they could be poisonous!"

He tapped a seedpod still on the bush. "See that thorn? It's so they don't get eaten. It's protecting its seeds, and if they were poison, it wouldn't need to."

"I wouldn't trust that reasoning," said Ricardo.

Victor shrugged. "We're going to need something to eat, and we haven't seen anything else so far."

Ricardo straightened his hat. "Well, that's because I've only been looking for water up until now."

Sometimes Ricardo has his Aussie accent, sometimes not. I wonder when he's being the most genuine?

"I'm hungry," said Cydney. "Really, really. Can I have some?"

"Not yet," said Victor. He popped the last two seeds in his mouth. "Let's walk a while and see if I drop dead or not."

She looked at him anxiously, so he smiled as though he had made a joke.

I hope they're not poisonous. I would hate for her to lose her big brother.

They drank from the cold trickle one last time and started westward again. Ruby clucked at him like a mother hen for testing the brushbeans, but Ricardo solemnly put his hand on Victor's shoulder and squeezed once.

It was a compliment of sorts.

Chapter Six

The brushbeans did not kill Victor, and Ricardo found nothing better.

When they came to another patch of the brushbean plants, everyone pitched in to gather more, although after pulling off a dozen pods, Cydney slowed down and rested more than she gathered. She opened the pods and ate the seeds as she harvested them, so by the time they stopped for the night she had no pods left to contribute. She wrapped her foil blanket around herself and lay down on a mat of green under a shrub while Ricardo gathered wood and Victor started a fire.

Using the flat edge of the screwdriver to scrape the metal hot stick on his souvenir knife, he sparked a flame from tinder and built up a pleasant fire, a fire with strange aromatic smoke from the broken brush. The evening was warm but having a fire was comforting and might keep away bugs and dangerous things. Or attract them.

He roasted some of the brushbeans by laying them on a flat rock near the fire. They softened inside and developed a pungent crust that made him wish he had some salt. He gathered more until the light failed, laying them around the fire for the next day.

Ricardo stretched his legs out towards the flames and turned to Victor. "That was heads-up of you to get that screwdriver from the pod. Do you know why every ship in space now carries a screwdriver and pliers near the controls?"

"In case they're needed?"

Ricardo shifted his feet. "You were supposed to say, 'No, I don't.'"

Victor cleared his throat. "No, I don't. Why does every ship in space carry a screwdriver and pliers near the controls?"

Ricardo nodded. "I'll tell you why. It goes way back to Rosie Pony, a woman who was mining rare earths from the Arcadia asteroid belt."

Ruby spoke up. "You mean Rosita Poña."

"I'm telling this story. Anyway, her donkey pod had a full bin and she tried to fire up the engine so she could start the three week return to base. Turns out, she had an electrical short under the control panel. All she needed to do was to remove the cover plate, trim the wires, reset the breaker, and she'd be on her way. Trouble was, she had no screwdriver."

Ricardo tossed a branch on the fire. "The pod was new and everything was ship-shape, but the person who had screwed on the cover plate was some muscular guy who tightened the screws in tighter than a...." He glanced at Cydney. "Well, they were tight. Rosy couldn't loosen them.

"They found her dead months later, her ship drifting among the asteroids. She had tried everything, edges of cans, her belt buckle, even her fingernails which were torn and bloodied."

"Couldn't she radio for help?" asked Victor.

"The radio was powered by the same circuit. Anyway, every since then, there's not a ship that sets out without having pliers and screwdrivers somewhere easy to get to. It's no comfort to her, I suppose, but by her death Rosie has saved the lives of several crews." Ricardo stroked his mustache thoughtfully. "True story. I usually stretch it out for the tourists, add a few details, and I've had some in tears at the end."

"It is sad," said Cydney, as she leaned against Victor's shoulder. She popped a couple roasted beans in her mouth.

"It's often the little things that cause trouble," said Ruby. "If Oscar had left earlier and gotten the sweeper working, it would have cleared the orbit and we'd still be at the Casino."

"Yes, and if that little bit of rock had missed our ship, I'd be leading a safari right now, probably telling that same story for big tips."

"A little thing got me in trouble once," said Victor, and immediately regretted it.

"How's that?" asked Ricardo.

"Oh, back in grade school." He shifted his feet. "It was on Septimus, you know, the big mining colony."

Ricardo sat up. "You were on the planet Septimus? The one that had the Collapse?"

Victor nodded. "Yes. This was before that, the little thing that caused trouble. Anyway, the teacher passed out math workbooks the first day of the school year, so I took mine home, and started it. I kind of zoned into it, I guess, and I finished it late that night. Next day, I handed it in and she starts yelling at me. Turns out it was supposed to be for the entire school year, and I was only supposed to do a section a week, but I hadn't heard that part. So then she wanted me to erase everything I had done, because they didn't have an extra book to give me. I wouldn't do that, though, and...." He stopped and watched the flames dancing over the branches. "So that was it, kind of a small thing, I guess."

"How did you manage to do a year's work in one night?" asked Ruby.

Victor shrugged. "It wasn't that hard." He spoke slowly, trying to explain without making them concerned. "I kind of get into things sometimes and my brain starts going a kilometer a second. But I'm okay now."

"I'm sleepy," said Cydney. She lay down again and pulled the foil blanket over her head. "Everybody stop talking."

Ruby rolled her eyes and made a face, mouthing words at Ricardo.

Victor put some thicker branches on the fire and patted the cargo pocket that held the screwdriver and pliers.

Thank you, Rosie.

He pictured her in her small cabin, having tried everything, waiting for her air, food, or fuel to run out. What thoughts did she have? Did she write letters? Did she curse the man who screwed the panel on so tight, or did she have a family that she prayed for?

He was surprised to find a tear sliding down his cheek.

The pills are wearing off. It's been years since I've cried.

He turned away quickly so the others wouldn't see and found a soft place on the mat of vegetation near the fire where he settled down for the night. His thoughts turned to his uncle, with his thinning hair and his quick laugh, the uncle who had found him in prison on Septimus and had cared enough to get the doctor from St. Jude to figure out what was wrong with him. His uncle, who had died of explosive decompression when a meteoroid that shouldn't have been there tore through their ship.

He couldn't remember the last time he had cried himself to sleep.

*

Something blinked at him.

Dawn had not yet arrived. Only the planet's faint ring and the shepherd moons overhead cast light, but it was enough that Victor could see two eyes reflecting in the foliage.

He had risen early, and in a restless mood had walked away from the others who were still asleep. His eyes had adjusted to the darkness and his pockets were full of raw brushbeans he had idly gathered as he walked.

Something else, it appeared, was gathering brushbeans.

That something else slowly reached down and picked up a stick. It tapped it against the thick stem of the tall brush next to it.

Is it warning me to go away? It is about to charge? Or is it calling others?

A familiar acrid smell at the back of his throat signaled that his hyper-D was active again, something the pills had long held in check. The creature's arm moved in slow motion as Victor's brain sped up.

It's a red ape.

He could just make out the two-legged creature, the long arms with too many joints, a bean pod in one hand. He couldn't quite see the serrated biting ridges and the folds like lips that surrounded them, but he could picture the face from the nature video in his room. Was this a small female or a large aggressive male? Was it a creature like this that had torn apart one of Ricardo's friends?

Victor's emotions, newly awakened, began to surge. Fear and anger flowed together; part of him wanted to run away, part of him wanted to attack. Why had he foolishly walked away from camp without his gun belt? He had let his newly-wakened emotions cloud his judgment, had gone into the brush without precautions.

He held still. It was up to the red ape to make the next move. It tapped a few more times and stopped, staring at him.

Victor remained motionless.

Its eyes closed and there was a rustle of leaves. It was gone.

He exhaled and wiped the sweat from his hands on his shirt. He wanted to charge after the creature, to challenge it, to learn more about it. The sensible part of him prevailed, however, and he turned and began walking back to camp.

He ripped a bean pod off a brush and shelled the beans. He popped one into his mouth and surprised himself by laughing aloud.

My beans. Not yours, you big red hairy ape. So there!

He returned to the camp in a noisy good mood and stoked up the fire. He strapped on his gun belt and folded up his survival blanket. By the time the others had grumbled themselves awake, he had a belly full of roasted beans and was whistling an old mining tune. He didn't mention the encounter. No reason to make them concerned.

Not long after starting out again, they found the remains of a beast that looked somewhat like a rhino, if a rhino had flat grinding plates instead of teeth and short coarse hair. The carcass was torn open and partly consumed.

Victor tapped the black horn on the snout with a stick. "What killed this?"

Ricardo took off his hat and squatted down to examine the remains. "Could be...um...well, red apes might do this, but I haven't heard of it. No, look at the neck. It wasn't apes."

Victor pointed with a stick. "You mean here? Something bit it."

"Something with actual teeth, and the red apes don't have separate teeth, just ridges like saw blades. I haven't seen that before."

The video back on the space station – I remember that the mounted red ape had serrated ridges instead of teeth. It would make a different wound than this when biting flesh.

Ricardo stood up and looked around him, his brow furrowed. "There's something big hunting around here that I haven't seen before. The sooner we get to Horseshoe Station the happier I'll be."

Victor looked at Ricardo, dressed in his cream-colored safari outfit. The man was experienced, but they were in new territory, unknown territory. Ricardo was uncertain but trying to maintain a brave front.

Ruby, on the other hand, was weighed down by her loss of the casino. She was also burdened by Ricardo's presence. She argued with him, and seemed angry with him, but Victor now realized that all her movements during the day centered on Ricardo. She was clearly attracted to her old fiancé and angry with him at the same time.

Cydney, of course, was useless.

He tossed away the stick and circled the kill in a fruitless effort to find prints in the ground. It was up to him, he decided. He was the one who could look at the world around them with heightened senses, with unbiased eyes.

He would have to take care of everyone else.

*

Oceans are the same everywhere on earth-like planets. The ocean that separated the two halves of the Horseshoe continent was salty from ages of evaporation as rivers carried minerals to the sea and clouds brought fresh rain back to the

61

mountains. Breakers roared as they rolled against the sandy shore, a shifting layer of grains too large to wash away and too small to resist the grinding waves.

They stood on the beach and looked at the distant horizon, lost in the mist thrown up by the crashing surf. Victor could taste salt on his lips from the spray of the waves.

"Okay," said Ricardo. "It looks like we couldn't walk straight to Horseshoe Station if we wanted to. We must have landed on the eastern leg of the horseshoe continent, and the station's on the western leg. We'll have to go south, then north. This could take longer than I thought."

"I want to play in the ocean!" said Cydney, spreading her arms in the hot sun.

Ruby shook her head. "You want grit and salt all over you the rest of the day? There aren't any showers on this beach, you know."

"There's fresh water in the streams; they can wash afterwards," said Ricardo. "Let the kids have some fun."

I didn't ask to play in the ocean.

Ruby frowned. "Oceans on Earth have sharks and jellyfish. What's on this planet? Do you know what's living in that water?"

"Okay, okay." Ricardo gave up a fight he couldn't win. He turned to Cydney, who was pulling off her boots. "Hold your horses, young lady. We'll walk until we get to a bay or someplace with clear water. If we stay close to shore, it should be safe to swim a bit."

Ruby folded her arms. "Should be? Should be? Have you ever taken tourists swimming?"

"Well, no."

"Then you have no idea if it's safe or not. Don't promise what you can't deliver." Ricardo clenched his jaw and his face darkened. Ruby ignored his response and looked to the south. "We need to go that way to find the other rescue pods, but we'll get burned if we walk along the beach all day."

"It looks like jungle to the south, though," said Ricardo, his voice tightly controlled. "Red ape territory. I'd rather risk sunburn than walk through there."

"You've got a rifle. Why should you worry?"

"They hunt in packs. I could shoot half a dozen and the rest would still pull me apart."

Cydney had her socks off and her boots tied around her neck, where they bounced on her chest with Peggity. She stood where the waves ran up onto the sand, letting the water flow over her feet. She grinned at Victor. "It's not cold."

He swallowed his pride and pulled off his boots. The two of them splashed through the surf, their pants rolled up, while Ruby and Ricardo walked on the dry sand and argued.

Large white birds, or what looked like birds, waded and dipped in the ocean waters. The birds had no fear of humans, and Victor got a close look as he walked past one. What passed for feathers was actually sleek hair, and the bird had slits on its neck that opened and closed. It puffed its neck and squawked at him. Cydney grabbed his arm and huddled close, but the bird merely went back to wading.

Ricardo pointed out a plate crab, brilliantly blue with numerous black legs, moving slowly along the edge of the ocean.

Victor remembered that plate crabs were edible. "Can we have some for dinner?" he asked.

"Sure, mate," said Ricardo, "but I'll have to show you how to crack 'em. They're a bit of work."

Cydney made a sour face. "Ewwww."

At a fresh water stream, Victor and Cydney washed off their feet and put back on their boots. Ricardo led them up into the brush, where they walked in the shade.

Taller trees appeared here and there in the brush, trees with slanted trunks. "That's what they do, those tangle trees," said Ricardo, ever the tour guide. "When they get thick they lean against each other and reach way up, high canopy. That's where the apes hang out. They don't travel in the brush, but pretty soon we're going to lose our brush and then we need to keep a lookout."

But the apes do gather food in the brush. We need to keep a lookout here as well.

63

Victor touched the handles of his guns just to reassure himself.

He wanted to walk slower. The butterflies clustered thick around the upper branches of the brush, where small red flowers attracted them. Miniature versions of the reaper that had reached into their pod clung on the upper branches, their tiny bodies and tentacles camouflaged a mottled green. They lay motionless beneath the red flowers, ready to snare a careless butterfly.

"Don't touch 'em, mate," said Ricardo. "You'll get a rash. Of course, those butterflies aren't harmless, either. They'll sting if you try to catch them. Yep, like that. Told you."

*

The evening mealtime was when disaster struck.

Ricardo and Victor had spent more time than they had expected gathering four plate crabs, one for each of them, and they returned to the chosen campsite to find Ruby arguing with Cydney.

"You've got to pitch in and start doing some work around here," said Ruby, her arms folded. "We have a long hike ahead of us and you've got to do your part."

Cydney stuck her lip out. "You can't make me! You're not my Mom!"

"We can't keep carrying you. You've got to start…."

"You're not carrying me! I'm walking all by myself!"

"I meant that we're doing everything for you. You need to gather firewood if you want to eat. There's only four of us…"

"That's dirty work and I won't do that! I won't wash or cook or clean. Other people do that."

"There are no other people to do it. You've got to get firewood."

"I won't!" She planted her fists on her hips. "It's scratchy and heavy and someone else can do it!"

Ricardo put down his crabs, still waving their dozens of legs slowly in the air. "What's all this?"

"I'm not going to do all the work while this girl sits around," said Ruby, her eyes blazing. "If she wants to eat dinner she can go and get some firewood."

Ricardo put on a conciliatory smile and turned to Cydney. "Listen, little lady, if Ruby says..."

"No!" shouted Cydney. "I won't and you can't make me!" She turned and ran into the forest.

Ruby sighed. "I'm sorry, Ricardo. I don't know how to deal with children."

"No, no, it's not you." He stepped next to Ruby and gave her a sideways hug. "You've been a good sport, you have, better than a lot of tourists I've had to swag around."

"Don't be patronizing," said Ruby, removing his arm from her shoulder.

Victor pulled his attention away from Ruby and Ricardo. They were distracted by each other. He needed to follow Cydney.

He walked towards the forest, following the path she had taken. She had been running but he knew that she would not go far. She had no destination; she just wanted to make a statement.

I bet she's thrown a lot of fits on stage when she wanted her own way.

Theatre people would give in to her, of course. She was their bread and butter. That was the problem. She didn't know how to make herself do something that she didn't want to do, even if she knew she *should* do it. There was always someone else to do it for her.

The tall shrubs gave way to tangle trees. They were sparse at first, scraggly but further ahead he could see that they grew much higher. As he walked into the trees, he picked up the sound of sobbing, and followed it into a clearing made by a fallen tree. On the tree sat Cydney, her face in her hands.

She hadn't responded to threats. Probably logic wouldn't work either. Perhaps he needed to be a friend to her. He stayed at the edge of the clearing. "Cydney?"

"Go away." She kept her face in her hands, her sobs suddenly louder and more dramatic.

"Come on back to camp. I'll help you gather wood." Something tickled at his brain, but he concentrated on Cydney.

"No. Ruby's mean and she hates me."

"She doesn't hate you."

"Yes, she does. She wants me to be a little servant girl and do what she tells me to, and I won't do it."

"That's not what...." He suddenly realized what his subliminal senses were telling him.

They were surrounded by red apes.

Motionless, their fur blending into the dark colors of the tangle trunks, only their blinking eyes gave them away. Cydney had not seen them as she ran into the clearing and sat on the fallen tree. Victor had not spied them either, his concern centered on Cydney.

He felt his brain accelerating, the sour smell rising in the back of his throat and the clearing coming into tight focus.

If I tell Cydney she's surrounded by apes, she'll scream and run, and they might attack.

"Cydney. You need to come with me right now. It's important."

"No."

A tapping sound started. One of the apes had a stick in his hand. Quietly, slowly, another started tapping, and another. A tiny ape huddled in a ball, its remarkably long arms wrapped over its head.

"I'm not kidding, Cydney. Come here."

"No. I won't, and stop making that noise!"

The tapping got louder, but to his mind it also got slower. The one advantage of his condition was that in a situation like this he had time to think, and he was now thinking furiously.

Every ape had a stick and was tapping on a branch or a trunk.

What does that mean? Why are they doing that?

He swallowed, his mouth dry. Should he grab Cydney and carry her away before they attacked?

A branch snapped outside of the clearing, and the tapping stopped. Every ape turned its head in that direction.

66

With a roar, a scaly creature with yellow eyes crashed into the clearing, knocking one of the smaller apes to the ground. With dagger-like teeth it bit the ape's throat, cutting off its screams. It reminded Victor of the odd-looking dinosaurs that paleontologists reconstructed from earth fossils, and though it was only slightly bigger than the apes, it was far more muscular and deadly, a true carnivore.

Cydney leaped to her feet and shrieked, her shriek echoed by the screams from the apes, as the clearing suddenly exploded with motion. Apes leaped into the overhead branches, their many-jointed arms pulling them to safety. One snatched up the baby and carried it upwards.

Another red ape, the largest in the clearing, leaped up onto the fallen tree beside Cydney and wrapped an arm around her waist. Cydney screamed, "Victor! Help meeee!"

Victor drew his guns, but before he could shoot, the ape lifted the struggling Cydney into the branches. The last he saw was her eyes white with terror.

The yellow-eyed carnivore raised its head, and focused on Victor. With a snarl, it left its kill and charged, its open jaws displaying rows of bloody yellow teeth.

Victor swung his guns and fired rapidly, again and again, the pistols bucking in his hands, trying to stop the predator that sought his blood. He fired with concentration and deadly accuracy.

The creature fell at his feet, bit at the air, and died.

He looked up into the branches. Screams echoed among the treetops as the troop of apes ran away, Cydney's screams mingled with them.

He pulled the empty clip from one gun and began thumbing bullets into it. Something ran up behind him and he whirled, but it was only Ricardo and Ruby.

"What happened?" cried Ruby. "Why were you shooting? What was all that screaming?"

Ricardo put his hand on Victor's shoulder. "You killed one of those things! The predator! Look at those teeth!"

Ruby pushed past them. "Where's Cydney? Where is she?"

Victor finished filling the clip and slid it back into the gun. He holstered it and with grim efficiency pulled the other gun and began reloading its clip. "Cydney was taken by red apes."

"Dear lord!" Ruby put her fist over her mouth.

"No. Oh, no." Ricardo pulled off his hat, his face stricken. "You don't mean it."

Victor nodded. "She was sitting on that log. One of the large apes hauled her up into the branches."

"Then she's dead," said Ricardo. "She's dead. I shouldn't have let her run off." He crushed his hat in his hands. Ruby tried to speak, but she fell to her knees in grief.

Victor snapped the clip back into the gun and the gun back into its holster. "She's not dead."

"What do you mean, she's not dead? I've seen them kill!" Ricardo's voice shook with emotion. "One of them ripped a partner of mine to pieces, and he was a strong man! She's just a little girl! She's dead!"

"You don't know as much about these apes as you think you do and I don't have time to argue," said Victor. "I'm going after her."

"That's madness! They'll kill you, too. I won't let you do it!"

Victor turned and faced Ricardo directly, his fists clenched, trying to control the anger boiling inside of him. "Listen to me, Ricardo. You do *not* know what you're talking about! I know more about them already than you've learned in months of hunting them, and one thing I'm certain of is that Cydney is not dead! I'm going after her."

Ricardo reached out to grab him by the sleeve, but Victor knocked his hand away. "Don't touch me!" He pointed his finger like a gun. "I'm off my medication and you have *no* idea how dangerous I am right now!" He stepped back from them and glanced up at the branches, gauging his climb. "Go back to camp. If I'm not back by morning, break camp, fire once into the air, and head south. Shoot in the air at noon also. I'll find you, don't you look for me. Do *not* shoot when you find a place to camp for the night; you could attract another predator and I don't think you could handle it." He stepped up onto a slanting trunk and grabbed a branch.

Ricardo and Ruby stared at him, their mouths open.

"I'll be okay." He tried to reassure them with a humorless smile. "I'm just going to get my little sister."

He jumped up onto the branch, and disappeared into the tangle trees.

Chapter Seven

Victor climbed from branch to branch, his boots finding purchase on the trunks. The sun was near the horizon and the upper canopy was still in full light.

Scratches on the tender branches revealed the flight of the apes. They had been spooked by the scaly predator and probably by Victor's gunfire. They were digging deep and moving fast.

He reached a height where the troop of red apes had stopped climbing and started moving forward through the trees. The branches were uneven, and he had to move carefully as he followed the signs of their passage. At this height, a fall could be fatal.

The foliage thickened, but as he squeezed between two branches, he stumbled into a hollow area and stood there dumbstruck. It was not just a hollow. It was a tunnel, a tunnel high in the treetops shaped by the growth of the tangle tree branches.

The tunnel was large enough that he could run through it standing upright, if he didn't fall between the branches. Two people could run side by side, because the tunnel was wider than it was tall.

How was this made? Who made it?

He walked slowly to the north, his hands touching the leafy ceiling in wonder. The floor, the walls, the ceiling were not solid; they were just branches of the trees that grew around the tunnel. At any point, he could step out of the tunnel, or fall through the gaps if he wasn't careful.

But why did the tunnel exist? Why didn't branches grow through and block it? Did giant snakes slide through here, or monstrous swarms of insects?

The apes with Cydney had passed through here. Signs of their passage were evident: more fresh scratches on the younger branches. He couldn't tell if they had headed north or south, so he chose north at random and began moving.

How far do these tunnels extend? Has anyone seen them before?

Ricardo had probably not seen the tree tunnels. In fact, as he thought about the safari expeditions with their wealthy patrons led by Ricardo, a crawler following behind with luxuries, he was sure the guide had not bothered to scale the trees, had not bothered to follow the apes into their natural habitat.

The scaly predator with the yellow eyes – it did not look like it could climb trees. In the trees, the apes would be safe, unless there were yet other dangers. There might be things like tree snakes that could prey on the young. He looked carefully as he walked, wary of some alien species lying in wait for a passing ape, a species that might also strike at a passing human.

Through a space between branches, he saw that the sun had sunk below the horizon. He ran his fingers over the branches around him, looking for signs, but he didn't know what he was looking for. He did know, though, that in a strange place one should first study what is normal, and then be suspicious of anything abnormal.

He turned around, traveled past the point where he had left the ground, and went further south. The branches here had no fresh scratches on them, so he reasoned that the troop had headed north, and he turned around again. He moved as fast as he dared, listening carefully for cries or screams, anything that might give away where the troop might have gone with Cydney. At any point, they might have left the tunnel.

Something below his feet caught his eye, something different in color caught between two branches. He knelt, reached down, and pulled up Peggity Polybot.

71

Cydney was carried this way. She wouldn't deliberately drop Peggity. Unless she wanted someone to see it, in which case she's smarter than she lets on.

At least now he was certain that he was headed in the right direction.

The tree tunnel seemed endless, but the twilight was not. His foot slipped and he fell between two branches, barely catching himself from a nasty fall. He pulled himself up and lay on his back, waiting for his heart to stop racing and listening to the sounds around him. Among the ratchetings, the whistlings, the roars, and other strange noises, he heard nothing that sounded like a troop of red apes.

He had no choice but to wait until morning; it was too dark to continue. He did not even dare descend and look for water.

The night was long, noisy, and quite uncomfortable.

*

At dawn's first light, he headed north again, moving faster as the dawn spread over the skies and illuminated the tunnel. His feet became sure on the branches, and he developed an uneven gait that kept him going as he trotted through the passageway. He could gauge the spaces between branches well enough that he could keep watch for signs.

Why was I so sure that Cydney was not dead when I argued with Ricardo?

He replayed the scene in his mind: Cydney on the log, the predator crashing into the clearing, biting the throat of an ape. Cydney shrieked, and the apes shrieked. The littlest ape had a high-pitched cry, and it was picked up and carried to safety.

Cydney certainly did not look like an ape, but neither did she look like a predator. She had two arms and two legs, her girl's voice was high-pitched, and she was small. To the instincts of the large red ape, Cydney was just another baby calling for help.

They would not kill Cydney.

They might, however, abandon her, drop her somewhere, especially if she started acting like a spoiled child.

72

I'm so thirsty I can't swallow, but I could lose an hour going down looking for water and Cydney might not have an hour left.

He heard noises behind him and almost slipped off a branch as he stopped. Turning, he saw three red apes swinging up the tunnel towards him. This particular stretch of tunnel ran straight, so they were still a distance away.

I'm glad I didn't run headfirst into them, or surprised them by going around a corner.

He thought about pushing out of the side of the tunnel and running, but he did not know if that would set off the apes' instincts. It might cause a rampage. The safest strategy seemed to be to look harmless.

Squatting down and turning to the side, he reached between two thick branches and pulled off a twig with leaves. He pulled off one leaf and held it to his mouth, pretending to eat.

The sounds of feet and heavy breathing approached him, and then the feet stopped. Victor peeked over his shoulder, then quickly looked back at the twig and pulled off another leaf. They were standing behind him.

What should I do? Are they going to rip me apart? I am such an idiot; why didn't I run?

He put the leaf into his mouth and crunched it, ignoring the vile taste.

See? I'm just sitting here eating. Nothing to see here; keep moving, keep moving.

A branch broke behind him, and then he heard a tapping sound.

Again with the tapping. Why, why, why are they....?

He turned his twig around, and tapped on the thick bole in front of him with the stem. He tried to match the rhythm he heard behind him.

Tap. Tap. Tap. Tap.

He almost cried out as an ape thrust a branch in front of his face. It had round bluish balls on it the size of plums. His hands trembled with adrenalin as he pulled one off and bit it, hoping it was edible.

Okay, okay, we're doing social interactions here instead of ripping me into pieces. That's good. I tapped back so maybe they don't think I'm a predator or a member of a competing tribe. I'm funny-looking to them, but I tapped, so they offered me fruit. Does tapping mean "I'm not dangerous" or does it mean "Do you have any fruit?" Maybe it means "Fatten me up and kill me later?"

He turned sideways and held up the branch with leaves as an offering.

Each ape tugged a leaf off the branch and put it into their mouths. The larger ape squatted low and looked closely at him with large black eyes, eyes that had intelligence behind them. "Churrrrrrit?"

He debated making a high-pitched cry like Cydney.

No way. I am not going to make a sound. Any noise I make could be insulting or sound like aggression or something.

He took another bite of the fruit, which turned out to be quite sweet. The moisture satisfied his thirst.

The ape uncurled its arm, a multi-jointed arm that reminded Victor of the neck of a swan, reached out its two fingers, and touched Victor on the nose. "Churrrrrit?"

That's right, I have a nose and you don't. I'm ugly.

The other two apes, branches of fruit in their arms, chattered at the one crouched in front of Victor. It stood up, laid its branch over its shoulder, and led the others down the tunnel.

Victor exhaled. He had negotiated the first steps of apehood without being ripped apart.

They're social. If I only knew their social behavior, I could fit in. I could be just an incredibly ugly ape.

And if I made a wrong move, I could be dead.

The apes headed in the same direction as the troop that took Cydney, so he followed. One ape glanced back idly, but otherwise they ignored him.

When the tunnel divided, the apes took the right-hand fork, which led away from the coast. Victor looked at the scratches on the branches, and concluded that Cydney's troop of apes had taken the same fork. The scratches were faint; perhaps the troop had calmed down at this point of their flight. Perhaps the three apes were part of the same troop, if he were lucky.

The sun was fully risen when the apes dropped down through a gap in the tunnel. Victor stood at the gap and listened carefully.

He heard a sob.

Cydney.

She was alive, and hopefully uninjured. Who knows what sort of a night she had spent, trapped amid a troop of alien creatures?

He climbed down behind the three apes, who were tapping as they approached. The troop was on the ground but wary.

The largest ape, its face fringed with brilliant red hair, received one of the branches with fruit on it. It pulled some of the fruit off, gave one to the baby ape that was clinging to its chest, and another to Cydney, who sat at its feet.

She was slumped, and though her head was down, he could see a cut on her nose. Her wavy brown hair, dirty and bedraggled, was now short and irregular as though a blind barber had been clipping it. She ignored the fruit.

Victor stopped short of entering the small clearing. If Cydney saw him, she would cry out and run towards him. The apes might attack. He would have to warn her to sit still, and to let him mingle with the troop.

He climbed higher until he was out of sight, and then called softly. "Cydney?"

"Victor?" He heard rustling sounds and pictured her standing and looking around. "Victor!" she said louder. The apes began to stir.

"Be quiet, Cydney! Sit down! They'll carry you away again!"

He heard more rustling, and then her voice, quiet and trembling. "Victor? I'm so scared, Victor, please, please help me!"

"I will, but you have to sit calm. Eat that fruit."

"I don't want to. She bit me."

"Shhh. Eat it."

"Okay."

He wished he had a branch with fruit to bring, but the foliage around him had nothing. He pulled off a thin branch with leaves to carry down.

"Victor?"

"Yes?"

"She bit me on the nose."

"That's because they don't have noses. She might have thought you had a, I don't know, a giant tick or something."

He heard more rustling sounds down below, and then Cydney complained, "I screamed and it bled a lot. And then she bit off my hair!"

"Hush. I'm going to...." He heard a noise beside him, and when he turned, he was face to face with the same large red ape that had handed the fruit to Cydney. Its black eyes stared at him and the fleshy lips pulled back to expose the sharp ridges that took the place of teeth. Bright red hair stood out like a halo around its face.

Very carefully, Victor tapped the branch he was holding.

The ape grabbed the branch from him and broke it. It leaned closer and ran its two-fingered hand down Victor's face, sliding its fingers slowly over his nose. "Churrrrit Chrrt?"

His mind raced. There was only one thing he could think to do. He reached up, ripped off a leaf, and stuck it into his mouth. Ignoring the rancid flavor, he pulled off another leaf and held it out towards the ape.

The ape stuck out a blue-stained tongue. "Ptthhht." It slid back down out of sight.

My offering was rejected.

Somehow, he felt insulted.

He climbed down to the floor of the clearing, where the apes merely glanced at him and returned to snacking on the blue fruits. He sat by Cydney, who flung her arms around him and buried her face in his neck, sobbing.

He held her, waiting for the sobs to subside. The large red ape crouched down behind them and stroked Cydney's hair with her two fingers and then offered him a blue fruit.

76

He took it, bit it, and then lifted up Cydney's chin. "Here. You should eat some more. You need it, and it will make him happy."

Cydney looked at the fruit with puffy eyes, and then took a small bite. "Her."

"What?"

Cydney glanced at the red ape behind them. "That's a her, not a him. See her baby?"

"Ricardo said the big ones were males."

"Ricardo's stupid." She finished the fruit and tossed the pit. The baby pounced on it and sucked on it, removing the remains of the fruit from the large center seed. It brought the clean pit back to Cydney and handed it back to her.

Cydney tossed it again. The baby went "Chee!" and did a backwards flip. It leaped on the pit and then hopped around, waving the pit like a trophy. It fell down, bounced back up, and bounded back to its mother.

"Oh, hey," said Victor. "I found this on the trail." He reached into a cargo pocket and pulled out the polybot doll.

"Peggity!" Cydney brightened up and reached for the doll. "I dropped her and they wouldn't let me go back to get her! Thank you!" She brushed off bits of leaf from the doll, pulled its arms long, and then clipped them around her neck. She hugged Victor and planted a kiss on his cheek.

"Yea, yea, don't get them upset." He wiped his cheek. "Remember, they killed Ricardo's friend. If we scare them or do something wrong, they could kill us."

She nodded and huddled, hugging Peggity to her chest. "I know."

"They're kind of like that bird we saw that wasn't afraid of us because it hadn't seen anything like us. We don't look any of their enemies, but we're not exactly like them, either. I think they'll ignore us if we ignore them."

At that moment, the baby ape climbed over Cydney's back and into her lap. It turned around and wrapped its arms around her, tucking its head under her chin.

"Victor?" She squeaked, her eyes huge with panic. "What should I do?"

Victor looked at the mother ape, who was smacking her lips and staring up into the foliage. "Nothing. Don't do anything. The mother's not mad. Is it hurting you?"

"No."

"Just be still then. Pretend you're a baby sitter." He changed the subject. "I'm sorry about your hair. What happened?"

Cydney shivered. "She, the momma ape, she carried me here when they all ran away and then she held me, even when I screamed, so I couldn't get away." She hesitantly stroked the baby's back. "Then it got dark, and they got together and went to sleep, and I was tired and I couldn't get loose so I slept too. This morning she started poking at me, and bit my nose. I screamed and she stopped, but then she yanked at my hair, and then she started biting it off, big chunks of it. I didn't know what to do." She looked pained. "Can't we leave now? Please?"

"Soon. I think we can walk to the edge of the clearing and sit there for a while. If they don't get upset, we might be able to slip away."

"What was that big thing that made them run away?"

Victor shook his head as he touched the back of the baby ape, curious to see what the hair felt like. It was soft, more like fur. "A predator. It actually had teeth, the first animal I've seen here with teeth. Ricardo hadn't seen one before either."

"Like I said, he's stupid."

"No, he just doesn't know as much as he thinks. He's never been around here before. Let's go sit over by that tree and maybe we can get away."

They walked to the slanting trunk of a tangle tree and sat uncomfortably. "What's the baby doing?" asked Cydney. "I can't see his face."

"Sleeping, I guess. His eyes are closed."

"He smells like cinnamon, sort of. He's...." Cydney stroked the baby's back. "He's soft. I'd much rather have him for a pet than a robodog."

"I don't know if he's toilet trained."

78

"I'd put a diaper on him, like they do on chimps." She sighed. "It's my fault, isn't it?"

"What?"

"Us being here. I got us into trouble, running away, because I was mad at Ruby."

"Yes, actually."

She nodded, her eyes bleak. "I'm sorry."

"Listen, Cydney. You lost your parents, and I lost my Uncle. Ruby lost her casino. We all have big hurts right now."

Cydney closed her eyes and nodded again.

"But we've got to work together if we're going to survive. I know you and Ruby don't get along, but when she asks you to gather firewood, you need to do it."

"I'll do it if you ask me to do it."

"Okay, fine. Will you do chores if I ask you to do them?"

"Yes, 'cause you came to rescue me. Not them. Just you."

That's better than nothing. If she'll help out, maybe this group can hold together until we get to Horseshoe Station.

Group or gang. Same thing. I no sooner go off my medication than I'm part of a gang again.

He looked up at the slanted trunk. "Can you climb this?"

She patted it and nodded. "I'm a good climber. In Cydney and the Pirates, I had to swing on ropes and climb all over things. I can even dance on a beam. I should have gone to the Universal Olympics."

"Whatever. Go on up. Let's see what they do."

Cydney pulled herself up the trunk, and Victor had to admit that she had not exaggerated. In a moment, she was up in the foliage and out of sight. The large ape, the mother, turned over the fruit branch, looking for any blue fruit she might have missed. The other apes were lying around and grooming each other.

Victor moved up the trunk as quietly as possible.

Cydney stood in the tree tunnel, gripping a branch for balance. "Victor? What do I do with the baby?" The tiny ape was still clinging to Cydney, its eyes still closed.

"I don't know. I should have had you leave it down there. The trouble is, if you wake it up and try to push it away, it might cry, and then we'd be in for it."

Three red apes popped up from below. One chirped, tapped Victor's nose, and ran hooting down the tunnel. The other two followed, glancing back at Victor and Cydney.

"I think I saw those same three earlier. They're headed the direction we need to head," said Victor. "I suppose we should take the baby back down."

The large female ape climbed up, stared at Victor, and then tugged at the remains of Cydney's hair.

"Ow!" complained Cydney.

The mother ape patted her, and then followed the first three apes.

"Or not," said Victor. The troop was on the move and headed south, which was in the direction of Ricardo and Ruby.

"Should I keep the baby or not?"

"Keep him for now. Can you move fast?"

"He's hanging on tight. I could run if I wanted to."

"Don't run; you'll break a leg. Go as fast as you feel safe, and I'll keep up."

She smiled, a touch of sunshine on her cut and dirty face. With a hand on the side branches, she started running down the tunnel.

Victor followed, again impressed at her agility as she jumped from branch to branch. He didn't know anything about making vidstreams, but it sure kept Cydney in good condition.

He relaxed into the run, letting his muscles work out their stiffness and their kinks, letting the flashes of the morning sun illuminate his mind. He could hear the sounds of other apes following behind. For the moment, he and Cydney were part of a troop of fierce red apes, racing through a tunnel in the trees of an alien planet.

And at that moment, he understood how the tunnel was made.

Chapter Eight

When the tangle tree tunnel crossed over a rocky stream, Cydney demanded that they stop.

The two of them dropped down out of the trees, looked carefully for anything dangerous, and walked over to the water. Several of the small males came with them, and a mother ape with a baby larger than Cydney's.

Victor sat on a ledge with his feet in the water while Cydney rinsed her ragged hair, getting what she called ape spit out of it. "I can't believe that momma ape chewed my hair off," she muttered to herself. "I'm lucky she didn't bite my fingers off or something."

"I figured out how the tunnels were made."

"What?" She looked up at him, her face dripping.

"The tunnels up in the trees. The apes make them." Cydney went back to scrubbing her hair, so he continued. "I don't think it's a deliberate thing, though. Any little twig that starts to grow into the tunnel eventually gets snapped off by the apes, but I don't think they know they're making the tunnels. I pulled off a branch myself when I came to get you."

Cydney shook her hair and wiped water from her face. "Huh."

"It's ecology," he said, more to himself than her. "The trees grow around the tunnels because they're reaching for the sun and the apes prune the inside. I bet the ape droppings even help the trees grow better."

"Eww." She sat down beside him and spread her arms to let them dry. "So where's Ricardo and Ruby?"

"South of us, probably. I told them to keep moving."

"You told them? All of a sudden you're the boss?"

"It was an emergency, remember? Did you hear a gunshot this morning?" He watched Cydney's baby ape fighting with the larger ape. They wrapped their gooseneck arms around each other and kicked with their short legs, rolling around and hooting. The little one would break loose and flee to Cydney, cling for a minute, and then run back to fight. The mother that bit off Cydney's hair was nowhere to be seen.

"No," she said. "Was I supposed to?"

"I told them to shoot once when they left camp, and once at noon." He looked up at the sun, almost overhead and pouring down heat. "If we stay by the coast and go south, we should catch up with them eventually."

"Think they're still arguing?"

Victor's laugh was short and bitter as he stood and buckled on his gun belt. "Arguing's not their problem."

"What is?"

"Chancel Corporation and Belle Enterprise. Those two companies are fighting and there's no law out here. Ricardo's taking us to Horseshoe Station, but it's owned by Chancel."

"So?" Cydney ran her fingers through her ruined hair and her shoulders sagged.

"Chancel's not going to help Ruby. She believes that Chancel Corporation sabotaged the sweeper satellite, which would mean that they wanted her dead."

"That's horrible! Why would they want her dead?" She ran her fingers through her hair again, as though trying to pull it longer.

"Money, probably. There's big money in those safaris, big money from rich people like my Uncle and you and your family, and money's everything to the sort of people Ricardo works for. Ruby was going to take some of that money away with her casino, and she also wanted to stop the hunting."

"My hair's driving me crazy. I've always had pretty hair and now it's all ragged!"

Victor sighed. "I can trim it a bit, if you need me to." He pulled out his knife and unfolded the blade.

"Just the long parts, to make it even? It's all strings now. And don't pull when you cut it."

He took hold of a long strand of hair and tried to judge how much to shorten it. "You know, it's ironic that the *Nairobi* got hit after Chancel sabotaged the sweeper. That's how we all wound up on Belle's Casino with Ruby. Hey, did you know that Ricardo and Ruby almost got married once?"

"No! Really? The way they argue?"

"Stop moving your head or I'll cut your ear off. I guess they didn't argue at first. Anyway, now Ruby knows it was sabotage, and she's sure Chancel did it, and if there's one thing I've learned is that people like Chancel Corporation don't want witnesses, so now they've got two reasons to kill her. I'm done. If I cut any more you'll be bald."

She ran her hands over her head and shuddered. "Thanks, I guess." She fastened on her hiking boots. "Do you think Ricardo would hurt Ruby?"

"Not deliberately and not physically. They still love each other. Can't you tell?"

"They don't love each other. All they do is fight."

"They just won't admit it. Too proud, too many walls built up." The baby ape suddenly raced up Victor's back and scrambled down his front, followed by the larger, both of them yipping and hooting. "Agh! Shoo!" he yelled.

They squealed and leaped away in both directions. The baby climbed up Cydney and hid its face in her neck.

"There, there, Scampy," said Cydney, stroking its red fur. "It's okay, it's okay, the big nasty mean man didn't mean to yell at you."

"Scampy? You named him Scampy?"

"That's better than what he just called you. Don't you yell at him."

"Well, tell him not to climb all over me."

"It's what he does. He was just playing."

Victor huffed and watched the surf breaking in the distance. The stream they had stopped at splashed down

83

several rock ledges before wandering into the ocean. The noise of the stream, the surf, and the playing apes could mask a distant rifle shot. "Let's get back up into the trees. If Ricardo fires, we won't hear him down here unless he's close."

When the apes entered the tunnel again they continued heading south, so Victor and Cydney traveled with them. Sometimes they moved ahead of the troop, sometimes the troop rushed past them.

Cydney stopped to look at the distant ocean between two widely spaced branches. "Victor?"

"Yes?

"How old are you?"

"Sixteen."

She squinted at him. "You seem older. Sixteen year olds don't talk like you do."

He shrugged. "I used to read a book every night so I could sleep. I was taken out of public schools when I was ten. Prison ages you pretty quick, too."

"You were in prison?"

"I didn't mean to say that. Don't tell anyone, okay?"

"I won't. What happened?"

In the distance, a rifle went off. Victor froze, trying to tell the direction. The sound echoed off the foothills, and he was not sure if it was to the south or to the north of them. "Cydney, point to where that came from?"

She hesitated. "Maybe there?" She pointed south.

"I think so, too. Let's keep going."

The apes clustered around them, chirruping nervously and patting each other. The big red mother ape plucked Scampy off Cydney and licked him. The baby ape squirmed, and when the mother ape released him, he climbed back up onto Cydney.

Victor held still, letting the apes mill around him. "They didn't like the rifle shot. It made them nervous."

"I can't blame them."

"But Ricardo said that they haven't hunted here. Maybe it sounded like thunder to them."

The apes quieted and started moving again, and Victor and Cydney moved along with them. "Victor?"

84

"Yes?"

"Why were you in prison?"

They trotted around a turn in the tunnel before he answered. "I was thirteen, living on the planet Septimus. I had a good friend, her parents were from India, and she lived near us. She went to a public school and I had my, um, my special school, but we used to play games afterwards and talk a lot.

"There was this big senior guy, he...well, he hurt her one day, pretty bad, and I got mad. I found him outside the school with a couple of his buddies and I tore into him. Blackened his eyes and broke his teeth, and I would have stopped there but a couple of his friends grabbed me and tried to hold me."

Cydney glared. "That's not fair!"

He laughed, another humorless laugh. "Actually, it was fair but they didn't know it. I lost it, then. I broke one guy's arm and the other's knee. Then I broke both of the senior guy's arms."

Her jaw dropped. "You're kidding. How could you do that?"

He looked down at his hands. "It's my condition. To me, they were moving in slow motion. Then the police took me away and put me in prison. Seems I had disabled a couple star players on the football team, so they had to make an example. I broke out, then the Collapse hit Septimus, and I spent a couple years in prison or on the streets."

"They put you back in prison?"

"A few times. My mom died, things were pretty crazy. I got caught in a sweep, the military would sweep the streets, and then I broke out, and then they caught me again. Then my Uncle found me, and, well, anyway, that's why I was in prison."

"That's awful."

"Yeah, but that's history. Look, the apes have stopped."

In the heat of the afternoon, the older apes rested while the younger went foraging. Victor took Cydney down to the shrubs, where they ate some brushbeans and fed Scampy, who was expert at popping the beans from the pod into his mouth.

They climbed up on a rock outcropping, but could not see smoke or any signs of Ricardo or Ruby.

Cydney chattered on about trying out for the vidscreens at age seven, when she was good at tap dancing and singing. Her mother watched over her career when *Cydney and the Pirates* became popular, and her dad quit his job and got fat.

Victor nodded and tried to look interested as she went on about the guest stars, the exotic locations, and the different costumes. He was grateful when the apes showed signs of moving.

That night he took the time to put piles of branches on the tunnel floor. The mother ape kept trying to throw the branches to the ground, but Victor had Cydney lie on them while he gathered more. The apes went to the lower branches to sleep. Victor laid his gun belt over his boots, and Scampy snuggled up to Cydney.

They fell asleep once it got dark, but Victor was disturbed in the middle of the night by a flash of light. He sat up, rubbing sleep from his face, wondering what had awakened him.

Another flash of light lit up the sky, coming from overhead.

He walked carefully up the tunnel in his bare feet until he had an open space overhead. He pulled himself up to a higher branch where he could see the stars and the planet's faint ring. A brilliant meteor streaked overhead, lighting up the sky. "Yes!" He clapped his hands. The display was fiery and bright, and it struck a chord inside him.

A smaller meteor streaked a different part of the sky, and something hooted beside him. One of the red apes had climbed up and was sharing his branch.

They sat together, watching the sky, until two brilliant meteors raced by at once, and Victor cheered. The ape beat his hands on the branch, either excited or frightened.

Other heads popped up into the high canopy.

The meteors came faster and in greater numbers, and the apes became more agitated. One whacked a stick on a branch, and immediately there was noise all over, the banging of sticks, not a gentle tapping, but a pounding that fell into an urgent rhythm.

The ape beside Victor dropped down, and Victor felt his branch vibrate as the ape pounded on the tree trunk.

"What's happening?" cried Cydney from below.

"Meteor shower! Come on up!"

The flashing from the sky was now almost continuous. Whether it was meteors pulled down by the planet's shepherd moons or the falling remains of Ruby's Casino, a mass of objects was vaporizing itself in the planet's atmosphere and the apes were going mad from the display.

Cydney secured herself on Victor's branch, and he shouted, "Stay here! Hang on! I'm going to move around!" He dropped down and saw the larger apes with clubs, pounding on the thick trunks of the tangle trees as though trying to pacify the frightening lights in the sky.

The trunks of the larger trees must have been hollow, because when struck they gave out with a resounding "Whoooommm!" Smaller apes raced up and down the tunnel in the flashing light, their eyes wild and white-rimmed.

Whooom. Whooom. Whooom.

Victor leaped up and hung from an overhead branch. A passing ape grabbed one of Victor's legs, swung in a half circle, and raced back the way he came.

Victor reached out his hand to the next ape that came by, and they swung around each other, screaming, then separated and swung up into the higher branches.

Whooom. Whooom. Whooom.

The overhead sky became a mass of flashing lights as meteors ripped the sky with blazing fingers, and the tops of the trees held a riot of screaming, racing apes. Victor let go of his veneer of civilization and reverted to his primal instincts, screaming face-to-face with one ape and then another, grabbing two-fingered hands and flinging himself from branch to branch.

Whooom. Whooom. Whooom.

Something deep inside him woke up and rejoiced, reveling in the chaos and the emotion, in the racing and the screaming and the blazing sky. Time had no meaning, he had no name, and in the tops of the tangle trees that night nothing was more primitive than the beast that used to be called Victor Benningham.

*

Cydney crouched in the morning light, her back to a branch. "Are you okay?"

Victor pushed aside a couple of apes that dozed on top of him and lifted himself up. "Uh." He stretched, feeling sore all over. Bloody scratches covered his arms and his feet. "Yea, I guess. What happened?"

"You went crazy. They all went crazy. Scampy and I were scared to death."

"Sorry. Where am I?"

"You're in a pile of apes. I wish I had my camera. You looked dead. I was afraid you were dead."

He stepped carefully over to Cydney and leaned against a tree. A wind had picked up overnight, swaying the branches. "I'm fine. Wow. All I can remember is a meteor shower."

"Look at you. You're all bloody scratches and everything."

"Where are my boots? My feet hurt."

"Up there in the tunnel."

"That was really something." He climbed up and found his boots and gun belt.

"You're scary, Victor. You know that? My agent would probably put you on the 'not approved' list."

He laughed and tugged on his boots. "He'd be right, I think."

"She."

"She'd be right. Don't worry, Cydney. Your big brother isn't crazy. Last night I just whooped it up with the boys, I guess."

A gunshot rang out, followed by rustling and screeching from the apes.

"That was close," said Victor. "That way. I think we can catch up with them." A second gunshot echoed through the trees, and he grabbed Cydney's arm. "Hold on! That means trouble. Ricardo wouldn't waste ammunition like that. We'd better go in slow. There might be a predator or something."

The tree tunnel did not extend the way they wanted to go, so they wound up carefully jumping from branch to branch. When their path through the trees could go no further, they descended to the ground.

"Are you sure the shots were this way?" asked Cydney, adjusting Scampy's arms around her neck.

"Pretty sure. We're almost up against the mountain, so we can't be too far off." A fine dry grass crunched under their boots. Long-legged hairy birds ruffled by the wind stepped gravely through the undergrowth, darting their yellow bills down to snare small creatures.

Victor spied something shiny in the distance, which resolved itself into the top of a rescue pod. "I think that's got to be the pod the engineer took instead of waiting for us," said Victor in a whisper. He looked for cover; he did not want to approach out in the open.

Tangle trees and a different tree with denser foliage grew together to their left, and they angled towards them. They crept to the edge of the trees and looked towards the pod.

In front of the pod, a man with a rifle stood over two bodies on the ground.

"That's Ruby and Ricardo," said Cydney in a choked voice. "He shot them!"

Chapter Nine

Victor put his hand over Cydney's mouth. "Shh! They're not dead. He's got them lying down so he can guard them. Be still." He pulled her down low. "Look over there, on the beach. It's a gunship."

The logo on the side of the gunship proclaimed it the property of Chancel Corporation. Angular and black, the gunship looked capable of wiping out a rebellious village or crossing oceans to rescue survivors of a downed pod.

Looks like they are prepared to drive away any competition. I bet they keep that ship out of sight of the tourists.

Fighting in the woods was not the same as street fighting, but Victor knew enough not to let Ruby and Ricardo remain prisoners. Waiting would only make the situation worse. He checked the pistols on his gun belt and waved for Cydney to stay put. "I'm going to sneak up behind him," he said, his lips close to her ear. "If he turns around, it might come to shooting. Stay down."

"You're crazy! We should run away! We'd be safe!"

"No. He might still try to kill them, and I'm not going to let that happen. Now be still." He moved forward slowly, staying crouched in the grass. He was grateful for the wind to cover the sound of his movements.

Someone was inside the pod; the man guarding Ricardo and Ruby kept looking towards it. The man with the rifle had

90

an angular face, a Stetson on his head, and leather cowboy boots.

He's dressed like a vidstream cowboy. Probably to give the tourists the flavor of the wild frontier.

Where was Gary the engineer? Was he the man inside the pod? And why was the cowboy holding Ricardo as well as Ruby at gunpoint? Ricardo worked for Chancel Corporation, not Belle Enterprises.

Unless Chancel considered Ricardo too much of a witness.

Victor placed his feet carefully, gauging the distance. When he got close enough, he would tackle the cowboy low, which would knock the muzzle of the rifle up towards the sky.

He started to plant his feet when he heard a voice behind him. "Hold it right there, kid. Don't move a muscle."

There was a second man! How could I be so stupid?

The cowboy he was about to tackle turned around, a grin on his face. He had dark eyebrows and thin lips that curled into a sneer. "You were right, Gary. They came a'runnin' when they heard the gunshots. Good job." His rifle pointed at Victor's midsection. "Unbuckle those guns real slow, kid, and drop 'em. You've got two guns aimed at you."

Victor hesitated, still trying to figure out some way to take down the cowboy. He debated dropping to the ground and letting them shoot each other, but they were too calm to fall for it. He unbuckled his gun belt and lowered it to the ground. "Ricardo, Ruby, are you okay?" he asked.

"Shut up, kid," said the cowboy. "Everybody's fine, just fine. Now you step over by the pod and sit."

Reluctantly, Victor walked to the pod door and sat on the trampled grass. Standing under a tree, where Victor hadn't seen him, stood Gary the engineer with a rifle. Ricardo, his hands behind his head, looked at Victor and shook his head.

"Gary, make that girl get over to the pod, too," said the cowboy.

"Stand up!" Gary brandished his rifle at Cydney. Her face pale, she stood and started to walk past him towards the pod. Gary grabbed Scampy and yanked him off. "And get rid of this filthy little thing!" The baby ape screamed and tried to

91

bite, but Gary flung him to the ground and pointed his rifle at him.

"No!" shouted Cydney, diving headfirst into him. His shot went wide.

Victor started to jump up, but the cowboy swung his rifle to cover him. "Sit!"

Gary slapped Cydney across the face, knocking her to the ground, and aimed at Scampy again.

Before he could fire, a long red arm swept down from the overhanging branch and wrapped around his neck. He choked and tried to turn his gun upwards, but he was yanked off his feet and pulled kicking up into the tree.

Victor heard the rifle go off, a desperate scream, and then thrashing in the branches.

"Damn it!" The cowboy fired wildly into the trees, cursing. "I told him, I told him, don't stand under any trees! Idiot! You, girl, get over there before I shoot you between the eyes!"

Scampy jumped onto Cydney, and Cydney ran to Victor. A man with a thick black mustache stuck his head out of the pod. "What was that?"

"That stupid Gary went and got himself killed by an ape. Are you done? I want to get out of here, now."

"He's dead? Just like that?" The man with the mustache climbed out of the pod. "Yea, I'm done. Put them in and let's get out of here."

"Grab those guns on the ground and go start up the gunship. We could be attacked by apes any moment." The rustling in the trees continued, and Victor knew it wasn't the wind.

The man with the mustache picked up the gun belt and ran down towards the ship.

"Get up," said the cowboy, prodding Ricardo. "Both of you, now! Into the pod."

"Listen, Sam," said Ricardo as he stood up, "you and me have been partners on lots of trips. You don't need to hold a gun on me."

92

"Shut your face, Ricardo, and get in the pod. The kids, too. Hurry!"

Victor climbed in and helped Cydney up. He would have dawdled, hoping the apes would attack, but the man that Ricardo called Sam had been shaken by Gary's death and would likely not hesitate to shoot. Ruby climbed in, followed by Ricardo.

Ricardo turned and asked, "Why are you..."

Sam slammed the door shut and it locked.

"What are they doing?" asked Ruby. "Why in the world would they put us in here?" Victor heard shots, muffled by the armor and insulation of the pod walls.

Ricardo grabbed his shoulder. "I'm glad you two are all right, but your timing was sure bad. You would have been better off staying away."

"This doesn't make sense," said Victor. "Why lock us in here? Ruby, you opened up the other pod; isn't it the same code for this door?"

"Yes, but it doesn't sound safe outside. Those are gunshots."

"They've stopped." Victor put his ear against the door and felt a rumble that made the pod vibrate.

"The gunship's taking off," said Ricardo, looking baffled. "Why didn't they rescue us? Gary must have called them when his pod landed. They came all the way here to get him, and he gets himself killed, and then they leave without us."

"Serves him right," said Ruby. "I can't believe he pulled a gun on me."

"What happened?" asked Victor.

"He was polite to us when we showed up," said Ruby, "and he apologized for leaving us behind and said that he panicked. Then he called Horseshoe Station and told them we were here."

"This pod had the equipment that ours didn't," said Ricardo. "So we told him we were hoping you kids would find us soon, but when that gunship landed he pulled a rifle on us. What I don't understand is that I've worked for the company now for two years. Why would they leave me behind?"

93

Victor snorted and pushed away from the door. It was no mystery to him. Ricardo was so caught up in being the great safari leader that he was overlooking the obvious. The real question was, why did the men from Horseshoe Station shut them up in the pod? "Ruby," he asked, "could you enter the code and unlock the door? They've gone."

She frowned. "But those apes are still out there."

"The apes are not a problem. Trust me. Can you open it?"

"We have no guns," said Ricardo. "If the apes attack, we'll be helpless."

Victor growled and walked away, trying to keep his temper. He slapped the walls as he walked around the inside of the pod. Something inside him was shouting warnings about the situation. What good would it do to lock them inside the pod?

His mind made connections, and he froze.

He knew Ruby would not be able to unlock the door even if she tried. The man with the black mustache must have changed the code.

They weren't supposed to be able to get out. That meant that there was a reason why they would desperately *want* to get out.

His eyes swept the interior, looking for something wrong, something different.

And there it was, a black packet taped at ankle height to the central control column. He leaped over a railing and knelt by it. The packet was sealed in dense polymer, and a tiny red set of numbers was counting backwards.

As he watched, it changed from 3:02 to 3:01 to 3:00.

"We need to open the door now!" he shouted.

Ricardo furrowed his brow. "What's the matter?"

"There's a bomb here and it's going off in three minutes!"

"What? Where?" Ruby started up the aisle.

Victor stood and pointed at her. "Ruby, open that door now or we're all dead! Hurry!"

She whirled back to the door and tapped at the access panel. She pressed ENTER.

Nothing happened.

She started entering the code again.

As I expected, the code was changed. She'll never get it open.

The acrid smell that showed his hyper-D condition was kicking in rose in the back of his throat, and his brain sped up. He scanned the door, looking at the locking mechanism. Eight bolts secured the door, bolts that slid into the surrounding frame like a bank vault, making it secure for space travel. The bolts were controlled by a central mechanism that was connected by a cable to the code panel.

A panel covered the central mechanism, held in place by Phillips screws.

He yanked the screwdriver out of his pocket, flipped the Phillips head in place, and knelt down in front of the panel.

Thank you, Rosy!

Five screws held the panel in place. He leaned his chest against the handle of the screwdriver and twisted the first screw. Adrenalin lent him strength, and the screw came loose without stripping. He quickly spun each of them out, and then pulled away the panel and studied how the wires connected to the bolt mechanisms.

"Hurry, Ruby!" hollered Ricardo, looking at the explosive. "There's only two minutes left. This is a sealed mining charge he put here, I can't disable it, and it's going to blow this pod to scrap metal and everything in it!"

"I'm trying, I'm trying," Ruby said frantically. "It's not working!" Cydney started moaning in fright, and Scampy, still clinging to Cydney, squeaked a cry of distress.

Victor's hands moved with unnatural swiftness. He braced his feet and yanked the mechanism loose, ripping free the wires. With the screwdriver, he shorted the leads to the first bolt.

It slid back out of the frame.

When he moved the screwdriver to the second bolt's wires, the first bolt slid back in.

"Quit messing with that control panel!" he shouted. "I've disconnected it. I need some things, boots, cans, anything you can find to jam these bolts when I back them out!"

Ricardo stumbled to the storage panels along the perimeter and began yanking them open. Victor looked for anything, anything that could jam the bolts open.

Remembering Rosy, he ran to the control column and found the panel that carried a screwdriver and wrench just like the first pod. He ran back to the door, shorted the first bolt and then jammed it open with the pod's screwdriver. He shorted the second, but could not reach the gap. "Help me, Cydney! I can't make the bolt open and jam it open at the same time!"

Cydney grabbed the wrench from him and pushed it between the bolt and the frame.

Ricardo ran back with an armload of cans. "Here. Will these work?"

Victor shorted the third bolt, and Ricardo pushed in a can to hold it back.

"Only sixty seconds left!" cried Ruby. "Hurry!"

The fourth, fifth, and sixth bolts snapped back as he shorted their wires, and Ricardo quickly pushed in a can to jam them in place.

The seventh bolt crushed through the can and closed again.

Victor once more shorted the bolt and opened it. "Use my wrench," he yelled, pulling it out of his cargo pocket and handing it to Ricardo. "Jam it in!"

"Thirty seconds!"

Ricardo pushed the wrench in place, and it held.

Victor shorted the eighth bolt and Ricardo threw his shoulder against the door. It burst open, scattering the cans and wrenches, and Ricardo tumbled out onto the grass. "Go, go, go!" shouted Victor, pushing Cydney and Ruby out the door. He jumped out and helped Ricardo to his feet. "That way," he shouted, waving to the forest. "Run! Get to the trees!"

They ran, fear making them stumble on the uneven ground.

Cydney stopped and pointed at a red mound lying on the ground. "They shot the momma ape!" she wailed.

"Don't stop!" cried Ricardo, turning back to grab her.

The pod exploded.

The deafening shock knocked Victor down and rolled him over. Metal and deadly debris whipped past him. He felt thuds and crashes, the sounds of pod fragments striking the ground. A tree toppled, sliced by a fragment of the outer armor. Ruby screamed.

The sound diminished as smaller pieces and high-flung wreckage fell to earth. Victor held still, waiting for the rain of rubble to end, hoping nothing heavy fell on him.

When it quieted, he climbed to his feet and tried to see what had happened.

The pod was gone, pieces thrown in all directions like a shattered egg. The grassy meadow was torn and scorched; shrubs were flattened and tossed like tissue. Ruby, lying next to him, bled from a cut on her shoulder.

He staggered over to where Ricardo lay on his side. Cydney was getting up, crying, but Ricardo wasn't moving. He knelt down and carefully rolled Ricardo onto his back.

A stainless steel rod protruded out of Ricardo's chest, piercing his right pocket. Blood spread out on his shirt like a red blossom.

Ricardo blinked, shook his head, and looked down at his chest. "Uh. That, I think that's pretty deep. I feel..." He laid his head back on the grass and coughed. "That hurts."

Rudy knelt by Ricardo's head, ignoring the blood oozing from her shoulder. "Ricky, Ricky, don't move, you're hurt really bad." She cradled his head in her arms.

Victor used his knife to cut the shirt away from the steel rod. He could see a bone fragment from a fractured rib in the wound. "Don't pull out that rod," he said to Ruby. "He'll bleed a lot more if you do."

He had seen many wounds on the streets of Septimus. This one needed a doctor, a hospital, blood, sutures, everything they did not have. At least the rod had penetrated the right side of Ricardo's chest, missing his heart.

If he pulled out the rod, Ricardo would bleed to death. If he didn't pull it out, the man had no chance of healing and surviving. They needed a medical kit, but finding one in the wreckage, a kit that was intact, seemed impossible.

97

Ruby was useless; she was holding Ricardo and crying.

"Hey, Ruby girl, don't cry," Ricardo said in a weak voice.

"I'm not crying." She waved her hand at the bar in his chest. "Don't you dare die, darn you, not now!"

"At least it will get me…out of your hair, mate."

"Stop that! I didn't mean for us to be apart. It's all my fault."

"No, Ruby, you're fine, it was me that wandered off. Don't ever think it was your fault."

"But if I'd only…"

"Hush. There's only one thing I need. Lean down."

Ruby lowered her head and Ricardo kissed her cheek. She turned her head and tried to kiss his lips, but he sagged and his eyes closed.

"No, no, no," Ruby cried, wrapping her arms around his head. "No, not now, not this way!"

Cydney sat down beside Victor and began pulling open her doll. "Peggity can help," she said. She pulled the metallic polybot out of the doll and pressed some buttons on the surface. "If she can fix me, and they showed me how, then maybe she can fix him."

Victor cut off Ricardo's sleeve and pressed it around the wound to stop the blood flow. "He's almost gone."

Ruby kept talking to Ricardo and stroking his face, but he no longer responded.

"Okay," said Cydney. "She's ready. But you have to pull that thing out of him."

Victor grabbed the rod. "He'll bleed when this comes out. Be ready."

"Hurry. I'm going to be sick."

Victor pulled the rod out, dragging the chip of bone with it. Ricardo opened his eyes and cried out. Cydney pressed Peggity against the open wound, and the polybot changed shape, extruding crab-like arms. It sank into the wound and disappeared.

Victor leaned close to the wound and watched. Whatever the device was doing, it was doing it inside Ricardo's chest.

"It can really hurt at first," said Cydney. "Peggity doesn't have any painkillers, but she makes them when she's done and, um, I've got to throw up." She staggered a few steps away and emptied her stomach.

Ricardo groaned without waking. Whatever the polybot was doing, it was hurting.

When Cydney returned, Victor sent her to look for anything she could find in the wreckage, especially any water canisters or medical kits. Ricardo coughed up some blood, and Ruby wiped it from his lips with her fingers.

A long arm with two fingers slid over Victor's shoulder and touched Ricardo's chest. Ruby gasped, but Victor grabbed her arm and held her still. "Don't move. It's okay."

A red ape, a small male, looked quizzically at Victor. "Chiirrr?"

Victor nodded. "He's hurt."

The male touched the blood around the wound. It opened its lips and showed its serrated ridges, then stuck out its bluish tongue and tasted the blood on its fingers. It stroked Ricardo's nose, then patted Victor on the shoulder. With a rocking gait, it walked back through the grass and swung up into the trees.

"What was that?" whispered Ruby, looking so pale he thought she would faint.

"One of the red apes. We're friends."

"Friends?"

Victor nodded. "Sort of. They've never seen anything like us before, at least the ones in this area, so they're not afraid of us." The polybot emerged from the hole in Victor's chest, and its legs began pulling the skin over the wound. "Look at that. It's weaving the skin together."

"I thought that ape was going to kill us." She stroked Ricardo's hair. "Is he going to live, do you think? I don't know what I would do if he died."

Victor raised an eyebrow at her. "But you argue all the time."

"I've been happy these past two days, just him and me. When there is nothing interfering, nothing pulling us apart, I feel like we're one person." She pointed to Ricardo's chest. "Cydney's thing has stopped moving."

Cydney returned with an armload of rags and cans, and a scorched and dented box that looked like a first aid kit. She dropped them and sat down by Ricardo. "See? Peggity closed him up." She picked up the polybot and wiped it clean with a rag. The tiny arms had disappeared, and it looked like a shiny thick oval.

"Did it repair him inside as well?" asked Ruby.

Cydney shrugged. "I guess. I know how to start her, that's all. Now you need to lie down so she can fix your shoulder."

"What's wrong with my shoulder?" Ruby turned her head and was surprised to see the long bloody gash. She lay on her side next to Ricardo, and Cydney started the polybot repairing Ruby's wound.

Victor stood up, brushing debris from his clothes. Ricardo would die or he would not. Gary was dead, and the shuttle with the men from Chancel was gone.

He walked towards the dead mother ape, and then stopped. A large gray reaper had its tentacles around the body and was pulling it towards the shrubs.

It's a scavenger, and scavengers clean up the dead bodies. I don't want Cydney to see this.

He turned towards the remains of the pod, looking for anything useful that Cydney might have overlooked. He found nothing but a small cracked mirror. He carried it back to the group, where Cydney took it from him and looked at herself with dismay. She tucked the polybot back into her doll and hung it on her neck, then walked towards the shore carrying the mirror.

Ricardo was breathing easier and his face had more color. Ruby's cut on her shoulder was nicely closed. The polybot had no sutures; it simply wove the skin together in a line so thin that Victor couldn't guess if it would leave a scar or not.

Victor wrapped Ruby's arm with a bandage from the kit, and taped several layers of cloth around Ricardo's chest to protect the wound. He found no containers of water, so he took

100

an empty canteen that had survived and looped it over his shoulder. "I'll be back in a little bit," he told Ruby. "Make him lie still if he wakes up again."

She nodded, her face looking haggard.

I hope he lives, for her sake as well as his.

He walked to where Cydney was sitting on a rock near the beach, looking into the mirror. Her face was pretty, but her nose was scabbed and her wavy brown hair was just tatters.

She put down the mirror and looked up at him with forlorn eyes. "I can't be Cydney anymore."

He sat down beside her. "Sure, you can."

She shook her head. "No, I can't. Look at me! I'm too old, it'll take months for my hair to grow long again, and even with a wig I'd still be too tall. I can't be Cydney." She sniffed, her eyes growing wet. "Victor?"

"Yes?"

"I need to tell you something."

He nodded.

"My name," she said, her lips trembling, "my real name is Emily Miller." She seemed to shrink as she looked down at the broken mirror. "And I was b-born in Ohio."

Then Emily Miller put her face in her hands and sobbed.

Chapter Ten

Ricardo recovered consciousness that evening and complained of thirst. Victor had a canteen full of fresh water handy, and Ricardo sipped it gratefully. From the scorched medical kit, Victor salvaged pain pills, a tube of antiseptic ointment, and some antibiotic patches that he placed on Ruby and Ricardo's wounds.

"I'm okay when I lie still," Ricardo said as his head rested on Ruby's lap. "When I move around I feel like I can't catch my breath."

"Then lie still," said Ruby.

"You have a collapsed lung," said Victor. "It'll take a while, but your lung will work again. Just take it easy."

Ricardo looked at him quizzically. "Where did you learn medicine?"

Victor shrugged.

"And how did you learn to open a locked door like that?" asked Ruby.

"Oh, that." He rubbed the back of his neck. "When Septimus had the Collapse, I was on the streets for a while, and, uh, actually I ran with a couple of gangs. They taught me how to open doors."

And vaults and safes...

"That was pretty slick," said Ricardo. "Thanks. I owe you for that."

Emily brought up an armload of loose branches from trees that had been shattered by the explosion. She dropped them on the growing pile and added a few to the fire.

"Thank you, Cydney," said Ruby with a smile.

"Victor asked me to, um...you're welcome." She smiled back and sat down on a seat cushion. The campsite was surrounded by whatever they could salvage, including several ropes that were sealed in polymer, a handful of food cans, and two intact rescue pod chairs. "You can call me Emily."

"Emily?" Ruby looked puzzled.

Glancing at Victor, Emily explained. "I was born Emily Miller, but my agent wanted me to live my stage name all the time, so I became Cydney. But Cydney's supposed to be eight years old, and have long brown hair." She ran her fingers through her short locks self-consciously. "I'm too old and my hair's gone, and I can't be Cydney anymore." She smiled bravely.

"Emily," said Ricardo. "That's a nice name."

It's a name. You don't have to evaluate it.

Emily looked as though a weight had been lifted from her, though. A weight called Cydney.

Ricardo and Ruby were in a truce, but he knew that as soon as they had to decide on a destination, the quarreling would start again. Victor's brain kept working overtime. He felt in his pocket for his single remaining pill. If he took it, he could stop thinking so much, slow down, sleep easily.

On the other hand, if he had been taking his medication, they would all be dead. He would never have figured out how to open the rescue pod door in time for them to escape the explosion. He was riding a two-edged sword, and either way he suffered.

"I have to ask you, Emily," said Ricardo, "why in heaven's name are you carrying around that baby ape? If they caught you with one of their babies, they would rip you apart."

Emily stroked the back of the little ape. "This is Scampy, and I was helping his mother carry him. He likes hanging on to me, and those men shot his mother. He's an orphan now, like me."

103

Ricardo furrowed his brow. "Okay, now, none of that makes much sense. Slow down. You were helping his mother?"

She nodded. "The big ape. The one they shot."

"The big apes are males."

Emily rolled her eyes. "No, they're the mothers. The small ones are males. They bring food."

Ruby leaned back and glared at Ricardo. "You've been killing the females?"

"Ruby, she's got it backwards. It was a big one that killed my partner, a big male."

"Did you dissect it?"

"No. We just wanted them for trophies. Why would we dissect them?"

"So you wouldn't do anything harmful like killing the females," she said with heat.

"Emily is right," said Victor. "The big ones tend the babies and the smaller apes, the males, do the foraging. We didn't see any babies being born, and yes, these are an alien species, but the babies stay by the big apes and the big apes defend the babies. It was probably Scampy's mother that killed Gary when he attacked Cydney and Scampy."

Ricardo looked at Emily. "Well, then, if she's a mother, why didn't she attack you? You've got her baby."

"I told you," said Emily, rolling her eyes, "I was baby-sitting." She picked up a rag and tied it around her head pirate-fashion.

Ricardo inhaled and winced. "It still doesn't make sense."

"You're foggy," said Ruby. "As usual. I'll explain it tomorrow. Emily, I just realized, your hair is all cut short. When did you cut your hair?"

Emily pulled the rag off her head and ruffled her ragged hair. "The momma ape, she chewed it off. I guess I didn't look right."

"She chewed off your hair, and now you're baby-sitting her baby." She closed her eyes and rubbed her temples. "My head is still ringing from the explosion. I'm hoping I'll wake up back at my casino."

"We need to decide what we're going to do..." started Ricardo, but Victor interrupted. "Not tonight. A lot has happened. We should sleep on it."

Ruby and Ricardo both looked at him, looking surprised that he had assumed so much authority. He kept his eyes focused on the fire, and they let it go unchallenged. They had survived the day; it was enough.

Emily was restless. She dragged a large flat sheet of metal from the wreckage and stood on it as if it was a small stage. In the dim firelight, she tapped her feet on it experimentally.

"These aren't as good as my pirate boots," she said to Victor. "You should see what I could do in those." She ran through a few tap routines, and Victor had to admit to himself that she had talent.

She hummed, and then broke out into song as she danced.

"We're Cydney and the Pirates,
We sail the Seven Seas,
We go where 'ere the wind blows,
And take what 'ere we please!
We're Cydney, (boom!)
We're Cydney, (boom!)
We're Cydney and the Pirates! (boom!)"

"Those booms are cannon shots," she said quickly as she danced.

"We're Cydney, (boom!)
We're Cydney, (boom!)
We're Cydney and the Pirates! (ka-bloom!)"

"And then the cannon always explodes at the end and I might be hanging from a rope, or up a tree, or in a sink of dirty dishes, or something else each time. The pirates are funny and they're all animated but I have to climb up on things or get into things."

Whooom! Whooom! Whooom!

Victor turned around and saw apes beneath the trees, their eyes blinking red in the fire light. Some of them were beating on the trees in the same tempo as Cydney's song.

"They think you're tapping at them. Sing it again, Cydney," said Victor. "I mean, Emily."

She turned around to face the apes and sang it again, her feet tapping away on the metal sheet. The beaters kept time with the singing and the rest of the troop capered and shook their arms.

Emily finished with
"We're Cydney, (Whooom!)
We're Cydney, (Whooom!)
We're Cydney (Whooom!) and the Pirates! (Whooom!)"

The apes continued pounding the trees but Cydney pulled off her pirate's rag and drank from the canteen.

"Good night," Victor called to the apes. "Go home. The party's over. Go to sleep. Shoosh."

The apes' pounding quieted down to tapping, and one by one, they disappeared.

"I would never," said Ruby, "never *ever* have believed that if I hadn't seen it. What were they doing? What was that all about? Ricky, have you ever seen that?"

He shook his head. "Never. I had no idea they drummed and danced like that. Could I have that canteen again? My mouth is dry. I thought they were fixing to attack."

Victor handed him the canteen. "You want to see them attack? You pull out a gun and shoot at them. Then they'll attack."

Ricardo took a few swallows and handed the canteen back. "No, I don't want them to attack. But I'd still feel safer if I had a rifle."

Victor screwed the cap back on. "Gary had a rifle, for all the good it did him. Tomorrow I'll go look for it. What I'm worried about is another of those scaly predators finding us."

"I've never seen nor heard of those creatures before," said Ricardo. "The sooner we can leave this area the better."

They gathered torn blankets and made beds for the night. Victor peeled open a dented can of preserved meat and enjoyed it, but Ruby complained about it not being the quality she had ordered. Emily rejected it and Scampy wouldn't touch it, so Ricardo finished it off.

106

Emily lay down beside Victor, and just when he thought she was falling asleep, he realized she was sniffling. "Are you okay?" he asked.

"I miss my mom. I wish she could have seen me dance for the apes. I wish..." She sniffed again, and he reached out and put his hand on her shoulder. "I'm sorry I'm such a mess," she whispered. "You're a good big brother."

When they awoke the next morning, they found branches laden with blue fruits on the ground at Emily's feet, and Scampy was happily eating.

*

The warmth of the sun had dried out the dew when Victor returned from the trees. "Here's Gary's rifle," he said, leaning it up against a twisted fragment of the rescue pod. "It was up in the branches. No sign of his body except a boot."

Ricardo grunted. "They probably ate him."

"I don't think they eat meat," said Victor, pulling another blue fruit off a branch the apes had left them. "I know they eat fruits and brushbeans. What dragged off his body was probably one of those gray reapers."

"Let me see that rifle. I don't want to try to fire something that's bent or damaged."

Victor picked up the rifle by the stock and inspected it. "It looks fine to me, but you're not going to be firing it."

Ricardo scowled. "What do you mean?"

"I mean," said Victor, handing him the rifle, "your right arm needs to be in a sling for a couple weeks while your chest heals up. You try to fire that and you'll be bleeding again. You've got a fractured rib."

"He's right," said Ruby.

Ricardo fumbled with the rifle, opening up the chamber with his left hand. He glanced up at Victor. "And how do I know you can use a rifle? A pistol and a rifle are two different things, and you were pretty slow with a pistol."

Victor snorted and took the rifle. He put a fruit pit on the edge of the fragment of rescue pod. He walked a dozen meters

107

away, closed the chamber and aimed Then he lowered the rifle without firing. "No. If the apes are around, it'll upset them. You'll just have to trust me; if I need to, I can use a rifle."

Ricardo raised his hand in resignation. "You might as well carry the rifle, for now." He tucked a blanket behind him so he could sit up a bit more. "There's something else we need to discuss."

Victor sat by the dead campfire, knowing what was coming.

Ruby sat on a salvaged pod chair. "Yes?"

"Where do we go from here?" asked Ricardo. "Because we're in real trouble."

"I would have never guessed," said Ruby.

Emily sat down beside Victor and started playing peek-a-boo with Scampy.

Ricardo started to speak, coughed, winced, and started again. "We got left behind by the gunship, and I've been trying to figure out why. That man in the cowboy hat holding the rifle on us was named Sam, and he and I have gone on safaris together. He always handled the money end of it. I was the professional guide, the man with the stories, the man who knew where the game was."

"You mean the man who knew where the females were," said Ruby. "And I don't mean dancers."

"Okay, I'll admit I might have been wrong about the apes. Can we set that aside?"

He was pale and looking weaker by the minute. Victor tried to help the conversation move along. "So it was Sam that ordered us all into the pod, knowing it had a bomb in it? Sounds like you were being fired by the company."

Ricardo nodded and stroked his thin mustache thoughtfully. "Yes, but why? I was bringing in a new shipload of tourists before we got hit and had to make for Ruby's Casino. I was making money for them."

"Did Sam know that you and Ruby had a history?"

Ricardo glanced at Ruby, and she raised her eyebrows. "Yes," he said, and looked back at Victor. "It was pretty obvious to Sam that the rich young ladies in the expeditions

108

held no interest for me. He asked me why, so I told him about Ruby. He knew the connection."

Ruby's eyes widened and Victor knew this was new information for her. She must have been picturing Ricardo playing the part of a lady's man on the safaris.

"All right. Two things, then." Victor held up one finger. "First of all, Ruby Tierney represents Belle Enterprise, and you've told me that they don't get along at all. Secondly," he added the next finger, "the casino was destroyed by a deliberate act of sabotage, and they would presume that Ruby would know it and that you would know it, if only by association, and they don't want witnesses. Besides," he added the next finger, "they wanted her dead in the first place."

"That's three things," said Emily.

"Don't bother me. So that's why we all got thrown in the pod with the bomb. They left fast to avoid the apes, so they don't know that we survived."

"Hum." Ricardo scratched his head. "So what do we do next?"

"We can't just go waltzing into Horseshoe Station. They'll get rid of us some other way that can't be traced. We can't expect them to help."

"That does make sense," said Ruby.

"Trouble is," said Ricardo, pulling the blanket out from behind his head and lying flat again, "Horseshoe Station is the only way we're going to get off of this planet."

"What are our options?" asked Victor. "One would be to stay here. Someone would eventually come looking for us."

Ruby shook her head. "Only if they thought we were alive."

"They might find Emily's polybot," said Victor. "She said it has a chip in it so they can find her."

"Again, only if they try to look, assuming that they can search from orbit. They'll eventually learn that the *Nairobi* was destroyed, and that the casino was destroyed. And I hate to bring it up, Cydney, um, Emily, but I bet you were heavily insured."

Emily sighed and stroked Scampy's back. "Mom took care of all that stuff but I guess so."

"If *Cydney and the Pirates* was near the end of its run, there would be no reason to seek for a needle in a haystack if you didn't want the needle." Ruby glanced back at Emily. "Sorry."

Emily shrugged.

"I didn't say we should stay here," said Victor. "I just said it was one possibility."

"Any other options?" asked Ruby.

Victor looked at Ricardo, but Ricardo had his eyes closed. "We could go to Horseshoe Station under cover," Victor said. "Look at the situation, and then decide. We'll probably have more information then."

"I second the motion," said Ricardo without opening his eyes.

Ruby stood up and brushed her pants. She looked around at the shattered clearing as though hoping another option might present itself, but apparently she found nothing. "Well, I sure don't want to stay here. Emily, what do you think?"

"I think Scampy is just the cutest widdle thing there ever was, oh yes, he is!" She tickled Scampy under his arms, and the little ape wrapped his flexible arms around himself until he was a ball, and squeaked and wriggled.

"There it is, then," said Ruby. "We keep going."

"One more thing," said Ricardo, his eyes still closed.

"Yes?"

"We're going to have to figure out how to get past the volcano."

"The what?"

Ricardo swung his left arm to the south and pointed. "Remember that to get from the east part of the continent to the west part we have to pass the southern volcano."

Victor leaned forward. This was a new thought to him. "Yes, you showed us that through the telescope."

"Now, it's not an explosive volcano, it's mild-tempered, but it is active. Sometimes the lava flows south from the cone and sometimes it flows north. Ever since I first visited

110

Horseshoe, it's been flowing north, and when we looked down from the casino it was still flowing north into this ocean here. There's no way you can walk past it unless you can walk on lava."

"What does that mean, then?" asked Victor.

"We're going to have to cross a bit of ocean to get past it. Anyone here know how to build a boat?"

*

They shifted their camp away from the site of the pod explosion, just in case the people from Horseshoe Station returned. Victor erased the fire circle and any signs that they had survived. After a short walk, they arrived at a place where the foothills touched the sea, and there they found a sheltered cove with a rocky overhang.

Victor traveled on alone for a day to look at the land while Ricardo convalesced. The rocky coast continued south without a break, and when he stopped for the night, he saw a red glow in the distance that waxed and waned. The tectonic plates were separating, and new land was being created from the depths of the earth. Ricardo had been right; walking to the western continent wasn't going to work.

He spent the night in the trees, and picked up a rash on his arm from accidentally touching one of the small green reapers, the sort that camouflaged itself on tree branches and ate butterflies.

I wonder if these things even have names. We might be the first humans to see these little creatures, and things don't have names unless we give them to them. How strange. Without humans, a dog wouldn't be a dog. It would just....be.

He mulled that over as he took a scrub in ocean water to help ease the itching. He returned to find the group still trying to figure out how to build a boat.

"What have we got to work with?" asked Ricardo, his right arm in a makeshift sling. "We've got a screwdriver, a wrench, some rope, lots of twisted metal, and rubbish. Lots of rubbish, but no wood."

"There are trees all over," said Emily.

"No saws. No axes. Victor, you've got a pocket knife, but we'll grow old trying to cut a tree down with it, and then cut some planks."

"There are some trees down already," said Ruby as she tied her hair up. "I saw some that the pod knocked down when it landed. And when the pod exploded, another one came down."

"We're thinking too complicated," said Victor, who was used to making do with little or nothing. "We don't need a boat, we just need a raft. A couple of tree trunks tied together. The wind has been blowing towards the west ever since we got here. We can use a blanket for a sail."

"But how would we make a mast?" asked Ricardo. "How would we fasten it?"

"You're still thinking too big. Think something more like a kite attached to the front of the raft. A blanket and a couple of branches and ropes. We don't need speed. We just need to cover a few kilometers. Right?"

"That's true, mate, that's true. But remember, I've never been down here before, so you can't trust my judgment."

They returned to the pod site and examined the downed trees. They selected two likely candidates, and Ricardo suggested using fire to remove branches and to even out their length. They banked fires against the pair of trunks at the appropriate spots, and took turns tending them and foraging. A column of smoke marked their presence, but it was a risk they had to take.

The troop of red apes was gone. Victor speculated that they had headed north, probably bothered by the explosion, deaths, and blood. He kept the rifle handy, but saw no signs of a predator, at least none that were worrisome. A small hairy creature with claws circled the camp to catch one of the long-legged birds, but it was too small to be concerned about.

"They're different from Earth creatures, these animals and plants, and yet not so different," said Victor as he watched the bobbing heads of the white birds. "In the vidstreams, aliens from other planets have multiple eyes, parts that break off and keep on moving, and they drip slime, but Scampy would be right at home on Septimus or Earth, I bet."

Ricardo adjusted his safari hat and rubbed at the stubble on his cheek. "Writers try to make up something frightening. They never think about the environment their creatures would have to live in. I mean, once you've got depth perception, once you've got two eyes, what good would be more?"

Victor raised an eyebrow at Ricardo. "Spiders have extra eyes."

Ricardo folded his arms. "Now, that's a different thing entirely. The big eyes are for depth perception; the tiny eyes are for just for light and shadow. I know about these things."

"And starfish have eyes on their arms." Victor had never been one to let a point go unchallenged.

Ricardo shook his index finger at him. "Starfish eyes aren't real eyes, no lenses, again just for light and shadow, and there, you see, you've gone and named two Earth creatures with extra eyes, and if you'd never seen them before on Earth, if you saw them here, you'd think they were horrible aliens."

"I guess." He cleared his throat. "Was that why everyone guessed wrong about which was male and which was female on the red apes? Because they thought they'd seen that before on Earth?"

Ricardo dropped his hand and kicked the gravel with his toe. "I was told the sexes by the workers at Horseshoe Station. On Earth I used to do photographic expeditions, and the male lion had the big mane, and male gorillas were bigger than females, and such." He met Victor's eyes and said sincerely, "Yes, I'm guilty of assuming that things on this planet would be the same as on earth. Made a bit of an ass of myself, I guess."

The overhead sky blazed with deep oranges and reds from the setting sun, colors that reflected off the calm ocean. On the sandy shore, Ruby and Emily, mere silhouettes, tossed a branch back and forth while Scampy kept trying to intercept it. The smoke from the fires mingled with the salty smell of the ocean.

"I should have expected greater variety between worlds," said Ricardo. "The way evolution works, it's always trying out things in every direction. It makes an animal bigger or smaller, faster or stronger, darker or lighter. Sometimes the different thing fits, and the animal gets more successful."

And sometimes, the different thing doesn't fit. Like me.

"Little Scampy there," continued Ricardo, "has depth perception, like us, so he can swing through the trees. These birds here, though, have their eyes on the sides of their heads, to watch for predators, and only a little overlap in front."

"Is this what you teach the tourists?"

Ricardo laughed, coughed, and caught his breath. "Yes, sorry, I was teaching again. I only teach them a little bit; they're usually too busy eating, drinking, or sleeping. I tell a lot of jokes and they think they're becoming experts on the alien ecology." He rubbed his chest and winced. "I get good tips."

After the fires burned the two trunks to the same length, they used levers and rolled the trunks down to the shore. By digging small tunnels in the sand, they ran rope, wire, and tough vines under and over the trunks, around and around, until the trunks were secure. They cut long branches to spread the blanket for a sail, and tied on some boxes from the ruined pod to hold the food and canteens. The rifle they wrapped in the empty plastic bags that used to hold coils of rope, and lashed it to the fore of the raft. Then they lashed branches across the two long logs to make a rough floor, which they covered with blankets.

The tree trunks were long enough that two people could sleep on them end-to-end, and large enough that they came to Victor's shoulders.

"This ship needs a name," Emily said. "You can't sail the Seven Seas if your ship doesn't have a name."

"All right, mate," said Ricardo. "Give her a go."

Emily tied her bandana pirate-fashion again. She lifted a damaged can of processed meat product. "Give me a second." She looked up at the sky and mumbled to herself. "Okay. I christen thee, the *Bloody Dagger of Revenge!*"

Before she could bang down the can, Ruby said, "Hold it! I am not going sailing on any Bloody Dagger of anything. It's just a raft, for pity's sake!"

Emily started to pout, but took a breath and pulled her lip back in. "Okay, well, any suggestions?"

"She's going to be slow but steady, we hope," said Ricardo. "How about the *Tortoise*?"

Emily looked at Victor, and he shrugged. Without looking at Ruby, she raised the can again and shouted, "I christen thee, the *Tortoise!*" She whacked the can on the front end.

"Good show," said Ricardo. "Gather your supplies and get a good night's sleep. The *Tortoise* sails at dawn!"

Chapter Eleven

The *Tortoise* didn't want to sail at dawn. It was painfully heavy, and once the front end entered the water, the waves kept pushing the raft back onto the shore and the contrary wind did not help. Only with long poles, much effort, and some bad language from Ricardo did they get the raft beyond the surf and underway.

Emily clung to the ropes in the middle of the raft, and as they poled away from shore, she started to cry.

"What's wrong?" asked Ruby, too busy poling to go to her.

"I'm scared! I don't know how to swim!"

Ruby laughed with exasperation. "You could have told us that before we started."

"This thing looked bigger on the sand. I want to go back!"

"We can't go back even if we wanted to. The wind doesn't blow that way!"

Victor laid down his pole and knelt beside Emily. "You're supposed to be a pirate. Why don't you know how to swim?"

"I was only a stage pirate," she said, clutching his arm. "They taught me how to sing and dance, but there was never any real water."

"Real pirates never knew how to swim anyway," said Ricardo, trying to tie down the sail at the front of the raft with his left hand. His right arm was still in a sling, and the fitful breeze kept collapsing the sail.

The water was now too deep for poling. Ruby tucked her pole into the ropes and caught her breath. "They didn't?"

116

Ricardo pulled the knot tight and sat down, his hand pressing the bandage wrapped around his chest. "No, not most of them." He wheezed. "They learned how to sail, but not how to swim. No time for it. If you fell in, you got tossed a rope fast or you drowned."

"So what about Emily?"

Ricardo grinned a rakish grin. "Emily, don't fall overboard."

Emily huddled and sniffed, hugging Scampy for comfort. "That's not funny. This boat is too small."

"Then sit near the front. You'll have a better chance to grab hold if you fall in. Victor, can you swim?"

Victor nodded, adjusting the lines that controlled the sail's angle. "I'm good. I learned how to swim in New Zealand. We should have made a tiller for this thing."

"You can't steer a raft," said Ricardo.

"I don't know; the *Tortoise* feels more like a canoe than a raft."

As they got further away from the shore, the wind picked up and filled the blanket they used as a sail. Two poles tied in a V helped to spread the sail, and the lines from the tips of the V held it against the wind and changed its angle. Victor pulled the left-hand line in. Slowly, clumsily, the *Tortoise* swung left to a southerly direction and began paralleling the coast.

"Why not go straight across?" asked Emily, clutching the deck ropes with white knuckles. "We wouldn't be on the water so long."

Ricardo started to speak, but then he raised his eyebrows at Victor. "How would you answer that?"

"I would say," said Victor as he adjusted their heading, "that if we get in trouble, we don't want to be too far from shore. We don't have a compass to guide us across the open water."

"Spot on." Ricardo nodded. "The ancient mariners never lost sight of shore. They were terrified to be out of sight of land. You see, back before the compass was invented..."

"He's teaching again," said Emily.

"And for free, too. Shame on me." Ricardo smiled, abandoning his lecture. "Anyone bring fishhooks?"

Ruby leaned over and looked into the water. "Do you think there are anything like fish here?"

"The plate crabs feed on plankton. Plankton can support a food chain, so I would expect some things in this water."

"Big enough to pull us under, do you think?" Victor looked at Emily with mock horror.

"Stop it," snapped Emily. "That's not funny."

"Sorry." He couldn't help smiling. There was something invigorating about being loose on the ocean, being away from shore. He would try to hold down his euphoria for Emily's sake.

I'm not used to having emotions.

"I honestly don't know," said Ricardo. "We never did any fishing. People don't travel interstellar distances just to fish. I suppose there could be anything down there."

The breeze picked up and the swells grew, pitching the nose of the *Tortoise* up and down gently. Victor angled the craft more to the west, aiming for a rocky point he saw on the horizon. It would take them further from the shore for a while, but it would also cut down the distance they would have to travel.

Scampy wandered about the raft hooting with distress and kept returning to Emily to hide his head under her chin.

Victor looked back at the foothills and the cove. The philosopher inside of him stirred and whispered: he and the others were no longer masters of their fate; they had set themselves adrift on the wind and tide.

Except the Horseshoe Planet did not have a tide. It had two small shepherd moons that circled the planet along with a ring of debris, debris that marked either the death of a large moon, or the failure to coalesce into one. The shepherd moons, the shipboard channel had explained, helped keep the ring neatly defined but sometimes deflected debris out of orbit.

A planetary ring both beautiful and dangerous. If it weren't for a small piece of that ring I would be on safari listening to Ricardo's stories and my uncle would be preparing to kill a female ape for a trophy. Instead I am adrift on this ocean with my small gang of refugees, hoping to survive.

Something that looked like a floating bowl lay in the water ahead. Victor tried to steer closer as they passed.

"I haven't seen that before," said Ricardo.

"Is it alive?" asked Ruby.

"Can't tell, but it probably is."

Another appeared, and another, and then the ocean was rich with them, bowls half a meter across, pale green bowls with ruffled fringes that rippled in the breeze. Victor tied the sail lines down, leaned over the edge, and inspected one closely.

"I wouldn't touch it," said Ricardo. "Remember how jellyfish sting."

"Don't know, I've never been stung," said Victor. "And these aren't jellyfish. What do these things eat?"

Ricardo began speculating about ocean ecology and Victor tuned him out. The *Tortoise* plowed through the flotilla of living bowls easily. Some tore as they passed, showing the delicacy of their forms.

I'm sorry. We humans pass through and some of you die, and we move on.

From joy, to philosophy, to melancholy. I need to get hold of myself.

The number of bowls diminished, and Victor turned his attention back to the distant point, wishing it would approach faster, and yet not wanting the voyage to end.

"Ruby," asked Emily, "What are you going to do now with your casino gone?"

Ruby sat in the middle of the raft, her white blouse showing the dirt and wear of the past days, her brown hair tied and dingy. She wrapped her arms around her knees and looked at nothing in particular. "I don't know. I haven't given it much thought. We were insured; I suppose we could rebuild." Her face grew dark. "If we do, we'll have armed security and better sweeper satellites."

Victor tied the sail lines down. The wind was steady, and the *Tortoise*, true to its name, moved slowly but surely. He did

119

not need to correct its heading every moment. He sat down and splashed the water with his hand.

Ruby cautioned, "I wouldn't put my hands in the water, or my feet either. You don't know what's down there."

Ricardo huffed quietly.

Victor pulled his hand back out, unconcerned. The water looked clear. He began tying the leftover ropes together, end to end. "Ruby, do sweeper satellites really work?"

"They've had them on earth for ages. In orbit, I mean." She rubbed the back of her neck. "You know about all the orbiting junk from the early space program?"

"Yeah, I read about that."

"After a manned space station got destroyed by an old discarded rocket booster, they started putting up sweeper satellites with radar-guided lasers. They cleared out thousands and thousands of junk parts."

"What about something the size of that rock that hit your casino?"

Ricardo waved his good arm. "It just takes a little longer. Right, Ruby? You aim the laser at one spot, vaporize the material, and it acts like a rocket and pushes the rock away from the planet. Or slows it down and drops it in to the atmosphere to burn up. Either way, it's gone. Ruby's sweepers would have worked, if they hadn't been sabotaged."

"We'll rebuild," said Ruby.

Ricardo tensed and looked away.

Victor tied one end of his rope to the raft and threw the other end into the water behind them.

"What are you doing?" asked Ruby.

"Safety line. If Emily falls in, she can grab this before we sail out of reach."

"What if I miss?" asked Emily, her face filled with concern.

"We'll drop the sail, and I'll swim back and get you. Don't worry."

"Well, you better swim quick 'cause I can't."

The day stretched on. Victor played guessing games with Emily to while away the time, and then Ricardo told outrageous stories, ending with "Early one morning I shot a great red ape in my pajamas. What he was doing in my pajamas, I'll never know." He laughed at his stolen joke, clutched his bandaged chest, and said, "Ow!"

They nibbled on the cans of rations and tried to stretch out their fresh water. The journey seemed to take forever, but they arrived at the rocky point that afternoon.

The sea was calm and they poled the raft to the shore. Victor took the rifle and found fresh water for the canteens. Upon his return, he built up a fire while Ricardo found some more plate crabs.

"You say that you don't like canned meat," Ricardo said to Emily as he laid the circular creatures upside-down on the sand. "Do you like lobster?"

Emily nodded as she dumped a load of firewood on the pile.

"Come here and let me show you how to do this."

She made a face. "Ewww."

Victor knelt down by Ricardo and beckoned to Emily. "Come on, little sister. You can do this." She grumbled but knelt down beside him, her mouth grim.

"Now," said Ricardo, "you see how this hard cap on top of this crab has this groove all the way around? A sturdy knife would be better, but if I push this screwdriver in like this, and twist..."

Emily flinched at the popping sound.

"...then go around a bit and twist again, and again, and see how it's tearing loose? A few more times, and there. See how the belly plate lifts off?"

She made another face at the sight of the innards.

"This is the good meat here," said Ricardo, pointing to a pink circular ring inside the crab. "Here, Victor, you open the next crab."

Victor found it a bit awkward, but the plate eventually came off, though he had damaged the meat by pushing the screwdriver in too deeply. "Sorry about that," he said, touching the ring of muscle tentatively.

121

"No problem, mate, you've got the idea. It'll still taste good. Emily?" He handed the screwdriver to her.

Emily glared at Victor, took a deep breath, and poked tentatively at her crab.

"A bit harder," Ricardo encouraged.

She grimaced, pushed the screwdriver blade in, and twisted. The plate made a satisfying pop. She rotated the crab and kept loosening the plate, a frown of concentration on her face. This time, when the plate lifted off, the meat was perfect.

"Excellent job!" said Ricardo. "Couldn't have done better myself."

Emily looked surprised and pleased. She held the opened crab towards Victor. "See? My meat is good, not scratched up like yours!"

Victor made a sour face at her, but inwardly he was pleased. This had been a big step for Emily.

Ricardo put hot rocks from the fire into a leaf-lined pit, laid the opened crabs on top of them, and then poured water over everything. The hot rocks boiled the water, and Ricardo laid more green leaves on top of the crabs to trap the steam.

By sunset, he declared the crabs done and pulled them out of the pit. Using Victor's knife, he levered out the ring of meat from Emily's crab, and then Victor's. "It's hot, mates, so be careful. We should have a little drawn butter, but it can't be helped."

Victor blew on his piece of crabmeat to cool it. He knew it was not really crab, it was alien flesh, but he just was not going to think about it. He tasted it tentatively, and then took a real bite. It tasted more like fish than crab, but he had to admit it was excellent.

Emily's eyes grew round, and around a mouthful of plate crab she exclaimed, "This is sooo good!"

Ricardo laughed and helped Ruby get her meat out of her crab. There was no music, no fancy drinks from smiling waiters, but eating the crab meat while the stars came out and the planet's ring arced across the sky was something Victor tucked away in the part of his memory reserved for special occasions in his life.

122

Victor securely moored the *Tortoise*, and then retired to his blanket for the night. The sandy beach was far more comfortable than lying down on the raft. The next day would take them past the volcano, and they might have to sail through the night.

There was no hurry. No ship would be waiting for them at Horseshoe Station, just men who thought they were already dead.

I'll have to deal with that when we get there. Not Emily, not Ruby, and certainly not Ricardo. Me.

Emily was too young, and Ruby and Ricardo were not street fighters. Moreover, they didn't have a nervous system that could suddenly kick into overdrive. He had dealt with situations like this before, in a previous life on Septimus. It was really a matter of their small gang of four against the gang known as Chancel Corporation, only their gang of four was really a gang of one.

He sighed, and shrugged off his thoughts. Emily lay beside him, and she was still awake. "Emily?"

"Yes?"

"You said you couldn't be Cydney anymore. So how come you put on that pirate kerchief back there and did the pirate songs? You know, for the apes? You didn't do it before."

"I don't know." She was silent for a time. "I guess, maybe, it's because I don't have to be Cydney anymore. Being her was painful, sometimes. I was never allowed to be just me. Now, I can have fun with it." He heard the sliding of her blanket as she turned towards him. "That was the fun part, the dancing and the singing, and I was good at it, Victor, I really was. I still am. But the pressure's off now, and I can feel it, it's fun again. Yo ho! Plus Scampy likes it when I sing, don't you, Scampy?"

Scampy squeaked.

"He knows his name now, you know. I can say, Scampy, go get this, and go get that, although he doesn't really know the words, he just goes and gets what I point at, and then I give him hugs and tickles."

"Hm." The ebb and flow of the surf was settling his mind.

"Can you see the glow of the volcano against the clouds?" she said. "It gets light and then it gets dark, and I think of vids I've seen of volcanoes, where the lava suddenly bursts out. They did an episode once, where Cydney was on an island with the pirates and the island was a volcano that blew up, but it's scary being near a real one."

Cydney's chatter was relaxing, and he did not mean to be rude but he could not help but drift off to sleep.

*

"There it is," said Ricardo, pointing with his left arm. "The volcano."

A low black mountain far to the south sent up a plume of smoke as a thin red line snaked down its side. The mountain was barren of vegetation, and a black and varied plain separated the volcano from the surrounding forest.

"I thought it would be taller," said Ruby, clinging to a rope on the makeshift raft. "Like Mount Fuji or something."

Ricardo gestured broadly with his hand. "That lava's extremely hot and flows long distances. It spreads out instead of making a cone. I keep hoping a geologist will come out on vacation and explain it to me better so I can explain it to the tourists. There's talk of a science station opening up someday, but no government's put money into it yet."

Ruby shielded her eyes from the sun. "Look at that steam! The lava's flowing right into the water. Can you hear it booming?"

"Hissing, more like."

Victor spread his stance. "I feel it through my feet, like thunder rumbling through the water." He adjusted the sail of the raft, keeping them at a good distance from the plume of steam. He saw irregular blocks of floating pumice drifting in the water closer to the shore, and he wanted to avoid them.

The sea was choppy, more than yesterday; the *Tortoise* heaved and rolled as it pushed ahead. The wind was stronger the further west they got, and the swells seemed to come from

124

two directions. He felt as though he held the reins of a peevish horse that stumbled over uneven ground. If the raft had been larger, if it had been a boat, he might have gotten seasick. As it was, the salt spray kept him centered.

Ricardo kept trying to stand so that he could see the volcano clearly. Ruby remained seated, and Emily gripped the ropes that bound the *Tortoise* together. The rougher the sea got, the tighter Scampy clung to Emily and the tighter Emily clung to the ropes.

Victor caught sight of what seemed a sudden spray of water ahead.

Are there rocks there?

The spray subsided, only to be followed by another burst of water into the air. Victor tried to steer the raft more northerly, fearing there were rocks just under the water.

Ricardo finally caught sight of the turmoil. "What's that up ahead?"

"You mean that, where that spray just flew up?"

"Yes. Are those rocks?"

"I don't know." Victor watched the swells as they rolled through the disturbed area. "I don't think it's rocks. If that were rocks up ahead, every wave would crash on them, but it's irregular."

"Ricky!" said Ruby in a tense voice, "the water's red down below!"

Victor looked where Ruby was pointing. A red glow fluctuated deep in the water ahead of them.

"Okay," said Ricardo, "That's not good."

"What?" Emily gripped the deck ropes tighter.

"That's a volcanic vent." Ricardo dropped low on the deck and braced himself. "That's molten lava down there."

"Underwater?"

"Yes. Maybe it's a lava tube from the volcano, or else the fault's opening up here, but that red down there is molten lava."

"So that's wasn't waves crashing on rocks," said Victor, tying down the lines of the sail, "That was gas bubbling up."

"I think so," said Ricardo. "The sooner we get past this, the better."

As if to accent his remarks, a huge bubble of gas erupted off the right-hand of the *Tortoise*. The raft rolled dangerously, and Emily screamed.

"Everyone hang on!" shouted Ricardo. Sulfurous fumes wafted over the boat, and Victor flattened himself and grabbed the ropes next to Emily. If a large enough gas bubble burst under them, it could roll the raft and put them all in the water.

A wave washed over them, and Victor gasped. It was hot! They were now passing over the vent, and gas bubbles began bursting on either side of them, splashing hot water, rocking the raft, and spewing enough sulfurous fumes to make them choke.

The *Tortoise* kept moving, slowly and ponderously, but the wind was fitful. Through the steam and the mist, Victor could see clear water beyond, and ripples that indicated a breeze.

If we can just make it past this vent....

An enormous gas bubble erupted under the back end of the *Tortoise*, and raft dropped into the void left by the bubble, pitching nose-up and rolling to the right. Emily screamed as her legs slid off the side of the raft.

Ruby reached out to grab her, but lost her own grip. She clutched frantically at the ropes but water rushed into the void left by the bubble and the raft bucked.

With a shriek of dismay, Ruby slid off the raft and disappeared into the boiling sea.

Chapter twelve

Victor watched in horror as Ruby's frantic hands vanished into the roiling water. Gas bubbles sprayed acrid fumes and hot water all around them, tossing the *Tortoise* left and right. Ruby would not be able to swim in such turbulence.

He rose to his feet, thinking rapidly. Ruby had gone down *there*, and the raft was moving *that* way. There was no time to take off his boots; he had to act. He made his best judgment and dove off the end of the raft.

His outstretched hand caught the trailing rope as he plunged headfirst into the sea. The water stung him, scalded his skin, and swirled in violent motion. As he descended, he swung his free arm, trying to make contact with Ruby. He kept his eyes closed, but a red glow penetrated his eyelids.

Now that he was underwater, he felt the shock waves of the lava vent, the explosive rumble of volcanic gas and the hammer of steam implosions. If he had ever pictured Hell, it would be this.

His hand hit an object and he swung again, this time grasping an ankle which had to be Ruby's. She kicked and struggled as he pulled her close and wrapped his arm around her waist. He pulled hard on the rope, slid his hand up and pulled again, dragging them both back up to the raft.

When they broke the surface he pushed Ruby upwards, his eyes still closed. His skin stung so badly that he was afraid to let the water get to his eyes.

He felt hands grasp Ruby and pull her on board, and then Ricardo's hand grasped his, and he struggled up the back end of the raft.

"Rinse her eyes!" he shouted. "The water's like acid!" Still clutching the rescue rope with one hand, he reached down with the other and felt the water. It felt cooler, so he splashed his face and hesitantly opened one eye. The raft was still moving and in front of them lay calmer water.

Ricardo poured water from the canteen onto Ruby's face, but she twisted in agony. Victor staggered over to Ruby and slid his arm around her waist again.

"What are you doing?" cried Ricardo, but Victor ignored him. He lifted Ruby and fell back into the sea.

The water was cooler here and his skin stopped burning. Ruby struggled, but he let them both sink for a couple heartbeats to let the water rinse through their clothes before he pulled them back up again.

Climbing onto the raft again after Ruby was dragged back on was painful; he was exhausted and gasping for breath. He could see, though. His eyes no longer stung. Ruby lay curled up on the deck, coughing.

"Keep the raft moving," he rasped hoarsely as Ricardo drained the last of the canteen onto Ruby's face. The raft bucked again, but this time they all stayed on. The wet sail rippled as wind touched it, and the raft continued to move out of the boiling sea.

Emily anxiously wiped Victor's face with her hand. "I thought you were drowned!"

"Is there any water left?" he croaked. "My mouth tastes terrible."

Emily took the canteen from Ricardo and shook it. "No, sorry, there's no water left."

He waved his hand. "'S okay."

The *Tortoise* rocked and heaved, but they were out of the area of the bursting bubbles. He rolled to the side, scooped up a handful of seawater, and rinsed his mouth. The seawater was acrid but better than the nasty stuff he still felt in his nostrils. He crawled over to Ruby. "Is she okay?" he asked Ricardo.

"She's awake but burnt."

Ruby up looked at Ricardo with red and runny eyes. "I thought I was dead." She coughed. "How did I get back here?"

"Victor pulled you out," said Ricardo.

"Victor? Tell him he's my...." She coughed again.

"Rinse your mouth out," said Victor. "Even rinsing with seawater, you'll feel better. It felt like we were swimming in acid. Hot acid."

"You probably were," said Ricardo.

Victor's feet stung, and he pulled his boots off and dipped them in the sea, pouring saltwater from his boots over his feet. "We need to get to shore."

Emily put her head against his shoulder and gripped his arm. "I want to go home."

"Me, too." He slipped his boots back on and loosened the sail lines. He angled the *Tortoise* to the south, towards the shore. They were past the volcano and he wanted to get off the sea.

He looked back over his shoulder to see the swirling column of steam that marked the line of the lava vent. Why had he not seen it sooner? He had let himself get distracted, and it almost cost Ruby her life.

The wind picked up. The swells were higher, but not caused by gas bubbles any more. "Trees," said Ricardo. "Up there, to the right. That's only volcanic rock ahead of us."

"We've got to land," said Victor.

"Not here, not at the rocks. We'd be torn to shreds."

Victor hated to ask for help, but he could not continue steering. "Could you hold these lines, then, please? Swing us towards the trees?"

"Sure, mate. Sorry I didn't do it sooner." Ricardo took the lines from him and held them with his good arm. Victor collapsed on the deck.

What I wouldn't give for a great big, fresh, cold glass of water.

Emily put her hand on his shoulder. "You want to know something funny?"

With all the patience he had left, he asked, "What?"

"Look at Ruby's hair."

He rolled to his side. Ruby's dark brown hair had turned to uneven blonde streaks.

"You, too," said Emily. She straightened his hair with her fingers. "You're a blonde now, mostly."

He managed a coughing laugh and looked at his arms. The hair on his arms was white, and his skin was red. "I guess I look pretty bad."

"I'd ask for my money back if you ask me. That's a pretty bad dye job."

This time he did laugh as the absurdity of it all struck him. Minutes ago, he and Ruby had been on the edge of death, and now the worst effect seemed to be a change in hair color, though his burned skin still stung.

Ruby revived, but did not laugh when she looked at the strands of her acid-bleached hair. Her blouse was now stained yellow and ragged, and her dressy deck shoes were dilapidated. She huddled as the distant line of trees approached far too slowly.

Victor took over the sail as they approached the shore, guiding them further north until he saw a sandy beach. "Hang on! The waves are breaking, and they're going to toss us around."

"Just what we needed," said Ruby grimly.

Victor swung the nose of the *Tortoise* towards the center of the beach. "If you get thrown off, watch out for the undertow."

"Stop scaring me!" cried Emily, and she spread-eagled on the deck again, her hands gripping the lines.

The beach was wide with a gentle slope, and he was grateful that Ricardo had urged him to go beyond the volcanic area. Driftwood lay scattered on the dark sand above the wave line, proof of passing storms. The green trees looked like a mix of tangle trees and shorter trees with long fronds he had not seen before.

The landing was rough but the waves were predictable, and with a sliding crunch the raft nosed into the beach. They climbed off the raft and pulled it up further before the waves could pull it back out.

Victor saw no stream, not even a trickle, and he was so desperately thirsty that he grabbed the canteen and started to head towards the woods.

"Not yet, mate," said Ricardo. "I think the *Tortoise* is through."

"What do you mean?" asked Ruby, lying on the sand as if washed up by the waves.

Ricardo pointed up the beach. "We have to go north, now, and we can't steer the raft across the wind. We only got here because the wind was blowing this direction."

Victor heaved a weary sigh. "I think you're right."

"So we need to grab what we're going to carry, and leave it."

The *Tortoise* had done its job. Slowly and steadily, it had carried them past the volcano and past the unexpected underwater vent. Victor pulled out his knife and cut the sail lines loose. "We can't carry much. Some rope, blankets, and the canteen."

They removed the rifle from its protective plastic, gathered what they could, and set off northward along the beach.

It was hours, painful hours, before they found a sluggish stream. Ricardo followed it inland, and returned with a canteen full of tepid water. "This stream comes a long way," he said, "and I gave up trying to find the headwaters. I don't trust it to be clean. I filled this where it poured over a ledge. It will have to do."

They drained the canteen, and Ricardo went back up to refill it. They rinsed the salt and sulfuric odor from their clothes in the slow-moving water, but the sight of tiny wormlike things corkscrewing through the water prevented them from stepping in and bathing.

They sat in the shade of a frond tree, waiting for Ricardo to return. Emily straightened Ruby's hair with her fingers, muttering to herself, "I want a comb, I want a brush, I want some lotion, I want shampoo, I want..."

"Ruby," said Victor, "can I ask you something personal?"

"You saved my life. You can ask anything you want."

Victor almost stammered at the unexpected praise. "You and Ricardo almost got married? Is that true?"

Ruby exhaled. Victor couldn't tell if her red face was from emotion or just the acid burn. "You're right, that's a personal thing to ask, but yes, we did. Almost. But he was determined to keep doing safaris down here, and I was determined to run my casino. Neither of us would give up what we wanted so we could be together." A thin smile showed that she was amused at her own folly. "It became a matter of pride, I guess. His and mine. Easy on the hair, Emily."

"Sorry."

Victor was curious, and the talking helped pass the time. "So now maybe you'll get together?"

"I don't know. I don't like to think about it. Things really haven't changed."

"If you want my opinion," said Emily, trying to tie Ruby's hair more neatly, "you could do a lot better than Ricardo. I don't like him."

"Emily," said Victor disapprovingly.

Ruby laughed. "Well, you're honest, I'll give you that." Her face grew thoughtful, and she smoothed the dark sand beside her as though looking for answers. "Ricardo...has his limitations. He's got too much pride, like me. He's not as smart as he thinks he is, and he's not as brave as he thinks he is."

Victor raised his eyebrows. Ruby seemed to see Ricardo clearly. Why did she still care for him?

"And his mustache is silly," said Emily. "It doesn't fit his face."

"I happen to like his silly mustache, and I like his face."

"Sorry."

"And it's, well, it's a big universe, and there are not a lot of decent men in it, and for all his bragging and his fake accent and his weak points, he's still a decent man and if we could get past the pride, I'd put up with everything else."

132

"There." Emily finished tying Ruby's hair and leaned back against the tree. "Maybe you can fix him after you get married."

Ruby laughed again. "You're a young one, aren't you? You cannot fix a man after you marry him. You take him for what he is. Trouble is, we women often don't know our men before we marry them. We marry the man we hope he is, not the man he really is, and then we can't handle the disappointment." Her smile faded into thoughtfulness. "I've seen him when he was leaving me. He wasn't hurtful or bitter, just sad. Sad and determined. He tried to get me to come along with him, but I couldn't. Or wouldn't. So I don't think there's anything left about him that I don't know."

"So, are you going to get married now?"

"I said I don't know. I don't know what's going to happen about my casino. One thing I do know though – I won't stay on this planet and watch him hunt down those beautiful red apes. So..." She looked at her hands and brushed them together as though trying to brush away the dilemma. "...I just don't know."

"Hi, ho, mates!" hollered Ricardo, crashing through the underbrush with a filled canteen.

"Speak of the devil," said Ruby.

"Nothing worth eating that I could recognize up there, sad to say," he said, dropping down beside them. "We never came this far south from the Station. Cydney, I mean Emily, what does your dingus say about locating things now?"

"I forgot about that." Emily moved Scampy and unloosed Peggity from her neck. The baby ape curled up against her side, wrapped his arms around himself, and whimpered. "Scampy's really hungry. We've got to find him some food."

"It's a shame he's not older," said Ricardo. "He could lead *us* to food."

Victor rubbed his chin in thought, and then stopped in surprise. He had stubble! He had been using a cream on his face that was a hair remover, and although he still did not have much facial hair, it was starting to thicken. He smiled and rubbed his cheeks, enjoying the new sensation until the burned

133

skin complained. Ricardo's face was darkened with stubble, threatening to hide his carefully trimmed mustache.

A tropical vacation on the cheap, that's what we're enjoying.

Emily pointed up the beach to the north. "Up that way is a weak signal and also the signal you said was that station place."

"Ramon's capsule," said Ruby.

"Let's hope he made out okay." Ricardo stood and tossed the canteen over his shoulder. "Much as I could stay here for a while, it's not a good place. No food and poor water. Shall we head north?"

With little enthusiasm and much groaning and complaining, they crossed the tepid stream and marched northward. The only redeeming features were the ocean breeze blowing from the east and the blessed shade from the trees.

"Emily," said Victor quietly as they walked behind the adults, "these are tangle trees."

"So?"

"So, I'm thinking, if we don't find food, we might climb up and see if there's a tree tunnel."

"So?"

"So, we could hammer on some trees and see if we can call up some red apes."

She looked distressed. "Why?"

"Food for Scampy. They feed each other, we know that. They would know where food would be, and they would know what Scampy needs."

"If we have to. I don't like it."

"Maybe we won't need to."

"But Scampy's really hungry." At the mention of his name, the baby ape unrolled an arm and tugged on Emily's ear. He peeped a weak complaint. "We'll probably have to."

The problem with following the beach soon became apparent. Lava flows from ages past divided the shore into separate coves, requiring climbing over rough rock and further threatening to destroy Ruby's deck shoes. They spent more time walking in and out of each crescent beach then they did walking north.

Ricardo called a halt when they found a spring of clean water trickling from an eroded lava dike. He declared he was going inland to look for food again and picked up the rifle.

"Ricardo," said Victor, "be careful about one thing."

"What's that, mate?"

"If you run into some red apes, don't shoot. Put the rifle down, sit down, and put a leaf in your mouth."

Ricardo started to say something flippant, and then stopped himself. "You think that would be better than defending myself?"

"If you defend yourself, you're dead. These apes might have been hunted. We're closer to Horseshoe Station."

Ricardo looked thoughtful. "You might have a point there. Just one rifle might not be enough. I guess I'll sit myself down so they won't have to chase me to pull me apart."

"Don't be stupid," said Emily. "If you were smart, you'd do what Victor said."

Ricardo's eyes narrowed and he hefted the rifle. "I've lived on this planet a lot longer than you have, missy. Don't you ever forget that." He turned and walked into the forest, his back stiff.

When he was out of earshot, Victor turned to Emily. "Now see, you got his pride up. Don't say things like that to him. You'll get him killed."

"Well, you do know more than he does. I mean, even Ruby knows more than he does."

Ruby spoke up, one eyebrow raised. "I also know enough not to poke the bear, my dear." She held out her hand. "Give me your fire starter before you go, Victor."

He pulled out his knife with the hot spark from of his cargo pocket, along with the screwdriver. "How did you know I was going somewhere?"

"Because you didn't send Emily out for firewood. You're going to go look for food for Scampy, right?"

"That's right."

"Don't stay out after dark. I'll have a fire going, and if you happen to find anything, *anything* that vaguely resembles dark chocolate, I'll be eternally grateful."

Emily laughed, but Victor had already started up the trunk of a tangle tree, and she hastened to catch up.

They struggled through several trees and descended to the ground twice before they encountered a small tree tunnel. It led inland, where it joined with a wider tunnel.

"Let's see what happens," Victor said as he pulled free a club-sized branch. "Emily, you have a stick ready to tap if any apes come."

"I know, I know. Scampy's starting to whine again."

"Let's pray for luck." He found a thick trunk and whacked it. It did not ring loud enough, so he picked another. *Whooom.* "This should work. I just hope there are some close."

Whooom. Whooom. Whooom.

He thumped away, trying to keep the tempo he had heard from the troop of apes before.

They were on a different continent. Would the apes be different? Was the volcano enough of a barrier that these apes had evolved differently? Would they communicate by tapping? Or had hunting made them vicious and hateful of humans?

He kept up the thumping for a long time, eventually despairing of attracting attention.

"Victor."

At the sound of Emily's voice, he broke from his reverie and looked up the tunnel. A small troop of apes was advancing cautiously.

"Time to be harmless," said Victor. He sat by Emily and grabbed a branch of leaves.

It's a shame I don't have fruit to share. Of course, if I had fruit, I wouldn't be calling apes.

The troop advanced slowly, not full of bravado like the apes on the other continent. Emily and Victor sat facing each other, tapping small sticks. The apes, several small males, walked close to them and chirruped.

You're supposed to tap back. Don't you know that?

136

The apes chattered back and forth, unsettled. One red ape, his fur pale to the point of being brownish-gray, sat beside Emily and rapped on the branch with his knuckles.

That's a start.

Scampy reached out a long arm towards the male, but it backed up. Scampy whined at him, a high-pitched whine.

The troop backed away, making room. Victor looked up to see a large female, the largest he had seen yet, towering over them.

Victor tapped his stick, trying to make social contact, but the female reached down and ripped the stick from his hands, snapped it effortlessly, and threw it away. With her eyes glaring and the brilliant red fur around her head bristling, she spread her arms wide, bared her biting ridges, and roared.

We're toast.

Chapter Thirteen

The branches under Victor shook as the smaller apes scattered before the rage of the large female.

What can I do, what can I do?

The tactic of tapping and offering leaves had failed. This mother ape was not going to socialize. Victor's heart sank; Ruby and Ricardo would never know what had become of him and Emily. They would merely be two travelers that disappeared into the forest.

Scampy slid off Emily's neck, uncoiled his arms and raised them in the air. He shrieked the plaintive shriek that Victor had heard when the yellow-eyed predator crashed into the clearing.

"Don't move," Victor whispered to Emily, keeping his head down and his arms motionless.

Emily whimpered with fright, which turned out to be a smart thing to do.

The mother ape growled and swooped up Scampy. She inspected him roughly, tasting his fur with her tongue. Scampy whined and stretched his arms towards the mother ape. She grunted and allowed Scampy to climb onto her and cling.

Emily was choking back sobs. The mother ape reached out an arm and drew it back. With a huff, she turned her back and sat down, patting Scampy. Victor caught Emily's eyes, which were white with fear. "Hold still," he whispered.

The mother ape turned her head and snapped at them. Victor bit his lip.

The male with the faded fur sat back in a low crouch, watching them with an air of curiosity. Scampy whimpered and reached an arm out to return to Emily, but the mother ape held him close.

"He doesn't like her," Emily whispered.

"Doesn't matter. She won't hurt him. Probably."

The mother ape growled at them again. Victor lowered his head and made a "zip your lip" motion towards Emily to keep her from replying.

Scampy had deflected the female's anger. If they had not carried the baby ape, she might have torn them to pieces, even with Victor's hyper-D kicking in. Of course, if it had not been for Scampy, they would not have been up in the trees in the first place. They would have been down on the shore looking for plate crabs, or scouring the underbrush for something edible. Shooting game for food did not look like a good option, especially after what had happened to Gary when he tried to shoot Scampy.

Now he wondered if they were going to be stuck up in the trees as night fell. Scampy was still complaining, but the mother ape held on to him.

Two apes came charging back, each carrying something under one arm, their free arms alternating with their feet to move them down the tunnel.

Their burden was not the blue fruit for which Victor had been hoping. One held a branch with fruit like orange balls with dark stripes running from stem to apex. The other carried a branch with two brown hairy pods like long coconuts.

The mother ape grabbed an orange ball fruit and bit it in two. She handed half to Scampy, who squeaked and dove into it with gusto, biting off pieces of the inside and swallowing noisily. The mother leisurely ate the other half.

Scampy whined for more, and the mother ape gave him fruit after fruit until his midsection bulged.

Victor's stomach growled. Emily grimaced at him and pointed to her mouth.

He shrugged. They could do nothing; Scampy's needs came first. They could only hope there was food left over, and that the mother ape would leave them alone so they could eat.

Scampy belched, stretched, and climbed out of the mother ape's arms. This time she didn't try to restrain him. He was no longer in distress; she was losing interest.

When Emily had screamed because of the yellow-eyed predator, that mother ape had dragged her away and nurtured her briefly. It was instinct rather than intelligence, guessed Victor. Scampy would probably be ignored until he cried again.

The baby ape climbed into Emily's arms, snuggled under her chin, and went to sleep.

The mother ape looked at them, grumbled to herself, and waddled down the tunnel. Only then did Emily sob and slide up against Victor. She put her forehead against his shoulder. "She almost killed us. Why?"

Victor put his arm around her and gave her a hug. "The apes around here have been hunted, I think. Even the old guy is being careful."

"What old guy?"

"Him."

Emily lifted her head and looked where he was pointing. The faded male ape had scooted closer and was chewing on a twig while pretending not to look at them.

Victor pulled the branch with the brown pods on it close, and twisted one off. "Look at him. He's lost the bright red color. I think he's old. I wonder if he knows how to open these." He offered the pod to the ape.

The old male reached out and took the pod gingerly, bit at it without effect, stroked it with his two-fingered hand, and then handed it back.

Victor pulled out his knife and inspected the pod for a weak spot.

"Shouldn't we go back now?" asked Emily. "It's getting late." She picked up an untouched orange fruit, but it looked withered and she didn't try it.

140

"In a moment. Let me try something first. This old guy wanted to get into this and couldn't." He laid the knife where the pod had a thin seam, and tapped the back of the knife with the screwdriver's handle, driving the blade into the seam. He pulled the knife out, and then pushed the screwdriver's blade into the slot made by the knife. He braced the pod against his boot, and pushed and twisted.

The pod opened, revealing a pink pulp.

Emily pulled back in disgust. "Ewww! Worms!"

The faded ape grabbed the pod and threw it away. "Phbbbtbt," he said expressively.

"Spoiled," agreed Victor. "Let's try the other one."

The other pod split to reveal a red pulp, wormless and sweetly aromatic. The faded ape took one half and began digging at it eagerly. Victor carved out a piece of the pulp and tasted it carefully. It was watery, with a mild sweet flavor.

He cut a piece for Emily and she ate it slowly. "Watermelon's better," she said.

"Don't have watermelon." Victor dug out the rest of the pulp. He held up the empty pod shell and said to the faded ape, "If you can get us more of these, that would be great."

The faded ape held up his empty pod half and hooted, and then pitched the pod shell out of the trees.

"Let's go," said Victor, tucking away his knife and screwdriver. "Maybe Ricardo found something."

"Probably found something with teeth," said Emily as she started back up the tunnel.

"This is Ricardo's area. These apes don't like humans. That means Ricardo and his buddies have been around here, probably, and maybe Ricardo knows what we can eat. Or what eats us."

"He said he never saw one of those yellow-eyes before."

"That was on the other side of the volcano. And be careful not to criticize Ricardo, especially in front of Ruby."

"Phbbbbt," said Emily, sticking out her tongue.

"Don't say that." Victor picked up the pace. "You don't know what you just said. You might be teaching Scampy bad language."

141

"Phbbbt!"

*

Ruby brightened up when she saw them emerging from the trees. "I heard something roar a while ago. I was afraid whatever it was, it might have seen you."

"It saw us all right," said Emily, sitting down by the fire. "Scampy, you keep eating like that, you're going to get fat and hard to carry."

Ruby frowned. "It saw you?"

"Mother ape," said Victor, adjusting the fire. Ruby had let the center burn out. "She was mad at us, wanted to kill us, but Scampy distracted her." He wiped his hands and looked up at Ruby. "Ricardo shouldn't show that rifle around here; he'll get himself torn apart."

Ruby sat on a fallen log and folded her arms, rubbing her hands over her shoulders as though she were cold. "I'll be so glad to get off this planet." She picked at the ragged edge of her yellowed blouse, her acid-bleached hair looking forlorn.

Ricardo eventually returned from foraging, his pockets and shirt bulging from the same striped orange fruit the red ape had found. He grumbled when Victor asked him to set the rifle aside and cover it. It was only after Victor reminded him of the way Gary had died that Ricardo allowed him to cover the gun with branches.

Everyone seemed in a bad mood that evening. Ricardo spoke only in grunts and Emily retired early. Victor saw the faded old ape blinking at them from the trees, but despite Victor's tapping, the ape disappeared back into the forest.

*

They had just resumed their travels the next day when a piercing whine echoed through the forest of tangle trees. Victor froze, trying to judge the distance and direction.

"What was that?" asked Ruby.

142

Ricardo peered left and right, trying to see through the thick underbrush. "Electric rifle, not one of the tourist rifles."

"That way," said Victor. "To the left."

Ruby caught Ricardo's sleeve. "Could it be Ramon?"

He shook his head. "Emily says Ramon's pod is north. That sound came from the west. Unless Ramon's gone hunting."

"He wouldn't have a rifle. His pod was as empty as ours."

"Be careful," said Victor. He had been cautious on the streets when there were strangers. He always wanted to know who was who, and what gang they belonged to. Seeing without being seen was a survival tactic. "Go slow and quiet."

Ricardo nodded slowly. "They tried to kill me. Everyone stay behind me." He checked his rifle and proceeded carefully through the woods.

Victor stayed behind Ricardo, followed by Emily and Ruby. The rifle whined again, followed by shrieks.

"Are those people?" asked Emily.

Victor shook his head. "Sounds like red apes."

"You're right, and something's got them upset," said Ricardo. "It's the wrong time for a hunt. Too early in the day. What's going on?"

They crossed a stream with bad water and colorless stinging butterflies. The tangle trees became thick and then thinned out again.

Ricardo halted them with his hand. "We're almost there. Let me take a look." He moved slowly forward, pushing branches aside and releasing them carefully. Victor refused to stay put, and followed behind.

"There," said Ricardo. "In that clearing." He pushed up a branch so that Victor could see.

The clearing was wide and man-made, dominated by a crawler with several tracks. Attached to the crawler was a trailer filled with cages.

"What are they doing?" whispered Victor.

"Well, I'll be," said Ricardo quietly. "When I left to meet this last cruise ship, they were building a zoo so tourists could see live red apes without having to go into the jungle."

"You're kidding."

"Looks like they finally got around to stocking it."

Two men in western outfits carried a limp red ape to one of the cages and pushed it inside. "Look there," said Victor. "Some are awake but they're thrashing."

"They're drugged," said Ricardo. "I'm glad I'm not doing it; Ruby would never speak to me again."

"You better be sure Ruby doesn't go out there and start knocking some heads together."

"What about me?" Ruby saw what was going on and gasped. Victor grabbed her arm and shook his head at her, cautioning her to be quiet.

Emily came up beside Ruby and watched as the last cage was filled and locked. Over a dozen sturdy cages sat on the crawler's trailer. Emily hugged Scampy tight. "Oh, that's so sad."

"What are they going to do with them?" asked Ruby.

"Display them," said Ricardo. "They've got an enclosure with running water and live trees and grass, where people could look at them. It's for the paying guests who don't want to go on a hunt."

"That's horrid."

"Ruby, it's just a zoo. I was only a tour guide, remember, but this isn't the first zoo humans have made."

"Victor, look," said Emily, pointing.

"What?"

"They got the old gray ape in a cage."

"Oh, no." Victor leaned forward.

"The last one, the cage at the end."

The crawler began moving, pulling the trailer along, crunching effortlessly through the underbrush. The limp form of the old faded ape was clearly visible in the last cage.

Victor started to say something, remembered that a young lady was present, and bit his tongue. "Let's leave. We can't do anything."

"You knew that ape?" asked Ricardo.

144

Victor stood up and backed away from the clearing. "We shared lunch." He ignored Ricardo's surprised look and resumed walking north, his mood grim.

*

"That way," said Emily, as she examined the tiny screen of her polybot. "The signal's coming from over there."

"The other pod," said Ruby. "Now maybe we can find Ramon."

They had traveled in the morning sun away from the ocean and deep into the forest. The air hung hot and humid under the thick branches, without a breath of wind to cool their skins. Sweat made their clothes cling to their bodies, and Victor wished more than ever for a shower and a clean change of clothes. He would have preferred to be traveling through one of the tree tunnels, but in spite of repeated climbs up the tangle tree trunks, he found none leading in the direction of the pod.

The ground rose, the trees thinned out, and grass took over, knee-high grass with long narrow blossoms of many colors. Stinging butterflies were thick, and small furry jumpers leaped up from the grass in attempts to catch an unwary butterfly.

Long trails through the grass showed evidence of a passing herbivore, something that chewed the grass low to the ground, but Victor saw nothing that was making such a trail. He nudged Ricardo. "So what is it that makes these trails?"

Ricardo pulled his hat off and wiped sweat from his brow with his sleeve. "No idea, mate. Something that moves at night, probably, or in the twilight. Never saw anything during the day."

"And no yellow-eyed predators."

"Not around here, not where we've been camping or hunting. We ought to run across one of our own roads, I would think."

"Roads?"

"Tracks, really, just the tracks from our crawlers. We cover the same route, often. It makes a trail for the horses. Tourists aren't into rough riding."

"Are there seats on the crawlers?" asked Ruby.

"Sure. Some guests don't like to ride horses, and some are a bit old for it. A crawler's air-conditioned and has a bar and a bathroom for the guests."

"I have a question, if you don't mind me being nosy."

"Sure," said Ricardo.

"Everyone I've seen so far is dressed to fit the Wild West theme. How come you're in a safari outfit? That's not western."

"Oh, that." Ricardo fiddled with the button on his shirt pocket. "Tourists trust me when I wear this during the trip here from their home planet. It's what people wear today when out in the wilds. It makes them feel I'm a professional hunter."

"You wish," said Ruby.

"I am so! I hunt and I get paid for it. That makes me a professional. But, once we land at Horseshoe Station," he said without pausing, "I put on a western shirt just to go along with it. By then, the tourists know me by name and think it's just good fun. You need people to have confidence in you if you're going to keep them safe."

Victor looked back at the forest. He missed the faded ape peeking at them. "Do you hunt at the same place each time?"

"No, we vary the location. We send someone out a couple days before with fruit, and...." He paused. "The apes are around when it's time to hunt."

"And what?"

"Nothing."

"You started to say you send someone with fruit, and....what else?"

Ricardo shrugged, his face guarded. "We lace the fruit a bit. It makes the apes more active and less cautious."

Ruby stopped dead. "You *drug* them?"

"No, we don't *drug* them," he said sharply. "It's more like, oh, giving them a couple of shots of whiskey. They stand

146

in the trees and shriek at us. Before we did that, they would just disappear."

Emily asked, "Is that what they did to those apes we saw them put in the cages?"

Ruby narrowed her eyes. "I'm ashamed of you, Ricky."

Ricardo looked as though he had been slapped. "Ruby, it's what we did. The hunt wound up the same way, with some trophies for the tourists but without a long and dangerous hunt. We were protecting people and providing a hunting experience."

"You hear that, Scampy?" said Emily. "He'll get you drunk and some fat man will shoot you." She hugged the baby ape protectively and glared at Ricardo.

Ricardo clenched his jaw and turned away, striding in the direction of the pod signal.

"You hurt his pride," said Victor quietly, as they followed.

"I don't care," said Ruby. "I can't believe he drugged them. That's not hunting, that's, that's shooting clay pigeons. No, worse than that. Sitting ducks. Bottles on a rail."

"It made money."

"So does...." She glanced at Emily, and began again. "There are lots of ways to make money that harms things, and ways that don't."

"No wonder that momma ape wanted to kill us," said Emily.

Victor looked at Ricardo walking ahead of them, his back stiff. "If he goes under any trees carrying that rifle the way he is, he could be in trouble, but if I try to tell him different right now, he wouldn't listen to me. Let's try to stay out of the forest."

*

Ramon's pod lay in a clearing, its tattered parachutes hanging from nearby trees. The door of the pod was clear, though it lay tilted on uneven ground. The grass around the pod was trampled, but there were no fire rings.

"Do you think he's gone?" asked Ricardo.

147

Ruby looked around the clearing for any signs. "Maybe that Chancel gunship picked him up."

"No," said Victor. "There would be burn marks."

"But there's not much sign of him being here. The grass is beaten down around the pod, but that could just be curious animals."

They found the door of the pod closed but unlocked. Ricardo put his hand on it and looked at Ruby. She nodded. With the rifle ready in one hand, Ricardo swung open the pod door.

From inside came a hoarse scream of terror.

Chapter Fourteen

The inside of the pod was dark, and Victor couldn't make out the person who had screamed. Ricardo shielded his eyes and called, "Ramon? Is that you?"

A quavering voice cried out, "Help! Who is that? Help me!"

Ricardo pushed the pod door fully open and hoisted himself inside. "Ramon? Are you okay?"

Victor saw the short heavy worker stagger forward, his eyes wide with fear. "Thank God you're here! You're here! I was so afraid...." He stumbled; Ricardo caught him and held him upright.

"We're here," said Ricardo. "Me, Ruby, Victor, and the little girl. We've also got a gun."

"I didn't know anyone else had survived," sobbed Ramon. "My pod ejected just before the casino was hit, and I landed here, but there was no food, no water, just those horrible things...."

Ricardo helped Ramon sit in the doorway of the pod, and Ruby took Ramon's hand. "I was worried about you," said Ruby. "We couldn't wait for you, but we were glad when we saw your pod take off."

Ramon wiped sweat from his brow. "The pod worked okay, but Ruby, there was no food or water! I didn't have any food or water!"

Ruby sighed. "We weren't open yet, Ramon. The pods hadn't been stocked or updated. We didn't have anything in our pod either. I'm sorry."

149

"And I tried to go look for water, and found a little in a stump, but then there were those things...." Victor passed the canteen up to Ramon. He grabbed it and drank greedily, whimpering between swallows.

"Things?" prompted Ricardo.

Ramon lowered the canteen and gasped. "Those apes, horrible killer apes, they stood up in the trees and shrieked at me, and there was this thing with tentacles, and even the butterflies, they stung me..." He sobbed, and Victor felt embarrassed for him. "Nothing to make a fire, no gun, I couldn't even lock the door, I was just going to hide in here and die, and then the door started to open and I thought one of the apes was going to..." His eyes fell upon Emily, and he cried out, pointing with a trembling hand. "It's on you! One of them!"

"This is just Scampy," said Emily, putting an arm around the small ape clinging to her neck. "He's only a baby."

"It'll kill you!" cried Ramon, sliding backward. "I've seen the vidstreams! They'll tear you apart, the others will see you with that baby and they'll tear you apart!"

Emily rolled her eyes and sat down in the shade of the pod. "Don't listen to him, Scampy. He's just crazy."

"Calm down, Ramon," said Ruby. "Ricardo's got a rifle, and nothing's going to hurt you. Here, we've got a little bit of fruit from breakfast." She held out the last of the orange striped fruits towards him.

Ramon took another swallow from the canteen and wiped his brow. Warily, he slid down from the pod and accepted the fruit.

Ricardo went into the pod to see if there was anything worth salvaging besides the Rosy Pony tools. Ramon took a bite from the fruit and spat out peel with a sour look.

"Don't eat the peel," said Ruby. "Just the inside."

"Now you tell me." He tore the fruit open and hungrily devoured the inside. "More?"

"No more," said Ruby. "But we'll get more food. Ricardo knows this territory and what's edible."

150

Ricardo jumped down and clapped Ramon on the shoulder. "Tough go, mate. Sorry we weren't all together, but we've had a rough time ourselves. Had to build a raft and all that. Almost drowned. Have you seen anyone since you landed?"

Ramon shook his head. "Nothing. No one. Didn't think I ever would. I had given up hope."

"Never give up," said Ricardo, straightening his hat like a tour guide. "There's always a way out. Well, now, that's that. We're headed to Horseshoe Station to see if we can hitch a ride off-planet. Are you up to walking?"

Ramon threw the peel into the brush and nodded. "Anything's better than being trapped in that pod. I never want to see one again. Ruby, what happened to your hair? And the little girl's hair?"

"Oh." Ruby self-consciously touched her yellowed locks. "I fell in some acid water with sulfur or something in it, and it got bleached. And an ape bit off Cydney's hair."

"Hah! You expect me to believe that about the ape?"

"That's what happened," said Victor, beginning to dislike Ramon. "It's a strange world."

Ruby put her hand on Ricardo's sleeve. "Why didn't the gunship come to this pod like it did to Gary's?"

"Because Gary called for them," said Ricardo, hefting the rifle. "He was working for them, remember, and he had a communicator. They weren't looking for distress beacons; they couldn't care less about this pod lying here, they probably don't even know it's here. I suppose we ought to be grateful for that."

She dropped her hand. "I can't believe they're so…uncivilized."

"They're in it for the money, I guess, and that's all," said Ricardo. "Wish I'd known that before I signed up with them. Shall we keep moving? Ramon, anything to gather?"

"Nah. Just what I'm wearing. Sorry if I don't smell so good."

"We'll find a stream soon. We can do a little foraging as we go."

151

Emily groaned dramatically and pushed herself to her feet. Ricardo led them northward, his face relaxed. Victor assumed that Ricardo had gotten beyond the morning's argument about drugging the red apes before hunting them. He was leading the group, a natural position for the man who pretended to an Australian hunter, and he was in familiar territory. Ramon kept up a litany of complaints to Ruby, who tried to look sympathetic.

Victor looked back to where the pod had landed. Ramon had been lucky; he could have landed on any of the continents, or with the door underneath, as they had.

"Hold!" said Ricardo, putting up his hand.

Everyone stopped, wondering what he had seen.

"There," he pointed. "A gray reaper." Resting in their path lay a tentacled reaper only slightly smaller than the one that had reached into their pod when they first landed.

Ramon whimpered and grabbed Ruby's arm. "Yes! I saw one of those outside! Horrible!"

"They are deadly, mate," said Ricardo, setting down his gun, "but nothing that a real man can't handle."

Ruby rolled her eyes. "Oh, for pity's sake."

Emily put her hands on her hips and glared at Ricardo. "Don't you dare pull that stunt again. Ramon's not up to it."

"Up to what? Up to what?" cried Ramon, looking at the reaper with terror.

"Stand back," said Ricardo, flexing his arms. "I can handle this."

"Oh, no, you won't!" said Emily. She grabbed a stick from the ground and ran at the reaper. "Get out of here! Shoo! Shoo!" She whacked one of the thick tentacles with her stick.

The gray reaper hooted, jerked its tentacle away, and began writhing into the underbrush. "Go on!" Emily shouted, tossing the stick at it. "Go bother somebody else!" Victor grinned at her spunk. She may be spoiled but she wasn't timid.

Ruby clapped her hands and cheered for Emily, who came back with a satisfied smile on her face. It was all for nothing, though. Ramon had fainted, and was lying face down in the rough grass.

152

*

The vegetation grew sparse and the dense tangle trees dwindled to tall shrubs. Ricardo pulled some gray roots that made for a bland dinner. Ramon ate root after root, all the while complaining about the lack of salt and pepper.

"Some people sure gripe a lot," whispered Emily to Victor.

Victor shrugged and tossed the stems from his root into the brush. "He's just not a pirate like you."

She flashed him a smile and nodded.

I wish Emily could have seen herself when I first met her. She's come a long way now that she's on her own, no agent, no parents, no one to pamper her, and not being forced to be Cydney all the time.

He thanked Ricardo for finding the roots and then asked, "How far is it to Horseshoe Station?"

Ricardo raised an eyebrow. "You mean, 'Are we there yet?' No, we're not there yet, but we should reach it in a few days. I recognize those bluffs there." He pointed past the low shrubs to some rocky bluffs that glowed red-brown in the setting sun.

Emily asked, "Is the Station there?" She scooted next to Victor and waited for Ricardo's answer.

Ricardo shook his head. "No."

Before Ricardo could give further details, Victor said, "When we get there, we can't just walk in. Right?"

"I don't think so." Ricardo fiddled with the collar of his safari shirt. "Obviously, my former partner tried to kill me, to kill all of us, I mean, so I don't think they'd welcome us with open arms. When we get to the Station, we'll have to see what the situation is and then figure out what to do."

Ramon wiped juice from his mouth with the back of his hand and furrowed his brow. "You said that before when we were walking, but it didn't make sense. So how come he tried to kill you?"

Ricardo recited the story of the Chancel gunship at Gary's pod, how Gary was killed by the red apes, and how Sam had locked them all in the pod with a mining charge on a timer.

Ramon didn't look convinced. "I've got friends at Horseshoe Station. It's hard to believe they would do things like that."

"I would have agreed with you up until a couple days ago. I've changed my mind since then. They didn't want any witnesses." He pointed to the bluffs again. "Emily, those bluffs are only a day's journey from Horseshoe Station by crawler, which means we have a couple more days on foot at least. It's dry and dusty there, but I was told they chose the spot because it was away from the jungle and safer. Better for the horses, easier to protect, more scenic."

He put his hands together at the wrists as though cupping a large ball. "Horseshoe Station is surrounded by bluffs like those, only redder. There's an old model western town they've built there, false fronts, dirt main street, watering troughs, just like the old vidstreams, only the women they've got aren't as good-looking as Ruby."

He winked at Ruby, who had joined the group to listen. She startled, started to say something, and then looked away, fighting a smile.

She likes him. If Ricardo would only compromise with her a little....

He drew a deep breath and pushed it from his mind. That was their problem, not his. His concern was to get everyone back into space and headed towards their homes.

Homes?

He didn't know if Ricardo or Ruby had permanent homes. Emily didn't have a home anymore, not one with parents. His own uncle was gone, so there wasn't much for him to go home to. None of them really had homes to return to. And Emily was now his adopted little sister by the Law of the Jungle or something, so he had to take care of her especially.

Things were too complicated.

"....landing station on the other side of the bluff," continued Ricardo, pointing to the outside of his left hand, "and

154

there's a stage coach to bring the passengers to the hotel right down Main Street. They've got a couple of professional ladies and a wait staff, one good chef and a gaming table in the casino. They're trying to grow the trade to where the town will look active. Right now, in between ships, it's a bit quiet."

"Is that why they wanted to stop my casino?" asked Ruby.

"I honestly did not know they were going to do that," said Ricardo, closing his hand into a fist. "And they *didn't* have to do that. More people were coming. The ship I was on was headed down to Horseshoe Station with guests before it got hit." He relaxed his fist and tapped his head. "They sure weren't smart in their timing when they sabotaged that sweeper satellite, destroying the very ship that had more of their own customers. I'll lay odds they didn't mean to do that."

"We both could have prospered," said Ruby with sadness. "Tourists who couldn't handle full gravity or didn't like the outdoors could have stayed in orbit at my place while their friends or family went down to the planet."

"To hunt drugged apes," added Emily. She stroked Scampy, who was restless and probably hungry again.

"You're right, Ruby," said Ricardo. "But then, if we hadn't had that accident, I wouldn't have gotten back with you again. We wouldn't have had this outing together." He smiled an exaggerated smile at her.

"I've been on better dates than this one, 'mate.'" Ruby poked Ricardo on the shoulder for emphasis. "It's not my idea of a good time to be dragged through acid water, to sleep on the ground, and to wear the same clothes for a week. Plus the entertainment around here leaves a lot to be desired."

"I could sing for you," said Ricardo.

"Shoot me first," said Emily, and she wandered off to look for food for Scampy.

*

A bath in a sandy stream helped Ramon clean up, and a meadow of beanpods eased everyone's hunger. The tangle trees were gone; the land was drier and rockier. A predator with a mournful yelp chased stilt-legged animals across the weedy hills. Ricardo assured the group that they were in no danger from the yelpers, but that they mustn't try to pick up any of the slow-moving creatures that looked like oysters with thick legs. "You'll lose a finger just like that," he said, snapping his fingers. "Those legs are sharp near the shell, and they pinch like pliers."

"I hate this place," growled Ramon, slapping at an insect. They were rationing the canteen and following a faint crawler trail through the low brush.

"On the contrary," said Ruby, "I actually like it. Look at those pink clouds over the hills, the way they catch the glow from the rock. It's a wide-open world, and mostly untouched. I'm surprised it isn't filled with immigrants already."

"Too new," said Ricardo. "No hospitals, no jobs, nothing to start with except what pioneers carry with them into a new frontier. Horseshoe Station is the beginning of a colony, but only that."

"Aren't there any valuable minerals here, rare earths and such?" asked Victor. "That would bring people."

"Remember that the value of some metals dropped when they found them in the asteroid ring around that star, I forget its name."

"Alexandra." Victor spread his hands. "Those asteroids around Alexandra caused the Collapse on Septimus that I got caught in."

"What do you mean?" asked Ruby as she stepped around a slow-moving land oyster.

"Septimus had a huge mining industry," explained Victor. "I was going to school and I remember hearing the ships taking off all the time. Then they found a way to harvest and transport metals from the Alexandra asteroids instead of lifting them off the planet. The economy of Septimus collapsed overnight and the bosses left, leaving the workers and their families with no way out, no jobs, no economy, nothing. That's why they called it the Collapse."

"I remember watching vids about that," said Ruby. "You were actually there when it happened?"

"Yes." He shrugged; there was no need to go into details. They would just try to offer him sympathy, and they wouldn't understand what it was like anyway. "I survived. My uncle finally came and got me."

"How did you survive? Were there farms?"

"No." He kept his eyes on the trail ahead. They were paralleling the red bluff. "Whatever food we got, we had to scavenge. They didn't have farms. I got pretty good at finding food."

"What about your parents?"

"Dad died in a mine explosion while I was in school. Mom...didn't survive the Collapse."

"What happened?"

"Not much to tell. There was nothing left but gangs when ships finally began returning. Our housing complex was burned down in a territory dispute. My uncle looked for her, Mom was his sister, of course, but he found nothing. I think she died in the fire."

"I'm sorry."

He shrugged. "A lot of people died."

"You were in one of the gangs?" asked Ricardo.

"I'd rather not talk about it, actually."

I'd rather not explain how I learned to break into anything, steal anything, survive at all costs. And how good I became at it.

"Sorry, mate. Didn't mean to pry."

"That's okay. It was a couple years ago."

Before my uncle got me to Saint Jude's, before the medicine that slowed me down.

He saw some edible roots alongside the crawler furrows and he pulled a few for dinner at sunset.

*

"My feet hurt," complained Emily.

"We're almost there," said Ricardo. "When we get to the top of this ridge, stay low. They can see you against the sky real easy."

157

"I still think we should walk in and talk to our friends," said Ramon, "instead of all this sneaking around." He was sweating and drinking more than his share of the water.

"I keep telling you," said Ricardo, "none of us are welcome. Clayton Chancel and his men consider us witnesses and they want us out of the way. In fact, they think we're dead. Remember, they blew up our pod, thinking we were in it."

Ramon said nothing.

"Get down," said Ricardo, "and move up here slowly."

Victor spread out like a crab and inched up the slope, putting his head beside a rock to avoid skylining himself.

Below him lay the model western town called Horseshoe Station.

It was as Ricardo had described, a single long Main Street, lined on both sides with stores and establishments. The town was surrounded on three sides by red sandstone bluffs, leaving the only entrance to the west. Their group had come up a winding ravine on the eastern side, and Ricardo had said that to the north, over the red sandstone ridge, was the spaceport with its gunship. "They keep the gunship on the other side of the hanger from the shuttle landing. It's not something they want to display for the tourists."

"Look at that," said Ruby with wonder in her voice. "You could shoot a vidstream here. They've got watering troughs and everything. And their own casino, I see."

"Remember," said Ricardo, "there's a huge mythology about earth's Old West. You build something like this and immediately people know what to expect and how to have fun. Nostalgia sells."

A man wearing a Stetson hat and a plaid shirt rode up to the front of a store marked "Dry Goods" and dismounted. He tied his horse to the rail and walked up the dirt street, dust rising from his boots with each step. He pushed through the double doors of a gaudy building that called itself the "Purple Sage Saloon."

"They've got their own well," said Ricardo, "and a power station by the spaceport. If you go out the town entrance and turn left, you'd see the corral and a herd of horses."

"Horses don't make sense," said Victor. "Even during the Collapse, the vans would always run. You just had to know where the hydrogen depots were and how to access them. Horses get sick and break legs."

"I like horses," said Emily.

"We went with horses because it's a western theme. For most of our tourists, this was their first time riding a horse. Plus, once you have a herd of horses, they keep making more horses. A herd of vans won't make any more vans."

Victor snorted, not wanting to concede the point.

"They've got a load of tourists in," Ricardo continued. "Hear that honky tonk piano? And the stage coach is in front of the hotel. I bet they've got the crawler out on a hunt."

"Where's the zoo?" asked Ruby.

"They were building it next to the corral when I left," said Ricardo. "Outside the entrance. That's where the well is, with some shade trees. It's all nicely laid out. They really did a good job, Ruby, even if there were abuses. Remember, a business like this grows by reputation; they needed to impress the tourists."

Ruby harrumphed. "They better not ask me for a reference, not as long as they kill people and red apes."

"I see a Sheriff's office down there," said Victor. "Hotel, tavern, barber shop….where do the bosses stay?"

"See the entrance, the beginning of Main Street?" Ricardo pointed. "You see that ranch house with the porch, couple of trees in front? That's where Sam and I stayed between hunts, and where the big boss would give us our assignments."

"Big boss?"

"Clayton Chancel, part owner of the Chancel Corporation and boss of Horseshoe Station. That's his house. A head for business but hard as nails. You never wanted to cross him."

"Too late for that," said Ruby. "I'd bet he's the one that told Sam to eliminate any survivors from my casino."

159

"The problem now," said Victor, "is what to do next. We need to get off this planet."

"I suppose so," said Ricardo. "I won't be working for Clayton anymore."

"We could hijack the shuttle. I bet I could find a way to break into it."

Ricardo ran his fingers through his hair, thinking. "Trouble is that would only get us back in orbit. We would have to convince the ship up there to take us on as passengers in order to get to a civilized planet. Remember, that ship is going to hang around until this load of tourists finish their vacation and go back up. If we take the shuttle, they've got no way to get back to the ship. Besides, that ship up there wouldn't let us in, coming up unexpected like that."

"I'm rich," said Emily. "Tell the captain I'll buy his ship."

Ricardo shook his head. "If I was the captain, and some people came up in a stolen shuttle, I'd call Clayton and ask what to do. And Clayton would tell him to keep the dock closed."

"Or he could come up in the gunship and put a torpedo into us," said Ruby.

"By the way, does anyone here know how to pilot a shuttle?" asked Ricardo.

No one answered.

Victor rested his chin on his fist and stared at the town. "What a mess. All this way here and we still don't have a clue what to do."

"Wait a minute," said Ricardo. "Where's Ramon?"

"Ramon?" Ruby called, turning around.

Ramon had disappeared.

"Bathroom break?"

"No. He always announced those. I bet he decided to walk in the front entrance and look for his friends," said Ricardo. "The man's an idiot and he's going to get himself killed."

"It's worse than that." Victor slid back from the ridge. "He'll alert them that we're here. We've got to stop him before he brings them down on us!"

Chapter Fifteen

Victor started running, not waiting for Ricardo or Ruby to come to a decision. Ramon was probably headed down to the town entrance, looking for refuge.

He had known people like Ramon, people who couldn't understand the viciousness of those in authority when things had gone wrong, who couldn't understand that sometimes people who should be your friends are the very people to be avoided.

On Septimus, after the Collapse, the authorities had become just another gang, only with heavier armament. Here on Horseshoe, something had corrupted the heart of the Chancel Corporation, and they had descended to evil.

Ramon was seeking refuge in the wrong place.

Victor kicked up gravel as he dashed around a shrub, looking for prints, but the ground was stony and prints were hard to see. He knew how to deal with gangs but he did not know how to track someone across rocky ground. Would Ramon have gone down the rocky slope directly into the town, or would he have circled around and come in the entrance?

Ramon had been refreshed by a couple of days of food and water, and he was a workman. He would be able to move fast when he wanted to, and Victor was handicapped by not knowing where Ramon was headed.

Forget trying to track him. I'll have to hope that he's headed for the town entrance and try to intercept him.

161

Victor raced along the base of the sandstone bluff, trying to stay close to the slope while dodging ravines and broken rock.

I have no weapon. They took my guns when they locked us in the pod. I should have taken Ricardo's rifle, but he wouldn't have let me have it without an argument. He grabbed a dead branch from a tree, but it shattered. He tried another, found it solid and heavy enough to knock a man out, and broke it to an arm's length.

In a fight, his hyper-D condition could kick in, allowing him to out-maneuver his opponents and disable them. He knew how to knock a man out. He knew where to hit, and how much. He had never killed anyone, but he had been in deadly fights. Ramon would be no problem. If he could find him.

The brush slowed him down, and landslides made him detour. The bluff diminished and the land became rolling foothills. Ahead he saw a windmill turning in the breeze, and he slowed and crouched.

Ricardo said, if you go out the entrance and turn left, you'll see the corral with horses and a windmill.

Victor walked slowly, keeping brush between him and whoever might be at the corral. Kneeling behind a low shrub, he finally got a good look. The rail corral had an Old West appearance, though it had probably been put together with power tools. Within the rail fencing a few red-brown horses flicked their tails lazily. The ground outside the fencing, where the horses couldn't stretch their necks to graze, was covered in rough gray-green grasses.

A cruiseship was in, so a lot of the tourists would be out on a hunting expedition and most of the horses would be carrying riders.

The tall windmill dominated the scene, its metal skeleton topped by a rotor with three blades, the thin kind used in generating electricity. The blades turned slowly in the gentle breeze.

A series of metal cages stood next to the corral, their machined appearance in contrast to the rough-hewn appearance of the wooden rails. Some of the cages held apes.

162

What caught Victor's eye, however, were the two men standing at the base of the windmill. One wore the flannel shirt and cowboy hat that seemed to be standard uniform at Horseshoe Station. The other wore work clothes and was wiping his brow.

Ramon.

I was too slow.

Ramon waved his arm towards the bluff behind Victor, but his words were too faint to hear. The man in the cowboy hat nodded and looked where Ramon was pointing. Victor carefully slid lower.

The man put his finger to his ear and took a couple steps away from Ramon, who shifted from foot to foot nervously.

Checking in with the big boss, I guess. What was his name? Clayton?

The man put his hand down and smiled broadly, clapping Ramon on the shoulder. He gestured towards the entrance of town, and the two of them began walking. Ramon had a smile on his face also, but Victor noticed the man in the cowboy hat casually touched the pistol at his hip.

Clayton told him to bring Ramon in, whether Ramon wanted to come in or not.

Victor cursed himself for not being more observant, for not tracking Ramon sooner. He had naturally assumed that after the "accident" that destroyed Ruby's casino, Ramon would have been a committed part of their group.

In hindsight, Victor wondered if Ramon might have even been on Chancel's payroll.

Would that save him?

Chancel Corporation had not had Ramon leave the orbiting casino before the sweeper was disabled. Nor had they searched to see if he might have survived in a rescue pod. Ramon would most likely be an inconvenience for Clayton Chancel. Ramon was a witness, and he had kept company with Ruby and Ricardo.

Victor could tell by Ramon's pointing at the bluff that he had betrayed the presence of the other survivors. Ramon would tell Clayton that Ruby and the others were in the hills of Horseshoe Station, and planning on going off-planet somehow.

It's too late to stop Ramon and that cowboy; Clayton already knows.

And what could Victor do anyway – tie them up? Have two prisoners to tend while still stuck on the planet?

Victor slid backwards into the shrubs.

If he didn't go back, Ruby, Emily, and Ricardo would worry, and they would be mad at him for letting them worry. But if he went back, they would still be without a plan to get off the planet. He could go forward, trailing Ramon and the cowboy, and see what happened. He was good at that, scouting and sneaking. Maybe he could learn something useful.

Forward it is.

He crept swiftly through the brush and small thorn trees, being careful not to bump against them, ignoring the occasional stinging butterfly.

Near the entrance of town he encountered another rail fence, with inconspicuous wires running along its length, probably meant to keep out wandering beasts such as the reapers. Nothing would spoil the illusion of the Old West like one of those tentacled creatures slithering down Main Street.

He hopped over the fence, being careful to avoid touching a wire. The entrance was narrow and bare of vegetation; he crouched down behind a tree while Ramon and the cowboy walked into the town. The only cover near the entrance was a wooden sign saying "WELCOME TO HORSESHOE STATION, POPULATION 850, MOSTLY HUMAN."

The pair walked up the path to the front of the bosses' ranch house. The cowboy held his hat in his hand and knocked. The door opened and a large man with thinning sleeked-back hair looked out, nodded, and waved them in.

When the door closed behind them, Victor took a chance and casually walked through the town entrance and behind the first building on his side of the street, a shack labeled "Doctor McGuire, Medicine Man." A man and a woman stood on the wooden sidewalk across the street, but were too engrossed in peering into the window of a clothing store to see him.

164

I need different clothes.

Ricardo wore a safari outfit in order to keep up the fiction that he was an Australian professional, though it clashed with Horseshoe's western theme. The outfit that Emily had bought for Victor had served well in their travels from the escape pod, but now he stood out, and it was stained and threadbare. He needed to look like either the cowboys or the tourists.

He wanted to cross the street and find out what was happening with Ramon, but he didn't dare cross in the bright midday. He was debating whether he should circle around the perimeter when some shouting began further down Main Street.

Creeping around Doctor McGuire's shack, which turned out to be a storage shed for tools, he peered down the street to see what the commotion was.

Two cowboys were squaring off in the middle of the street, preparing to shoot it out for the benefit of the tourists. One of them, a tall unshaven man in a black shirt, shouted, "They said you was the fastest draw in the west, Quickdraw! Prove it! I dare you! You're all talk and no action!" He sported a broad handlebar mustache that was darker than his hair.

Tourists came out of the saloon and candy shop to see the show. The other cowboy in the street, broad-shouldered, clean shaven, wearing a light leather vest over a gray shirt, laughed loudly. "You doubt me, Whisky Bill? I'll show you what I can do and then you can run. As usual." He called over a boy from the crowd and handed him a metal can.

Quickdraw joked with the bystanders about Whisky, and then teased the boy a little bit about tossing the can up in the air as high as he could and then flattening himself on the ground in case the gunfighter missed the can. After milking the situation, he stepped back, poised his hand, and called for the boy to throw.

The boy threw the can skyward and then ducked, to the laughter of the bystanders.

The laughter cut short as Quickdraw whipped out a pistol and shot the can repeatedly, keeping it in the air for several hits until it landed between himself and the other gunfighter. The crowd applauded and whistled.

Quickdraw held out his pistol to the boy. "Hold onto this for a minute, kid. Careful, it's hot! Don't worry, Mom, it's probably empty. Just don't make him mad." He waited for the laughter to die down. "I only need one gun to handle this turkey." He straightened up and faced Whiskey Bill.

A real gunfighter would have reloaded, but his other gun probably carries blanks. It wouldn't do to get them mixed up. And if this was a real fight, Whisky would have shot Quickdraw while he was shooting the can.

Victor took advantage of the distraction to walk casually across the street and step between two stores on the other side. He paused to see the outcome of the show.

The man playing Whiskey Bill shouted that he wasn't "skeered," and they walked a few steps towards each other for dramatic effect, hands poised over their guns. The crowd buzzed with excitement.

Whiskey Bill went for his guns.

Quickdraw was blindingly fast, pulling his single gun and snapping off four loud shots before Bill could fire. Whiskey put his hand to his chest, spun around, shouted "Argh!" and lay down in the dirt.

The crowd cheered. Quickdraw spun his gun and slipped it back into his holster. He turned to the boy and gave him a souvenir Sheriff's badge in exchange for his empty pistol back. The crowd applauded again, and a man dressed like an undertaker hefted Whisky Bill by the armpits and dragged him off the street.

Victor slipped between the buildings and walked back towards the ranch house.

The workmen who built the town had leveled the area between the bluffs and then left a space back of the buildings for the convenience of construction. Despite rock fall and the accumulation of scrap and debris, Victor was able to move behind the buildings with only an occasional scrape.

He stopped behind the clothing store. Next was Clayton's house, and it would be tricky going. He eyed the roof of the clothing store; it was solid, built to last. The buildings of Horseshoe Station looked ramshackle, but Victor could tell from exposed edges that they were built on sturdy skeletons of polycarbon. He tugged at the rough-cut boards that made up the back. On Septimus the hidden wall would be a solid sheet of polycarbon, easily produced on a civilized planet, and hard to break into. Here, it was just boards.

He could sneak into the clothing store and get some western clothes so he could blend in. The tourists would assume that he was a member of the staff; the staff would think he was a tourist. They would not be screening for unauthorized people. A resort reached only by spaceship and shuttle would not have unauthorized people wandering in.

Except for Victor and friends.

He debated loosening the boards, but he needed to find out what was happening to Ramon, and what the bosses might be planning. There wasn't time to go clothes shopping, and he wasn't ready yet to mingle. He moved on.

Clayton Chancel wanted his house to look nice, like a rich rancher's home. That meant greenery, and cover for Victor. Looking carefully for watching eyes, he moved out slowly from behind the clothing store. He knew the human eye was drawn to sudden motion. Moving slow drew less attention, so he looked intently at the ground in front of him, kept his shoulders slumped like a weary workman, and walked behind a strip of trees next to the ranch house.

The house had clear glass windows, but shades were pulled down and he couldn't see inside. That also meant that they could not see out, so he assumed no one had noticed him move from the store to the trees.

He crept closer, using neatly trimmed shrubs for cover. The yard was empty, but he could hear voices from inside the house. His heart pounded from excitement, and he felt the familiar exhilaration of invading the territory of a rival gang.

I'm enjoying this way too much.

On Septimus, food reserves had been guarded with deadly force, and stealing food and vehicles meant going up against people who were armed and experienced. Here, no one was on guard for someone sneaking in their midst. The people in the house had no clue that anyone would deliberately spy on them.

He lay flat and crawled the last meters to the house, then put his ear against the wall. Snippets of conversation came through.

"...do any good to put blame. Sam thought he'd eliminated the problem."

"I still say he shoulda stayed and watched until the pod blew. Probably somebody else opened the pod for them, or the door never really locked."

A sharper voice that Victor recognized as Sam said, "I wasn't going to sit there in the gunship waiting for that blasted pod to blow. It might have damaged the gunship."

"The gunship's armored, you fool."

"I didn't want to risk it. Besides, the door WAS locked, and I scanned behind as I left. I saw the explosion. They should be dead."

"I don't like it."

"Shut up, Pietro."

"You're in it with us, Pietro. All of us in this room. You'll be filthy rich like the rest of us, if you keep your mouth shut."

Filthy rich?

Tourists from Earth paid well to hunt game on an unregulated planet, but Victor couldn't imagine anyone getting "filthy rich" from it.

Scraping sounds suggested chairs shifting. The front door slammed.

From the front of the house came the loud voice of Quickdraw. "'Argh?' You don't say 'argh' when you die! Pirates say 'argh.' You oughta scream, or holler for momma, or say 'yuh got me!'"

"They applauded, didn't they? I'll die better next time."

"Next time I won't use blanks. Hey, what's this meeting all about?"

"Come in, Cocic, Bill." Victor guessed the voice was Clayton Chancel.

"Call me Quickdraw. Is there something wrong?"

168

"Sam here didn't do the job right."

"Hey!" objected Sam, but Clayton ignored him. "Ruby and Ricardo's still alive, and a couple of kids. They made it here, and they're somewhere in the hills around town."

"I can't believe it." A chair scraped. "How do you know?"

"They picked up another survivor who shouldn't have survived. He ran to us, told us about the others. We've got to take care of them right this time, and without disturbing the paying customers."

I was right. Walking in the front door wouldn't have been safe.

"Sam," continued Clayton, "you take Cocic and Bill...."

"Quickdraw."

Clayton snorted. "Grab some electric rifles and some horses and see if you can round up Ruby and the rest before they get into town." He paused. "There's a grave already dug over at Boot Hill just for atmosphere. Pietro, since you don't like the rough stuff, you can help me wheel the body over there. It'll look natural."

Body?

"The crawler's due back around seven, boss." Sam's voice. "How about I tell the ladies at the saloon to put on a show for the people here? Otherwise tourists might follow you to Boot Hill."

"Good. That's good. No one needs to see us bury Ramon. Move fast, men. Let's clean this mess up once and for all." Chairs scraped, people mumbled to each other, and the front door slammed as they left.

Ramon was dead.

169

Chapter Sixteen

Victor slid back from the wall, sickness rolling inside him. Ramon may have been foolish, but he hadn't deserved to die like that. If they had shot him, they must have done it while Quickdraw was firing his gun in front of the crowd.

He moved to the trees behind the house, looked around, and ducked behind the clothing store.

Ruby, Ricardo, and Emily don't know they're in danger. I need to get to them as soon as possible but I can't afford to be noticed and stopped. The clothing store will open, I suspect, when the crawler and hunting party return, so I better grab something fast.

He pulled the screwdriver from his pocket and loosened a couple of boards from the back of the clothing store. He couldn't risk being spotted, now that the street theatre of the shoot-out was over. He moved swiftly, his thoughts on his friends back on the bluff.

Funny; I've never met them before Ruby's Casino and now I'm going to risk my life warning them. I suppose we've become a gang of sorts, watching out for each other. Ramon never went through trials with us; he never bonded and he didn't stick. Now he's dead.

The store was still closed, and the only light came from the front windows. He quickly scanned the racks for something inconspicuous and in his size. He settled on a light blue flannel shirt with a western cut, and a pair of jeans with generous pockets. He kept his boots; in spite of the rough treatment, they had held up well.

He changed clothes and glanced in the mirror.

His hair was a mess, streaked with blonde because of the volcanic acid. He smiled wryly at his profile. He wasn't handsome as handsome goes, but he looked okay, considering, and thinner than usual. The shirt and pants fit him well.

He grabbed a belt with a silver buckle on his way out. Everything would be tagged, of course, and he would set off the alarms if he had attempted to leave through the front door. Apparently no one had expected a customer to leave through the back wall.

He transferred his pod tools into his jean pockets and left his rolled-up safari outfit behind the clothing store. He walked up between the stores to the wooden sidewalk and hesitated.

Sam might recognize him if he saw him, but no one else would. Sam had been sent to tell the ladies in the saloon to put on a show; Victor wasn't sure if he was still up in the saloon or not.

He stepped out onto the boardwalk, keeping in the shade, and looked quickly up and down the street.

I should have grabbed a hat.

Loud music rang from the saloon, and shouting and catcalls. Either the ladies were preparing to dance or were already dancing. He waited a few anxious moments more, and then decided that Sam had already come back from the saloon and had left with the others.

He scanned the bluff on the other side of Main Street, the bluff where they had first seen Horseshoe Station. Some broken rock behind the candy store looked like a pathway to the top. Going back out the front entrance of the town would be too visible and he might meet Clayton Chancel coming back from burying Ramon in Boot Hill.

He sauntered across the street and up onto the wooden sidewalk. The candy store was open and he looked into the window as he passed. Along with many types of candy treats, the store also sported souvenirs, games, toys, and snacks.

171

His stomach growled, and he wished he had some money. A woman in a checkered dress waved at him from behind the counter, and he smiled and waved back. He walked on, stepping into the alley between stores once he was sure no one was watching.

The broken rock was easy climbing, but the crevice further up was more difficult. He moved quickly but carefully. He was completely exposed and if he kicked a loose rock against the back of the candy store, the woman might come out and investigate.

He pulled at branches and roots to drag himself to the top, and then rolled on his back to catch his breath.

No time to waste. I need to find their tracks and follow them. I don't dare holler.

Sam, Quickdraw, and Whisky Bill would be on horseback by now, and moving fast. He got to his feet and began tracking.

The spot where Ricardo, Emily, and Ruby had looked over the town had footprints, and with three of them, the prints were easier to follow. They had moved away from the edge, and then milled around a bit.

Probably deciding what to do. I was gone by then. I'm glad I didn't wait.

The three tracks went down the slope, and then diverged from their tracks coming up. They had originally approached the town from the west up a gradual ravine. Now the footprints of the three followed roughly the same path that Victor had taken, though further downhill.

Victor started running. The tracks were faint but definite, and the route was easier. If he could only catch up to them and warn them, turn them aside, find a place for them to hide....

He heard noises up ahead, and he stopped. His muscles grew weak with despair and he lowered himself to the ground. It wasn't just the voices of Ruby, Ricardo, and Emily. There were other voices, harsh voices. He shouldn't have wasted time stopping at the clothing store; he should have risked getting caught in his ragged safari outfit.

Again too late, just moments too late!

172

Angry at himself, he crept close enough to see what was happening.

Ruby and Ricardo were sitting on the ground, their hands on their head. Emily was throwing a fit. "Shoot 'em and have done with it," shouted Quickdraw.

"You can't shoot a little girl," argued Whisky Bill. "You just can't."

"Clayton wants 'em dead. You want to argue with him?"

"That ain't the problem," said Sam, his eyes searching the surrounding brush. "Where's the kid?" Victor held still, grateful that he had been cautious in his choice of cover.

"What kid?" asked Quickdraw.

"They had a kid with him. He was old enough to use guns. I put him in the pod with the rest, and Ramon said the kid was with them just now. Ricardo, tell me where he is or I'll start shooting pieces off of you."

Ricardo swallowed nervously. "I don't know. He ran off."

"Which way?"

"I don't know. Maybe that way. He was following Ramon."

Sam shifted his electric rifle so it aimed at Ruby. "Ricardo, you've always been an easy liar. Tell me where the boy is or I'll shoot your woman here. Then I'll shoot the little girl."

"I tell you I don't know! I just don't know! If you can catch him, good luck. He's outdoor savvy. I never could keep up with him."

Sam spat and moved the rifle so it covered Emily, who kept her face in the ground and sobbed. "Ruby, where's the boy?"

In a weary voice, Ruby said, "Ricky's telling the truth. We don't know where he is. If you're going to shoot us, just shoot us."

"Sam, we're not shooting any little girls," said Whisky Bill.

Quickdraw leaned on the pommel of his saddle. "The thing is, Sam, with these three dead, we got nothing over the

173

boy. He could get to the wrong people, could cause trouble that Clayton doesn't want. Now, if you keep these three, lock 'em up, say, down in the ape cages, that boy might come looking for them. This batch of tourists is scheduled to take off tomorrow afternoon. After that, it don't matter."

Bill nodded. "Kid could be anywhere. Likely he run off scared."

Sam snorted. "He won't last long out there on his own."

Ruby laughed.

"What?" Sam looked at Ruby suspiciously.

"That 'kid' can live with the apes like they were his family. He won't die out there, and you'll never catch him. You'd be the one that would die trying."

Sam's face hardened. "Like hell. Stand up."

"What are you going to do, Sam?" asked Bill.

"Put them in the ape cages." Sam smiled a cold, hard smile. "Those cages were built to handle the big males, and they lock up good and tight. We'll use his friends as bait, like you said. If the kid's still alive, he'll come looking for Ruby like she was his momma."

"What about the tourists? What if they see them in the cages?"

Sam's horse danced as he answered angrily, "Hang the tourists! The zoo isn't open yet and the town gate is closed. They won't see anything. Get up, you two, and drag that girl by the hair if she won't walk. It's getting late. Let's go!"

Ruby and Ricardo helped Emily to her feet, and the three of them started walking ahead of the men on horseback.

Victor slumped to the ground and cursed himself, hurtful curses from the mines of Septimus. He had failed them, failed Ramon, failed himself. They had gone through jungle and ocean to reach this place, only to fail at the end.

He couldn't hope to overpower the three men with rifles. His friends would be guarded, and if he tried to approach the cage he would be playing into their hands. And who knew how patient Clayton would be? He might order their execution at any moment.

What should I do?

174

He grabbed a rock and threw it in frustration.

What should I do?

He stood up, despair and anger fighting for dominance. Aimlessly he retraced his steps, walking back up to the bluff overlooking Horseshoe Station. He crouched where he wouldn't be seen, and watched.

Clayton and a small thin man with black hair whom Victor guessed was Pietro walked back into the bosses' house. After some time, Sam, Quickdraw and Whiskey sauntered back into town. In the distance Victor could see the crawler moving, and a line of horses. The hunters were returning as the sun set.

Ramon is dead. Ruby, Ricardo, and my adopted sister are in a cage.

Bitterness and anger grew inside him, a deep anger he hadn't felt since the streets of Septimus, an anger that burned like fire in his chest.

You want to play rough, Clayton? You want to be the big boss? You picked the wrong people to go after.

He wasn't sure how, yet, but Clayton and the Chancel Corporation were going to pay, and pay dearly.

*

Night time.

The Horseshoe Planet's ring and the dome of stars shone brilliantly in the clear air. The town of Horseshoe Station resounded with music and celebration. The hunters had bagged several large red apes, and the tannery was preparing the hides to be taken with the tourists the next afternoon when their shuttle lifted them up to their orbital cruise ship.

No one noticed Victor as he moved from the back of one building to another, staying in the shadows. Skillfully his hands loosened boards and his eyes scanned for security. He took food from storage and ate well, then refreshed himself with carbonated juices.

The gunsmith shop was open as the tourists did some last-minute buying, and he saw from a casual walk-by that it was tightly secured. At the end of town, he broke into a warehouse and discovered mining charges, the same type that Sam had used to demolish Gary's rescue pod.

He paused.

Mining charges? Why were there mining charges?

There was no fake "gold mine" for the tourists as far as he could tell. The town had been built to fit into the bluffs; the charges hadn't been needed to make room for the town.

What are they mining, and where?

He knew mining charges – he had used them on Septimus. They were plentiful after the economy collapsed and mining had stopped. He could use mining charges as weapons.

He took two of the charges that were remotely controlled and checked to make sure the controllers were locked in the off position. He slipped the controls into his pocket and hefted a charge under each arm. Aware that he carried enough explosive to blow up half the town, he carried them to the broken rocks behind the candy store, and then carefully hauled them one at a time up onto the bluff.

He rested and studied the town again.

Clayton was being careless. He should have had guards watching the hills, but Victor saw only Sam stationed at the town entrance. A few other guards probably lay hidden near the ape cages.

I'm not some kid running for his momma.

Anger kept flaring inside him like a wildfire blown by gusts of wind.

I could handle one guard, but not two or more, not when they keep an eye on each other. I need to do what I do best; spread chaos.

When his eyes adjusted to the starlight, he picked up the mining charges and walked through the sparse brush and scattered trees towards the back of the bluff surrounding the town, moving carefully lest he step into a hidden ravine. He eventually came down to the flattened area that served as the spaceport for Horseshoe Station.

A wide metal shed separated the pad where the gunship sat and the larger pad where the tourists' shuttle lay. Victor watched for a long time to see if there was any movement, anyone guarding the gunship, but not even a glimmer of light betrayed anyone's presence.

Clayton's power resides in two things: this ship and his guns.

Silently he walked up to the large, heavily armored gunship and studied it. The door had a keypad covered by a panel, but he left it alone. Any pushing of the buttons would be sure to set off alarms back in town, and he didn't want to get inside the ship anyway. He had no idea how to pilot a ship.

He walked around the gunship until he found an access port low on the side. CAUTION was printed above it, and FUEL was printed below.

Just the right spot.

He slid the two mining charges under the fuel port and twisted the arming tabs on them until they each showed a tiny red light.

He walked back to the edge of the field and studied the distance between the gunship and the tourist shuttle. It was enough; Clayton had not wanted the tourists to see the heavily armed gunship, and so they were nicely separated. The shuttle from the cruise ship would be safe.

He walked back to the top of the bluff and down behind the candy store, where he hid one of the controllers, just in case. He wouldn't need to set off both charges; if one blew, it would set off the other.

He stole two more charges and their controllers. One he set up on the bluff near the entrance, and then he took a long hike around the town and set the other charge on the bluff behind Clayton's house. The charges wouldn't damage anything, but they would hurl dust all over the town.

One more charge he placed against the back wall of the gunsmith. By this time the shop had closed, and Victor chanced opening up a couple of the back boards to investigate.

Inside the front door small tubes faced each other, and similar tubes were arranged on the walls on both sides. Victor studied the arrangement. He was familiar with the tubes; they emitted beams that were invisible but would set off alarms if interrupted.

He dodged the beams and stepped inside.

Unfortunately the gunsmith shop didn't sell modern equipment but recreations of Old West weaponry. Under glass cases lay long rifles of ancient make, and ammunition. The prices were high but anyone who could afford to come to Horseshoe Station could afford to pay big money for quality equipment.

A pair of pistols caught Victor's eye. They resembled the revolvers used in the game in Ruby's Casino, the one he had played with Ricardo. It seemed like ages ago, back when he was still on his medication.

He used his screwdriver to disable the security on the cabinet, and then pulled out the pistols and the leather belt that came with them. The belt fit around his waist, though he had to use the last of the buckle holes to secure it. He needed to eat more; he was too thin.

He slid the pistols into the holsters, and then pulled them out several times to make sure there was no drag. The cylinders rolled smoothly, and the balance of the pistols was superb. He filled the chambers and put extra rounds in his pants pockets. He had no idea what he was getting into, but he didn't want to run out of ammo in the middle of it.

After stepping carefully back out and securing the boards, he looked at the charge set to destroy the gunshop and debated with himself.

I'm not going for revenge. I'm not just trying to be a spoiler. I want to hit Chancel Corporation hard so I can get my friends free, and I want to get us off this planet.

Even if he destroyed the gunsmith shop, Clayton's men would still have all the arms they would need, modern ones. He hated to destroy beautifully crafted weapons. But it would make a statement, and it would add to the confusion, and confusion was what he wanted. He growled to himself, armed the charge, and left it. Then he carefully distributed the controllers to his various pockets so he wouldn't get them mixed up.

The music from the saloon quieted and tourists walked or staggered back to their rooms at the hotel. Victor crept back up on the bluff and watched Sam guarding the entrance until the gunman was relieved by another guard.

Sam walked the circuit of Main Street, trying each door, making sure the town was secure. The man looked uneasy, often glancing up at the bluffs, but the lights from town would have ruined his night vision, and he had no chance of seeing Victor.

Victor sat and watched until Sam walked into the bosses' house. Lights came on and off and people walked from room to room, but the house never went completely dark. Prisoners were being guarded, and the few men who knew about it had to work in shifts.

He contemplated what he was about to do. Was he an evil person? He had often thought so, but now he was older and more experienced, and his actions made more sense to him. Back on Septimus he had been fighting for his life and his friends, meaning his gang. It was a matter of survival. Here, it was the same thing, and that was not evil.

It dawned on him that perhaps he was not a bad person; he was just someone who had been stuck with unusual traits. He was taking advantage of his skills and his traits to save the lives of his friends. He hoped.

Dawn was only a few hours away; he could smell it in the wind. He felt no need of sleep. He would move in at first light.

I'm not some kid running for his momma.

Chapter Seventeen

The sun rose slowly, lighting the sky before its rays fell into the sleeping town of Horseshoe Station. The door of the ranch house slammed, and Sam walked up the path to the sidewalk. He turned towards the entrance of town, running his fingers through his hair and yawning.

At the entrance he stopped suddenly and grunted. The man who was supposed to be guarding the entrance was tied up and gagged. Sam pulled a knife from a boot sheath and cut the man's bonds, letting out a string of curses and berating the man for being careless while on watch.

Victor, watching high above, didn't wait to hear the guard's defense. He smiled and eased his way down the bluff to the back of the candy store. It had been easy to move noiselessly behind the man in the early twilight, stun him with a blow to the head, and then tie him up. He had crept close enough to the cages to see that they were guarded by more than one man, both too alert to tackle, so he had retired to the top of the bluff to wait.

Now it was time to act.

He walked out into the middle of Main Street and looked around. Everything was quiet; the tourists were sleeping in from the revelry the night before. In the distance Sam yelled at the guard and waved his arms.

Victor pulled a controller from his pocket, making sure he had the correct one. After a deep breath, he set off the charge behind the gunsmith's shop. The building erupted; boards and dirt flew in all directions, and nearby windows shattered.

If anyone was sleeping in, they're awake now.

Sam started running back into town. The ranch house door slammed open and men tumbled out, belting on their guns. Victor pulled out two more controllers and touched their buttons.

Thunder blasted trees and dirt into the air above the ranch house, and a second explosion on the bluff across Main Street hurled debris and shook the town.

The morning wind swirled fine dust over Horseshoe Station, casting darkness over the town like an impending thunderstorm. Victor closed his mouth and breathed slowly, keeping out the grit.

Once the echo of the explosions had died away, voices arose, loud tumultuous voices from the hotel, the saloon, the workmen's quarters, and curses from the direction of the ranch house. Victor tossed the now-useless controllers aside, tucked the last one inside his shirt pocket, and waited for the dust to subside.

The particles in the air began swirling sluggishly and he felt his heartbeat settle. The familiar acrid smell began at the back of his throat. He was sliding into Hyper-D.

Slowly, four figures resolved themselves, walking towards him on Main Street, staying close to each other in the obscuring dust.

Sam was to Victor's left, his angular face red and his hands hovering over his revolvers. Next to Sam walked the shorter Quickdraw, his tan vest off-center. He looked puzzled and he glanced back and forth, apparently trying to figure out the cause of the explosions.

Next to Quickdraw was a nervous thin man with dark black hair, his single gun buttoned down in its holster. Pietro. At the end of the line walked Whiskey Bill, an electric rifle in his hands.

Victor's mind raced, and as Chancel's men slowly moved out of the roiling dust he had time to evaluate each one of them as an enemy.

181

Whiskey Bill hadn't wanted to shoot Emily, and wasn't happy about killing. He had that electric rifle, though, and one shot from it would take Victor down no matter where it hit. He would be the most dangerous.

Pietro still had his gun buttoned down. He wasn't a killer; he would likely surrender in a fight.

Quickdraw would be fast and accurate. He was a professional showman; Victor could only hope that he might hesitate when firing at a human target.

Sam was vicious. He would fire late but he would shoot to kill, and Victor thought a single bullet would not stop Sam unless it was to his heart.

I have never killed anyone and I don't want to start now. But how am I going to survive this?

Back on the ship Ricardo had said that this scenario never happened, that gunmen never walked down the street towards each other, waiting for the other to draw.

It was happening.

Sam stopped walking when he saw Victor, and the others stopped also. Whiskey Bill slipped his finger onto the trigger of the electric rifle. Victor wore guns, and it was obvious he had been waiting for them.

"Who are you, and what the blazes just happened?" said Sam with heat.

"I'm the kid you've been looking for. Remember when you locked me in the pod, Sam? I wanted you to know I was in town, so I made some noise." He folded his arms. "My name's Benny the Kid. I want to talk to Clayton."

Sam laughed without humor and glanced at the sidewalks. People were emerging from the hotel and trying to figure out what was going on. "Yeah, sure. Come with us, kid, your momma's waiting for you."

They don't want to gun me down in front of a crowd.

"I want to see Clayton."

"Mister Chancel's not seeing anyone."

Victor put his hand on his chest. "That's too bad. I was hoping I wouldn't have to do this." He pressed his finger against his shirt pocket.

A series of explosions shook the ground and echoed through the hills. People screamed and fell, clutching each other for support.

Victor risked turning away and looked behind him. Beyond the bluff that wrapped around the town, half of a gunship lifted into the air, spouting flames and smoke. It turned upside down and disappeared, followed by another rocking explosion.

"That was our ship!" shouted Pietro, clutching Quickdraw's arm. Quickdraw cursed and shoved Pietro away from him, and Sam turned red with anger. He opened and closed his hands, obviously fighting the urge to pull out a gun and shoot Victor down on the spot.

Victor unfolded his arms. "Take me to Clayton."

Sam found his voice. "Don't you move, you little…don't you move a finger! I swear I'll shoot you down right here if you even twitch!"

"What did he do?" asked Whiskey Bill. "How did he do that?"

"Shut up! Everybody shut up!"

There was death in Sam's eyes, and Victor felt time slow until it almost stopped. Dust hovered in the air, and Sam's glare of hatred froze. Victor could see Sam's hands, and Quickdraw's, and Whiskey's finger on the rifle. He calculated the sequence he would shoot them if he had to.

Unexpectedly, he found himself laughing.

"What?" Sam scowled. "What's so funny?"

"I fit!" Victor stopped laughing, but a smile lingered on his face. "I just realized it, I fit and you don't."

"What?"

A surprising peace washed over him. "This is where I belong. I'm built for this. You aren't. You're the misfits here."

"You're not making sense."

"What I'm saying is, drop your weapons. You're outgunned. This fight is over."

Whiskey Bill began looking right and left for other fighters that might be backing Victor.

"Fight? Don't be crazy, kid." From the way Sam's hands twitched, Victor could tell that he was no longer thinking of the watching crowd. "You go for those guns and you'll have more holes than Swiss cheese."

Victor quit smiling. "I've never been more sane in my life, or more serious," he said softly. "Drop 'em. Now."

"Like hell I will!" Sam reached for his guns.

Silence descended over Victor, all sound washed away by the acrid smell that filled his brain. His hands dropped and he pulled his guns.

It all comes down to this.

Quickdraw was grabbing his guns, but Whiskey Bill had only to lift his rifle and fire. Victor stepped to his left and fired both guns at the stock of the electric rifle. He was already swinging his guns towards Quickdraw when the rifle exploded. Whiskey screamed and started to fall backwards.

One down.

Quickdraw had his guns out and was firing. Victor leaned to the side and fired at Quickdraw's guns. He knew he would injure the man, but he had to stop the gunfighter fast.

One gun flew from Quickdraw's hand but his other gun fired again, too soon, too hastily. Victor actually caught a glimpse of the bullet before it whipped past his ear.

The gunpowder in the old style cartridges created a cloud of bitter smoke, and Victor stepped to the left one more time to get a clear shot. He fired again at Quickdraw's gun and hit the man's arm instead.

Two.

Sam fired and Victor felt a sting in his left shoulder. He reversed, threw himself to the right, and fired both guns at Sam. As he fell slowly to the ground, Victor saw that Whiskey was flat on his back, Quickdraw was clutching his arm and turning away from him, and Pietro had his hands up.

Three. Pietro's out of the fight.

Sam was still on his feet, one gun aimed at Victor.

I'm going to hit the ground with my shoulder. I've got to hold on to my guns or I'm dead.

But to his perception he fell slowly, and he had time to aim and fire one more time before he hit. His bullet shattered Sam's gun and also Sam's arm. As Victor landed on his side, Sam cried out and dropped to his knees.

Four...no!

Something wasn't right.

Quickdraw turned away. He has a hidden gun on him.

Victor pushed himself up on one knee and aimed at Quickdraw. The gunfighter twisted around, a small hideaway gun in his left hand, a single shot but still deadly. Victor fired, putting a bullet into Quickdraw's wrist and ending his career as a gun artist.

Victor remained balanced on one knee, guns ready, as the wind blew away the gun smoke and the dust. Pietro had his hands up, Sam and Quickdraw were no longer a threat, and Whiskey was out cold. The crowd applauded hesitantly, uncertain if it was a show or not.

He rose to his feet and took a step towards Pietro. "You want to live?" Pietro's hands were still up. He nodded, unable to speak.

Victor slid one gun into its holster and began pushing shells into the cylinder of the other. "Then pick up the guns from these men and toss them into the horse trough."

Pietro bent down, hastily picked up the pistols and rifle from the ground, and threw them into the water. Sam swore weakly at Pietro but Victor could tell by the gunfighter's wounds that he was no longer a threat.

He began reloading his other pistol. "Good man. Now go get the doctor and tell him he's got some patients."

"The doctor's right there on the sidewalk, Mister B-Benny."

A gray-haired man dressed in black and white with a thin black t-shaped bowtie stepped carefully off the curb. "I'm Doc McGuire."

"The medicine man. Howdy. I saw your shop." He snapped the filled cylinder back in place. "These men need attention."

"I'll see to it. Let me go get my bag."

"Just a second, doc." He stepped closer so only the doctor could hear. "These three are going to be in a lot of pain. Can you give them something to make them sleep for the rest of the day, if you know what I mean?"

The doctor nodded.

"I mean it, doc. If I see any of them walking around again today I'm going to have to kill them and then I'd have to kill you."

I've had to threaten death before, but never had to follow through. The threat is enough.

The doctor blanched, nodded more vigorously, and hurried off towards his office.

Victor turned towards Pietro. "Where's Clayton?"

"Back at the house. In the bosses' house. End of the road."

"What's he armed with?"

"Um. Shotgun. He never carries a pistol, but he keeps a shotgun hanging in his office. Double-barreled."

The crowd was milling and starting to ask questions; the people in the show were bleeding real blood. Had something gone wrong?

Victor ignored them. "Come with me," he said to Pietro. He started walking towards the end of town, and Pietro fell in with him. "You work for Chancel Corporation. Right?"

"Yes, I do. But I didn't sign up to kill people."

"How many of these men did?"

"Nobody, but Clayton...well, he got greedy. Some people went along with it."

Victor stumbled. He looked at his left shoulder, and saw that his sleeve was bloody. "Sam scored a hit on me."

"Sam was the killer." Pietro pulled a knife from his waist. Victor startled, but Pietro held up a hand reassuringly. "No, no. You need a bandage." Pietro swallowed. "You don't have to worry about me, Mister Benny. Your shirt's ruined; let me cut off the sleeve. You keep losing blood like that, you're going to go into shock."

Victor kept his right hand on his pistol while Pietro cut off his left sleeve at the shoulder and tied it around the wound.

186

Back up the street he could see the undertaker dragging Whiskey Bill away again, only this time Whiskey was a limp rag.

"You're going to need stitches," said Pietro.

"Later. I've got to finish this." He resumed walking. "If I go right to Clayton and I get killed, my friends will still be caged. I've got to get them out first." He looked over at the thin man with his shock of black hair.

How good are my instincts? Sometimes I have to trust someone I just met.

"Will you help me?"

"I won't shoot anyone," said Pietro.

"You won't have to. Listen. Chancel Corporation's done on this planet. I represent Ruby Tierney and Belle Enterprises. I suggest you switch employers."

I suggest you switch gangs.

Pietro nodded soberly. "You shot up his best men. And after Sam killed Ramon...."

"It was Sam that killed him?"

Pietro looked down at his feet. "Yes. When the street show was going on, back of the house. That did it for me, but I wanted out long before that, when I heard that Clayton was going after women and children." He lifted his head and looked Victor in the eyes. "Are you offering me a job?"

"Yes. Belle Enterprises is going to need some decent men, and I need you right now. No shooting required."

"Count me in, then."

"Are you doing this because I shot up some gunfighters or because you want out of Chancel?"

"I want out of Chancel."

"Done." He shook hands with Pietro, who had a firm grip. Then he took a deep breath. He was light-headed; his wound was starting to pain him and he had lost blood.

He turned to the right and led Pietro to the back of the clothing store. "We can't walk past the ranch house, not the front, anyway," he explained. "Clayton's going to be watching, trying to figure out why his men didn't come back or

187

call and what those explosions and gunshots were all about. We'll take the back way."

They walked next to the bluff, keeping landscaped trees between themselves and Clayton's house. They passed the sign saying "WELCOME TO HORSESHOW STATION" and turned left towards the windmill and the zoo.

"Are the men at the cages also gunfighters?"

Pietro shook his head. "No. They have guns and they do what they're asked, but if Clayton wants your friends killed he'll have to do it himself now that Sam's shot up."

"This morning I saw two men out here guarding the cage. Can you relieve one of them, tell him that Clayton wants him to give Doc McGuire a hand?"

"Sure, I can do that. But I have to ask, how did you manage that gunfight back there? I never saw anyone move so fast. And what did you set off, anyway? Sam nearly had a fit when the gunship blew up."

"I'll tell you later." He stopped walking. "Here's where you go on alone. Just settle down, talk to the other guard, and don't look at me if you see me coming." He slipped into the nearby vegetation.

Pietro walked past the corral, greeted the guards, and talked to one of them who nodded and hurried back towards town. In the cages sat several red apes and Ricardo, Ruby, and Emily, their heads down. Pietro sat on the rail where he could see the cages and began an animated conversation with the other guard about the explosions.

Victor quietly and carefully moved up behind the remaining guard, and was almost upon him when Emily squealed, "Victor!"

The guard whirled; Victor hit him on the jaw with a right undercut that turned the guard back around, then knocked the man behind the ear with a pistol butt. The man collapsed.

Pietro slid off the fence. "Good hit. I'll get the keys to the cage."

"Are you three all right?" asked Victor.

Ruby stood clutching the bars, Ricardo beside her. Emily had her hands over her mouth, looking at the unconscious guard. "We're fine," said Ruby, "but you've got blood on you!"

"I'll live."

"The keys are missing," said Pietro. "They should be hanging on this hook on the rail."

"Is he safe?" asked Ruby, tilting her head towards Pietro.

"He's an employee of yours as of today. He's safe."

Ruby pushed on the bars, and the cage door opened. "Then I guess we'll come out."

It was Victor's turn to look dumbfounded. Emily laughed at him and said, "Scampy fetched the keys when the mountain exploded. I told you he would fetch things I pointed to, so when the guards ran to look, I sent Scampy, and then we unlocked the cage but the guards came back so we've been waiting. And then you showed up." She threw her arms around his neck and kissed his cheek.

"Ow!" he said, putting his hand on his wound. His shoulder felt like it was on fire.

"Sorry, sorry," she said, almost patting his bloody bandage. "What happened? Did you get shot?"

Ricardo frowned at Victor. "You ran off and look what happened to you. You should have stayed with us."

"Someone had to go after Ramon. Ruby, this is Pietro. Pietro, this is your new boss."

Pietro nodded and touched the side of his forehead. "Ma'am."

Ruby looked puzzled. "Pleased to meet you?"

Ricardo shook Pietro's hand. "We've met before. Hunting guide, name's Ricardo."

"Oh, yes, I remember you." Pietro nodded. "The colorful one."

Too much time was passing. "Pietro," Victor said, "drag this guard into the cage and lock it up again. Ruby, could you give Pietro the keys?"

Ricardo asked, "Did you find Ramon?"

"He's dead. They buried him last night in Boot Hill. Sam shot him."

"Oh, no!" Ruby took a step backwards. "Why?"

189

"Same reason they blew up the rescue pod with us in it. Getting rid of witnesses."

Pietro dragged the guard into the cage and shook the door to make sure it was locked. "I heard Belle's Casino got blown up," he said. "You survived that?"

"It wasn't blown up," said Ruby. "Someone disabled the sweeper and we got hit by an asteroid."

"Same thing," said Pietro. "That's when I began looking for a way to leave Chancel Corporation."

"Victor!" Emily poked him. "How did you get shot?"

"There was a gunfight on Main Street with Sam and a couple others. We can tell stories later." Victor looked back at the town and steeled himself. "There's one thing more I have to take care of."

"What's that?" asked Ricardo.

"Clayton Chancel."

Chapter Eighteen

Ricardo picked up the guard's fallen rifle. "I'm going with you."

"No, you're not," said Victor. "This is something I have to do alone."

"Don't get all dramatic, mate, that's my routine." Ricardo straightened his worn safari shirt. "Of course having me with you would be better. Two against one and all that."

Victor shook his head. "Not this time. Now that you three are safe, Clayton won't have a bargaining chip."

"He'll shoot you down like an ape," said Ricardo. "You couldn't even beat an arcade cowboy, remember? You need me along to back you up."

Pietro spoke up. "He just outgunned four men at one time. Three, anyway; you can't count me."

"He's been shot, though. He's still bleeding."

"I'm okay," said Victor sharply. "I'll be worse off if I have to protect somebody else."

Ricardo furrowed his brows and looked insulted.

"How about a distraction, then," offered Pietro. "You go do what you're going to do, Mister Benny, and I'll walk in with Ricardo here like I caught him escaping."

"Now wait a minute!" Ricardo poked Pietro on the chest. "You were just in a gunfight with Victor and now you're on his side? I don't trust you."

"I was in that gunfight but I wasn't fighting. I wasn't hired as a gunfighter. Clayton was willing to kill women and children to get what he wanted, and I wanted no part of it, but until now there wasn't anyone else on this planet, in case you hadn't noticed. There was no place else to go except to die in the jungle!"

Victor closed his eyes against the pain of his shoulder and ignored the squabbling in front of him.

Clayton will have guards at the ranch house. The tourists are packing, getting ready to shuttle back up to their cruise ship, so the other employees will be busy.

I need to get to Clayton alone, and if Ricardo and Pietro can distract the guards...

"I can live with that," he said. He opened his eyes. "Ricardo, I trust him. And I think what he suggests will work." He turned to Ruby. "But you and Emily have to stay here. Seriously, if you walk into town before I'm done, I'll get killed trying to protect you. Promise me that you'll stay here."

Ruby took Emily's hand. "We'll stay, but I feel silly. This isn't really the Old West and I'm not helpless, you know."

Victor sighed in exasperation. "This has nothing to do with you two being women. Pietro here has got a gun and Clayton still thinks Pietro works for him. Plus Ricardo knows the men and they know him. All I need is a few minutes."

Ruby made a sour face and nodded.

"Maybe you could let the apes out," he suggested. "Help them get back to the tangle trees."

"Oh, no," said Emily. "They're really, really mad. I wouldn't go near 'em."

"What about the old gray? Let him out, if you can. I have to go."

Emily ran up and kissed his cheek again for luck, and hurt his arm again and apologized, and then he, Ricardo, and Pietro began walking back to Horseshoe Station. The sun was climbing in the sky, and the dry air smelled of dust.

"Pietro," said Victor, "unbutton your gun so it's available, and Ricardo, you should hand him that electric rifle." Pietro loosened his gun, and accepted the rifle from a sour-faced Ricardo.

Victor continued, "Let me go in first. I need to sneak around a bit, find out where Clayton is inside the house. Ten minutes ought to do it. Then you bring Ricardo to the front door. Clayton will have a guard there, maybe two. Ricardo, you try to talk your way out of it, you know, argue a lot, remember there will still be tourists so they won't do anything right there in front of the house. If you hear gunshots, Pietro, take out the guards with your rifle. On low power you can shoot them in the legs and they'll go down, you won't kill anyone."

"I thought you said no shooting."

"You volunteered. It's too late to stay with the women."

Ricardo snorted. "Bossy for a teenager, isn't he?"

"He earned it. Mister Benny, you can count on us."

"*Mister* Benny?" Ricardo raised his eyebrows.

"Thanks, Pietro," said Victor. "I really mean it. Here's the entrance. You two stay here." He glanced at his watch. "Ten minutes."

"You've got it."

"Good luck," said Ricardo. "You're going to need it."

Victor accepted the well wishes with a nod and a mumbled thanks. He walked behind the welcome sign, and stumbled on a rock.

Not now. I can't let the blood loss make me tired now.

He stiffened his spine and walked more carefully.

Into the entrance of the town he crept, and behind the landscaped trees of the ranch house. Honky-tonk music played at the saloon as tourists celebrated their last hours on Horseshoe. A couple of workmen with a wheelbarrow cleaned up debris from the remains of the gunsmith shop.

In front of the ranch house, on a white wooden rocking chair, sat a guard with a rifle. One of the window curtains twitched.

That's either a second guard or Clayton.

Victor slipped behind the house and saw no one patrolling the back yard.

They still don't realize that the bluff behind the house is no protection.

193

He crawled through the brush to a side window that had gotten overgrown by a shrub. He lifted his head slowly, carefully. There was no window shade; the overgrown shrub blocked the window. He eased his head up into the shrub, releasing a dusty cinnamon smell from the curled leaves.

Through the grime on the window, Victor saw a kitchen with modern appliances and western décor. The chandelier over the checkered tablecloth was made from a wagon wheel. On the table lay a double-barreled shotgun and a box of shells.

A heavy-set man sat at the table. He wore a tan shirt, his thinning hair was in disarray, and his heavy-lidded eyes glared at the cowboy standing in front of him.

That's got to be Clayton Chancel.

"...sign of him," the cowboy was saying. "We've been through every room in every building. The guard reported in from the cages, and said the kid hadn't shown up there. Sam, Whiskey, Cocic, they're still stretched out cold at doc's and shot up pretty bad."

Clayton cursed and slammed the table with his fist. "What's going on here? My gunship's destroyed, my best men shot up, and you can't find some stupid boy that's causing trouble. This town just isn't that big!"

He's angry. He's rattled. That's good.

And I am not some stupid boy running for his momma.

The cowboy didn't say anything; he just kept rotating his hat nervously by the brim.

Clayton waved him away. "Go back up front. When the tourist shuttle takes off, the town will be empty; he won't be able to hide so easy. Until then, keep watch out front. If you see him, shoot him."

The cowboy nodded and hurried back to the front of the house.

Victor slid down slowly and walked to the back door. The door's window was broken, shattered by the mining charge he had placed on top of the bluff. Two windows bracketed the door; one of the windows had its glass still in the frame although cracked. The back door opened onto the kitchen.

194

The door was just a wooden frame door with a simple key lock. Victor crept up to the door and turned the knob very slowly, just enough to loosen the door in the jam. It was unlocked.

An argument began outside the front of the house, and Victor recognized the voices of Pietro and Ricardo. He glanced at his watch.

Ten minutes gone already? Usually I move too fast; I must be tired. I've got to get in there before Clayton leaves the kitchen, and I can't use my left arm. I can only fire one gun.

Can't be helped.

Time to dance.

He stood up and kicked the door open as hard as he could. "Clayton!" he yelled, and then ducked low under the window by the door. A shotgun blast shattered the doorframe where he had been standing.

He reached up and broke the window glass with the muzzle of his pistol. Another blast blew out the window, scattering fragments of glass and wood.

He leaped to his feet and charged through the door and into the kitchen. Clayton was pushing a fresh pair of shells into the shotgun. "Freeze!" Victor yelled, but Clayton snapped the shotgun closed and began swinging it towards Victor.

Time slowed, letting Victor squeeze off three quick shots at the shotgun muzzle. Two of them hit the barrel, knocking the shotgun away. Clayton cried out, fell back against the wall, and then slid to the floor.

Victor shoved the table aside with his hip and stood over Clayton, his gun aimed at the man's face. Then he heard someone yell "Drop it!"

The cowboy he had seen before in the kitchen stood in the hallway, his rifle aimed at Victor.

It's an electric hunting rifle. He can't miss at this range.

It didn't matter how much time slowed, Victor still couldn't move faster than the man could pull the trigger. He had just turned away when he heard the shivering buzz of the rifle.

He felt nothing.

He was still standing.

The cowboy toppled forward, crashing to the floor at Victor's feet. Behind him stood Pietro, a rifle in his hands. "I told you you could count on me."

Victor turned back to Clayton, who was reaching for the shotgun. He kicked the weapon away and knelt down face-to-face with the heavy-lidded man, his pistol against the man's chest.

"Don't shoot me!" cried Clayton. "Don't shoot! Anything you want, boy, anything, just don't shoot me!" He winced and clutched his chest, his eyes wide with panic. "Just tell me what you want!"

"My name is Benny the Kid," said Victor, his voice tight, "and I want you and your men to get off my planet!"

"Your planet? Your planet? You...." He moaned. "Oh, man, you got me good." Blood began flowing between Clayton's fingers, trickling down his tan shirt.

NO!

He hadn't shot at Clayton; he had only aimed for the shotgun. How could Clayton be shot?

One of his bullets must have ricocheted off the shotgun and hit Clayton in the chest.

Don't die, don't die, I've never killed anyone before, please don't die...

"Help me lay him down," said Pietro, and then he pulled away Clayton's hand and ripped open his shirt. Dark red blood trickled from a bullet hole on Clayton's chest.

Victor struggled to regain his composure. He had seen terrible wounds before during the fighting for survival on Septimus, some of them fatal. The first thing to do was to stop the loss of blood. They needed a bandage, a piece of cloth, something to press against the wound to keep Clayton's life from seeping out. But this was a chest wound, and a chest wound would have internal bleeding that would be hard to stop.

"Go get Doc McGuire!" he yelled at Ricardo. Ricardo nodded and hurried out the back door.

"We need a bandage," Victor said to Pietro. He held out his right arm. "Cut my other sleeve off."

Pietro pulled his knife and hacked the remaining sleeve off of Victor's western shirt. Victor grabbed the cloth from Pietro and pressed it against the wound.

He heard a gasp, and looked up to see Ruby in the hallway. "You were supposed to stay at the corral," he said sharply, realizing how irrelevant it was as he said it.

"We walked to the entrance of town and then we heard shots, and Ricky had already knocked out the guard on the porch, so...."

Emily stood behind Ruby, her eyes round.

"Emily!" Victor cried. "Can we use your polybot?"

Emily looked at Clayton's bleeding chest, turned pale, and nodded. She moved Scampy over to her hip and unsnapped Peggity from her neck.

"What?" asked Pietro. "What are you doing?"

"Better medicine than Doc McGuire has. Hold Clayton down. This is going to hurt."

Emily slid the metallic polybot out of Peggity, pressed some buttons, and handed it to Victor. "You put it on him, I can't," she said, looking at the bleeding injury with nausea.

Hang on, hang on, prayed Victor as he laid the circular polybot onto the gunshot wound.

"You sure you know what you're doing, Mister Benny?" asked Pietro.

Ruby put her hand on Pietro's shoulder. "He does."

The polybot extended its miniscule legs and began burrowing into the wound. Clayton moaned and thrashed. Victor laid his weight on Clayton's legs, and Pietro held Clayton's wrists against the floor.

By the time the polybot began emerging from the wound, Doc McGuire had made his appearance and was digging through his black bag. "A polybot?" he said, raising his gray eyebrows. "I didn't know anybody had one of those yet."

Victor explained to the doctor about how the bullet had ricocheted off the shotgun and into Clayton's chest. Emily sat on the floor at the other end of the kitchen, trying not to watch. Clayton had quit struggling but was panting shallowly.

"There's the bullet," said Pietro. The polybot pushed a flattened slug out of the wound and began weaving the skin closed.

McGuire knelt down and pressed the area around the wound, being careful to avoid the polybot. "Hit a rib, looks like. The bullet probably flattened after ricocheting off the shotgun or it would have penetrated deeper. You're a lucky man, Mister Chancel."

Clayton coughed. He glared at Victor, his heavy-lidded eyes narrowed. "You win, kid," he said in a hoarse voice. "You can take your family and go. There's room on the ship. We won't touch you."

Victor turned a kitchen chair backwards and sat down, resting his arms on its back. He was weary to the bone but he knew a fight wasn't over just because the other party was down. "No. There's room on the ship for you and your gunfighters. I meant what I said. I want you off my planet."

Clayton tried to laugh, and wound up clutching his chest and gasping for air. "You can't just walk in here and tell us to leave."

"I certainly can just walk in here and tell you to leave. There's no law here. There's no law anywhere on this planet, and I know how things work when you make your own laws."

There was no law on Septimus when I had to survive.

"What you can take is yours," Victor continued, "and what you can keep is yours, and a gang that has principles will last longer than a gang that doesn't. You don't have principles, Clayton, and you don't have a gunship or any men left to fight for you. You've lost."

Ruby interrupted. "Doctor, take a look at Victor's arm. He got shot and he's still bleeding." The doctor cut away the improvised bandage on Victor's arm and began clucking as he cleaned the wound. Victor thought about using the polybot, but he didn't want to be distracted.

He grimaced, pained by the doctor's ministrations but too weak to complain. He fought off a wave of faintness and

198

continued. "Clayton, you had Ruby's Casino sabotaged and then you tried to kill off the witnesses. For some reason you didn't want other people moving to Horseshoe; you didn't want this planet to become civilized and regulated. It's not the tourist trade you were concerned about. What was it, Clayton? What was it you didn't want other people to know about?"

"Nothing. There wasn't nothing."

"You have mining charges, but you didn't need them to build this town. What are you digging up?"

Pietro rubbed his jaw and cleared his throat. "Mister Benny? You might want to take a look in that." He pointed to a sturdy metal footlocker against the back wall of the kitchen.

"Pietro," gasped Clayton, "I'll kill you myself, I'll, I'll....." He fell into a coughing fit.

Victor got up and walked over to the footlocker, followed by Doc McGuire who complained about patients that wouldn't sit still.

"Hold on, Doc, no stitches yet. Give me a moment." He studied the lock on the footlocker, and then pulled open some kitchen drawers until he found a skewer. He turned to the doctor. "May I borrow one of your needles, the stitching kind?" Doc McGuire handed Victor a needle from his bag. Victor slid the skewer into the keyhole, and then began poking with the needle.

"You know," said Ruby, "we could just get the keys from Clayton's pocket."

Victor almost smiled. "Yeah, I suppose we could, but...." He twisted the skewer, and the locker popped open. Victor lifted the lid.

Ruby gasped, and Emily scooted closer. "What are those?" she asked.

"Raw tourmaline and emeralds," said Pietro. "Turns out this part of the Horseshoe continent had lots of hydrothermal activity, which makes those gems."

"Hydrothermal. Tell me about it," said Ruby, touching her acid-bleached hair.

"They found a rich deposit up north." Pietro picked up a dull piece of purple tourmaline and held it up to the light.

"They take these to other planets and sell them to dealers to be cut into gems. It's all done on the black market. What started out as a tourist attraction became a cover for transporting these. If Horseshoe Planet ever became civilized, developed a government, then it would be smuggling." He dropped the gem back into the locker. "They've already hauled several loads this size, duty-free."

"So it wasn't the tourists being taken away by Ruby's casino that Clayton cared about," said Victor. "He just didn't want enough people moving in to form a government."

Clayton growled. "Pietro, you're fired."

"I already quit."

Victor felt the sting of a needle. Doc McGuire had a syringe in his hand. "Don't put me out, Doc!" he warned.

"Just a local anesthetic, don't get excited." The doctor pushed the needle into the other side of his wound and injected more painkiller. "A couple of stitches ought to do it. You'll keep bleeding until you pass out if I don't do this."

"Clayton," said Victor, trying to ignore the stitching, "you are leaving on this shuttle. You and Sam and Quickdraw and Whiskey, even if you have to be carried on. You can keep whatever money you have stashed elsewhere and go live on it, but you can't come back here, not ever again. Chancel Corporation is done; Horseshoe Station belongs to Belle Enterprises, lock, stock, and barrel. If I see you or any of your men back here again, I'll lock you in a cage with one of those red apes." He started to stand up and Doc McGuire yelled at him to sit down and hold still. Victor sat.

Clayton muttered something under his breath.

"It doesn't matter if you agree or not," Victor continued. "Doc, when you're done with me, give Clayton something for the pain, like you did with Sam and the others. Ricardo, you'll need to get a couple of strong men to help move them onto the shuttle. The undertaker looks like he's good at it."

Ricardo looked at Victor with one eyebrow raised until Victor caught himself and added, "Please."

"That's better." Ricardo smiled and walked slowly out the door.

Victor looked at Ruby apologetically. "I'm sorry; I didn't run in polite company for a few years and I guess I fell back to my old habits."

"It's been a rough couple of days."

Doc McGuire finished bandaging Victor's wound, and then he gave Clayton an injection. Clayton closed his eyes and his body relaxed. "There," said the doctor, "he'll sleep until tomorrow." As he packed his bag, he looked at Victor. "If we do get the law around here, I hope you'll give me some warning? Some of this stuff isn't exactly legal on certain planets."

"No problem, Doc."

The doctor left. Emily pulled up a chair and sat beside Victor. Ruby stood over the somnolescent Clayton Chancel. "So you're the reason my casino was destroyed, and all because of some stupid rocks. It was all about money."

Victor blinked, trying to stay alert. There would be time enough to rest after the shuttle left. "Ruby? I have a suggestion."

She turned towards him. "Yes?"

"You should stay here in Horseshoe Station. They've got a casino, actually a whole town here, and you and Ricardo could run it. It's yours if you want it."

She picked absent-mindedly at her hair again. "I don't know. I don't know if Ricky would want that. Maybe..." She shrugged pensively. "Let me think about it."

He heard the rumble of wagon wheels, and he looked out the side window. The stage coach was driving into town to take tourists to the shuttle.

Emily stood beside him and looked out the window also. "People are going home?"

"Yes. We made it just in time, Emily. The shuttle leaves today for the cruise ship." On impulse he tousled her hair. "You get to go home."

She leaned her head against his arm. "I don't have mom any more. It won't really be home."

"I'm sorry."

She looked up at him, her eyes sad. "What will you do? You're my big brother, will you come with me?" She suddenly looked like the younger Cydney he first met.

"No. I can't." He looked out the window again. "I belong here. This is my home, Emily, it's the only place where I fit."

She hurt his arm again by hugging him, her eyes wet. "I don't think I fit anywhere anymore."

Chapter Nineteen

Emily bravely fought back tears. The large, black and dusty stage coach stood ready, and the last remaining tourists milled around, waiting for the driver to let them in, to take them back to their ordinary lives.

Ruby squeezed Emily comfortingly. "They'll get you home safely, don't you worry. You've been a real trooper and I am going to miss you."

"Me too, mate," said Ricardo. "You sure you want to take that little ape with you?"

Emily sniffed and stroked Scampy's back. He reached up and patted her nose. "He's all I've got now that Mom's gone, and he needs me to take care of him."

She kissed Victor on the cheek again, and wrapped her arms around him, Scampy in between. "I have to go back to the studio, and I know my people will take care of me, but I won't have you to protect me anymore. I'm going to miss you terrible, Victor."

He patted her back. "You'll be fine. Hey, after all, you're Cydney. Everyone loves you."

"I'll send you vids. You better answer me back."

"I will. I promise."

Pietro joined them, his black hair neatly combed. "Did you know that one of the tourists had a recorder going this morning during the gunfight?"

Victor raised his eyebrows. "Really?"

"Yes, and I have a copy of it. I'm not proud of my part in it, but I'll show it." He pulled a rod from his pocket, and held it vertically. "I owe it to Mister Benny to let you people see this, because none of the rest of you saw what happened." He twisted a knob on the bottom, and the gunfight appeared in three dimensions above the top of the rod.

The sound was tinny, but they could hear Benny the Kid identify himself and demand that they throw down their guns.

I must have been stupid or crazy. Probably both.

Suddenly gunshots and smoke erupted, three men went down, and there was Benny the Kid on one knee, his guns pointed towards a man with his hands in the air.

The scene froze, and Pietro turned it off.

Ricardo whistled in appreciation, and Ruby shook her head in amazement.

Pietro handed the rod to Emily. "You take this home with you, young lady. I don't want to see it again."

"Thank you." She tucked it into her bag. "Oh, darn, I don't have pictures of the rest of you, I need to get a camera..."

At that moment the stage driver, having just stowed the last suitcase in the back of the stage, dramatically pulled a paper from his vest pocket and turned to the waiting crowd. "Now listen up, pilgrims," he drawled, "and listen tight. Before we load you up, we had some messages come in for some people, and if I call off anyone here, let me know."

He rattled off the names of several people, including "Sherilee Miller and her daughter Cydney."

"Oh," cried Emily, "I'm Cydney!"

The driver looked surprised. "Most of these people were on the *Nairobi*, which never arrived for some reason. How did you get here?"

"I came with them," she said, pointing towards Ruby and Ricardo.

"I see. I guess. Anyway, there's a message waiting for you." He pointed her towards the building labeled Wells, Fargo, and Company. "That's actually the communications center," he said as though giving away a secret, "and the man inside will help you. We'll wait."

Emily dashed across the street, her brown hair flying, and banged through the door. The other passengers grumbled and milled about, or went back into the Purple Sage Saloon for a final drink. Victor thought of following Emily into the communications building, but didn't want to intrude.

"When we get our girl Cydney off to the shuttle," said Ricardo, extending his arm for Ruby, "let me show you the town and I'll introduce you to the ladies." She looked at him with narrowed eyes, and he added quickly, "Strictly business acquaintances. That's all."

"Business acquaintances? You call fancy ladies business acquaintances?"

"No, they're not like that. Sure, they sing and they dance and wear mesh stockings, but you don't have to get upset about it."

"I haven't had a shower in days, my hair is a mess, my clothes are ruined, and you want me to go smile and get acquainted with some perfumed women in show dresses?"

"I hadn't thought about that, I...."

"I need a hot shower and something to eat and a place where I can change and do something to my hair, that's what you should be thinking about! Get me a room at the hotel."

"You can have the ranch house. It's all yours."

She tapped his chest. "And I can't even change clothes until I *buy* some clothes to change into, and I don't have any money, no ID with me to buy clothes even if I can find some clothes that fit!"

"Victor owns this town, now," said Ricardo. "I'm sure he would treat you to some clothes."

Victor turned away from their bickering and looked at the town for the first time without being in a battle.

The rough board sidewalks were covered with dust not only from the passage of the stage coach and its horses, but from the mining charges he had set off at dawn. The gunsmith's shop was a pile of rubble, and the stores around it had shattered windows and would need their walls repaired.

But the town was surrounded by lovely red bluffs, and when the walks were cleaned and the buildings repaired, it would be a scenic place for people to come to visit, a place where people could hunt apes with cameras and recorders and not with rifles.

And the trade in gems would keep the town prosperous.

Time stretched on, and the driver glanced at the modern timepiece on his wrist. "We're going to delay the ship if we don't get moving. Maybe I should go check on the young lady."

At that moment the door of Wells, Fargo, and Company banged open and Emily came running out. "I can stay! I can stay!"

Ruby turned from her badgering of Ricardo. "What?"

Emily ran up to Victor and slammed into him, hugging him like she'd been away for months. Scampy climbed up on her shoulders and complained and hooted. "I can stay here with you! On Horseshoe!"

"What was the message?" he said. "What took you so long?"

The driver shouted to the rest of the tourists, "Last stage is leaving! Everyone on board!"

As the tourists crowded into the stage coach, Emily explained, bouncing in her enthusiasm. "It was from my agent, she'd heard our ship had had an accident, so the man inside connected through the cruise ship and then through space and called her back. She thought I was dead and I had to tell her that Mom really was dead but not me," her face clouded, "and I cried, and I told her how I survived and Mom didn't." She took a deep breath and grabbed Victor's hand. "I showed her Scampy over the vid. She thought Scampy was darling."

"So that's what took so long," said Ruby.

"And then she told me that the producers had decided not to record any more episodes of Cydney and the Pirates, I'm too old now, so it's all going to be reruns from now on." She smiled bravely but her eyes were shiny. "I told you that was going to happen, but it still hurt to hear it. But then, but then," she started bouncing again, "I showed her the recording of the gunfight, and said that my best friend and big brother Benny the Kid was the one that rescued me from the red apes, and she

206

got all excited, because she's got this great imagination, that's why she's my agent."

"Go on," said Ruby with a growing smile.

"She wants to come out here with a camera man and shoot a pilot. She says there hasn't been a show lately with a western flavor, especially not recorded on an alien planet. She said with me acting as teenage Cydney, and with Scampy, and with wild apes and gunshots and blood and Benny the Kid, it could be a real hit!"

"Wait a minute!" said Victor.

Before he could ask a question, she rushed to a finish. "She'll be out here in a couple weeks, and I asked if I could stay here with you, Ruby, that you would be my foster mom, and she said okay, so I can stay!"

"What do you mean, foster mom?" asked Ruby.

Victor interrupted, "What do you mean, with Benny the Kid?"

"Well, um." Emily looked at Ruby, then to Victor, then back to Ruby, wringing her hands nervously. "I sort of told her that you had agreed to be my foster mom. There wasn't really time to ask, I'm sorry." She smiled a broad smile, her face desperately innocent.

Victor cleared his throat. "Benny the Kid?"

"Oh." She took his good arm as though he was rescuing her from Ruby. "She really liked the way you looked, all rugged and she said you had an interesting face, you looked dangerous. She asked about your hair style and I told her I did it to make you look edgy."

Victor ran his fingers through his acid-bleached hair self-consciously. "I don't want to be in any shows."

"No, it'll be real neat." She raised her hand and moved it like putting a title on a screen. "The Adventures of Cydney and Scampy!" Her hand lowered a bit and her fingers got closer together. "With Benny the Kid!"

Ricardo laughed and slapped his leg. "Benny the Kid in a vidstream! And you get billed below the ape!"

"No," said Victor. "Look, I'm glad for your sake, Emily, that they're going to try another series and that you get to stay here longer. But I'm not an actor."

"Not an actor." Ricardo snorted. "They can teach apes to act. They'll probably animate Scampy and he'll out-act the both of you."

"You ought to think about it seriously, Victor," said Ruby. "It would be good for you to have a job, and it would give you a chance to go out in the wilderness."

"I need to go out, but I need to go out alone."

I don't do good in civilization. Without the medication, I will need an outlet, I will need times to let the wildness in me come out. I can only be civilized in small doses.

Emily patted his arm. "You just want to run with the apes and scream at the stars again. I think you're half ape."

"What have you got to lose, mate?" Ricardo clapped him on his good shoulder. "At least try it out. It might do you good."

Should I? The worse that could happen is that I'll be a flop, and then they'll leave me out of the show.

No... maybe the worse that could happen is that it will be a success and I'll have to be Benny the Kid for years.

Would that be so bad? It would be better than being Victor Benningham.

He sighed, and nodded. "Okay. Maybe I'll do the pilot."

Emily clapped her hands and returned to bouncing. "Hooray!"

"Do you need to call your agent back?" asked Victor.

"No." She shrunk a little and toyed with her fingers. "I, um, I already told her you would do it."

"What?"

"Don't be mad at me!" She flapped her hands. "I was excited, and I really, really didn't want to go back."

Ruby frowned at her. "If I'm your foster mother, do I get to spank you when you're bad?"

"Oh! Um...you wouldn't really do that?"

"I need something to eat," said Victor firmly. "And then I need to go free the apes."

208

"Oh, the apes!" said Ruby. "Yes, we need to let them go."

"If the kitchen in the ranch house isn't all shot up," said Ricardo to Ruby, "I could whip up some sandwiches for everyone while you shower."

"I haven't had one of your sandwiches in years," said Ruby. "You don't have to ask twice. But don't think you can buy me off that easily, you and your professional ladies!"

*

"It'll be fun, you'll see," chattered Emily as they walked to the end of Main Street. Victor rubbed his eyes. He had fallen asleep half-way through his second sandwich, and had spent an hour on the large leather couch.

He awoke to find Emily watching him, Scampy asleep in her lap.

Ricardo and Ruby were going shopping to buy Ruby some new clothes. They invited Victor to come along, but he insisted on freeing the apes while it was still light.

Ruby, warming to her role as foster mom, admonished Victor to have Emily back before dark, but he said they wouldn't head back until the apes were safe in the tangle trees and it might take part of the night.

Victor touched his bandage, feeling the soreness underneath. "Maybe it will be good to have a job. I can earn my keep and visit the jungle now and then. I mean by myself, just to live with the apes."

"Do you think Ricardo will kiss Ruby now?" asked Emily.

Victor laughed. "I don't know. Who cares?"

Emily frowned. "I hope so. They'd be nice foster parents."

"I suppose."

"You know what else?"

"What?"

"When the show premieres, when *our* show premieres, people will want to visit Horseshoe Station, you know, to see the place where it's recorded, maybe get to see us and the red apes. We'll have crowds of people!"

"I don't know if that's good or not. Hey, there's the old gray! You let him out!"

The faded red ape sat by the empty cage where Ruby, Ricardo, and Emily had been imprisoned. He had a handful of grass, and was holding it out to a reddish-brown horse that had its neck stretched over the fence as far as it could.

Victor stopped and picked up a stick. He tapped a post of the corral a few times, and the gray ape rapped on the ground with his knuckles. "How are you doing, old fellow? Are you feeding that horse or teasing him?"

"He's feeding the horse, silly. It's what the males do; they get food and feed whoever needs it. He doesn't like grass but the horse does."

"Those apes have got to be thirsty and hungry." He took the keys from his pocket and stepped closer to the female's cage. She howled and reached for him. The other apes began shrieking and shaking the bars. He stepped back. "And you're right, they are mad. If I unlock the cage now, she'd rip me apart." He glanced at the sky. "The sun will set soon." He sat on the ground and studied the cages, pondering.

Emily wandered over to the horse and began stroking its forehead. "Victor, do you like horses?"

"I never rode one."

"Oh, you'd love 'em, I love horses, I used to ride them all the time when I was at the studio in Argentina. You're a nice horsey, aren't you? Such a good horsey. Scampy, don't grab its nose. You'll get nipped."

"Emily, maybe you could dance for them."

"Dance?"

"Remember the other apes, back when the pod exploded and you danced on that metal sheet and they began dancing also? Rhythm means a lot to them. Maybe we can settle them down."

"If you say so. Here, help me lay these boards down side by side."

They arranged a makeshift surface by arranging a couple of old boards from a stack by the windmill. Emily hummed to herself, counted down, and began tap dancing on the boards.

210

"We're Cydney, and Scampy, and Benny the Kid....dum de dum....I don't know how....to make it rhyme....but it will..."
She kept a simple time step going.

Victor didn't dance, but he shuffled a bit and beat time with a stick, hoping that no one would see them quieting down the apes.

The old gray sat down next to Victor and thumped the ground along with the beat. The caged apes looked up with interest; one of them hung from the top of his cage and bumped his feet on the bars in time to the rhythm.

Now for some friendly behavior.

Victor kept tapping the stick on the ground while walking to a nearby bush. He pulled off some branches and offered a twig to the old gray. The ape took it and bit it without enthusiasm.

He handed a piece to a small male in the end cage. The male took it and bumped it against the cage bar while Victor unlocked the door. With a grunt, the male leaped out of the cage.

Victor rapped the next cage with his stick in time with Emily's tapping, and then unlocked it. The male in that cage jumped out and ran to the first one. They wrapped their arms around each other and hooted.

The ape in the next cage got excited and began shaking the bars. "Yes, yes, you're getting out," said Victor, "just don't forget who's unlocking these cages."

The large female sat in the back corner while he opened her cage door, and then she shuffled with dignity over to Emily. She tried to pick up Scampy, but the little ape wrapped his arms tight around Emily and would not be removed.

"Gack!" said Emily, loosening Scampy's arms from her throat.

Victor quickly unlocked the rest of the cages before the occupants got too restless. The troop of apes gathered around Emily, who kept tapping and singing. They were shuffling, barely dancing as they patted each other, but their movements reflected Emily's beat.

"Victor," said Emily, "bring the horse."

211

"Why?"

"So we can lead them to the tangle trees. They're not afraid of the horse, and I'm about danced out."

"He doesn't have anything on his head, no straps or anything."

"There's a harness hanging on the shed. Bring it here." She skipped off the board, singing, and danced up to the corral. Victor handed her the harness, and she slid it over the horse's head and adjusted the bit. "I've never...done this...while dancing before!"

Victor led the horse out of the corral, closed the gate, and gave the reins to Emily.

"Which way should we go?" she asked.

"West. The land drops down, I can see tangle trees off that way, and there ought to be water."

"Let's mount up fast. They're restless." Emily leaped onto the horse, then half dragged Victor up behind her. "It'll be bony without a saddle, but you're tough." She clicked at the horse, shook the reins, and it began walking. Benny clung to her, trying to be calm.

The old gray ape followed alongside, shuffling his feet and rolling and unrolling his arms.

"Are they coming?"

Victor looked behind. "They're coming. Sing to them, Emily. The old gray trusts us, and they trust him. They're following him home."

Home.

I'm already home.

The entire planet was his home. It didn't matter where he was, he fit.

"Scampy, don't grab the horsey's ears," Emily scolded. "He's a good horsey."

Cydney, Scampy, and Benny the Kid put Horseshoe Station and the Old West behind them, and rode off into the brilliant rays of the golden sunset.

The End

Background illustration by NASA

Morgan Keyes has helped me greatly by critiquing my writing. She is the author of the new novel DARKBEAST which will be in stores on August 28, 2012, and I can vouch for the quality of this book. It is a traditional fantasy novel for young readers, and can be preordered on Amazon.

If you enjoyed BAD TIMES AT HORSESHOE STATION, you will also enjoy THE POCKET UNIVERSE, CHILDREN OF A DISTANT STAR, GOLDENEYES, ABOVE AND BENEATH, and CAPTAIN COSETTE.

Here is a bonus chapter from CAPTAIN COSETTE:

"In the depths of winter, I learned that within me there was an invincible summer that could withstand the slings and arrows of outrageous fortune."

-- Renée Chevalier, Planet Sorine, author of BLAZING HEARTS ON FIRE AGAIN.

Chapter One

No one helped Cosette cut the heavy vine of ambrosia fruit. No one helped her heft it to her shoulder, or helped her struggle to the end of the row and settle it into the cart.

Her step-brothers, Lucas and Claude, had their own quadrants of the family vineyard to harvest. No one helped them either, but they were twice her weight and half again her size. They whistled and called to each other, but not to her. She was the sibling by a previous father, she was small, and she was a girl.

I don't care. I can harvest my quadrant the same as them.

She carefully cut the next large branch from the vine, a sloping cut one inch from the divide, just right to encourage a

215

new growth next spring. She tucked the knife into the scabbard at her waist and heaved the vine over her shoulder, slowly so as not to bruise the dark red fruit, full of the juice so prized in the port city.

"Lucas," called Claude from his quadrant, "I'm on my last row. You need some help?"

Sweat from Cosette's forehead collected on her eyebrows, but she didn't wipe it off. She needed both hands to balance the load on her back. Each step took concentration; the ground was uneven, and a fall would be disastrous.

She had eaten an ambrosia fruit once, cutting it in half with her knife and sucking the juice. It was almost worth the whipping her stepfather had given her and the accusations that she was a thief and a waste. She protested that the fruit was as much hers as anyone else in the family, but that just brought on a few extra strokes. She never tasted the fruit again.

But that one taste had been heavenly.

Merchants at the spaceport paid well, and spaceships took crates of the ambrosia fruit to other planets, where the value increased greatly due to its rarity.

Cosette never saw the money, though. Auguste, when he did take time to speak to her, said only that the money had been invested in her future, and that after the bills had all been paid, there wasn't much left anyway.

Lucas and Claude always wore the best of clothes and never lacked pocket money when festivals were held. Somehow, even though Cosette was the oldest, Auguste had trouble dredging up a few coins when she asked for them.

She gently laid the vine in the cart, and walked wearily down the row for another.

"What do you mean, do I need help?" shouted Lucas. "I'm done! Finish up, you lazy carcass, and let's go swimming!"

Swimming!

She would give anything to throw off her work dress and fall into the clear water of the river that skirted the edge of their property. Several farms lined the banks, and on special days, such as pruning, thinning, and harvest, everyone would gather above the irrigation dam at the end of the day and swim.

Gregory would be there.

Her heart warmed and her step quickened. Gregory, the boy with the quick laughter, the sandy hair and the kind eyes, who didn't hesitate to talk to her and dunk her in fun. He was a decent soul, the only decent soul she knew, though she had to admit that she didn't know very many others.

Lucas and Claude met her as she carried back another vine to her cart. "Not done yet?" taunted Lucas, his dark curly hair half-hiding his eyes.

Claude, a year younger than Lucas but with the same dark curls and leering mouth, elbowed him in the ribs. "She was probably sleeping again."

Lucas elbowed him back. "She'll miss swimming! She'll break Gregory's heart!"

Claude clutched his chest and put the back of his hand against his forehead. "Cosette! Cosette! I will die without you!"

Cosette kept her face grim. Years of being taunted had built stone walls inside her. The taunting still hurt, but the hurt never got out for anyone to see. "You could help me with the last rows. I would appreciate it."

Lucas' face lost its humor. "We did our quadrant, older sister, and you can do yours. Fair's fair."

"I'll make it up to you."

"How are you going to do that? Wash our clothes? Cook our food? You already do that."

Claude elbowed Lucas again. "Stop wasting time. Let's go swim!"

They ran off, elbowing each other and laughing. The last thing Cosette heard was Lucas mimicking her voice, "I'll make it up to you!"

She added another stone to the wall inside her, but a tear of frustration got out.

She looked at the rows, and pushed back her short blonde hair.

I can walk faster.

217

After taking a deep pull of water from the bota on the end post, she ran back to the next vine, chose the branch with ripe fruit and cut it, after checking carefully for any of the large yellow spiders that would make her hand swell up. She hated spiders, and her stepbrothers would sometimes drop them on her hair for spite.

Hefting the vine on her back, she trudged quickly back to the cart. She laid it down, careless of the fruit. Let her get caned for the damage – if she could spend some time with Gregory, she would have memories to comfort her.

Back and forth she went, ignoring the complaints of her legs and back. She filled her cart, and then pulled it to the place where the merchant would park his truck, the whine of its turbine bringing everyone out to help load.

She grabbed another empty cart, and hurried back.

Gregory will be there, and he'll smile and wave, and I'll jump in the cool water and swim to him. He'll try to dunk me again, and I'll dunk him instead, and then we'll swim to the bank and chat.

She stumbled, lost in her reverie, and almost dropped a branch.

I'll be bold, I will, and I'll grab him and kiss him quickly, my first real kiss, and then he'll confess it was his first real kiss also, looking all shy. We'll be more than friends after that, we'll get married, we'll start our own farm and I'll have children, sweet children that I will teach never to bully each other.

And she would never have to see her stepfather Auguste again.

She was wringing with sweat when she finished. Flies buzzed her, attracted to the salt on her skin, but she didn't bother to swipe at them; she needed to get the last cart in place for the merchant.

Done, and the sun was still up. The rest of the branches wouldn't be ripe for another week.

She threw the harvest knife in the shed and ran towards the dam.

Trees softened the heat of fall as she left her property, and she slowed down and lifted off her work dress. Her underclothes, everyone's underclothes, were thick and served for swimming; only city people had bathing suits. Still, she was a lady, and she didn't like removing her work dress in front of others.

Her mother and father had cleared the land and planted the ambrosia vines. She was the only child her mother had; the sickness came and carried away her father, and when her mother married Auguste, her mother found she could bear no more children. Auguste already had Lucas and Claude from a previous marriage.

Her mother cared well for them, but she weakened and died when Cosette was twelve. After that, Auguste and his two boys acted as though they owned the property, and Cosette remembered no happy times from then on.

Still, legally, she would be the one to inherit the land because she was the oldest child. Eighteen times had the planet Sorine orbited its sun since she was born, making her seventeen standard Earth years. Lucas was sixteen Earth years, and Claude a year younger. It didn't matter that Cosette was a female; the planetary council had insisted that there be no difference between the legal rights of men and women on Sorine.

But she would happily leave the farm to Auguste and begin a new farm with Gregory. She wouldn't mind working hard, as long as there was love in her life, something to give it meaning.

Laughter echoed through the woods. People were still swimming.

I'm not too late! Gregory should still be here!

She paused where the narrow path left the woods, hung her work dress on a dead branch, and studied the swimmers in the water. The irrigation dam was an earthen dam but substantial, holding back enough water to swim in and to jump in from a rope swing. The swimmers were playing catch with an old leather ball, but Gregory wasn't there, just Lucas and Claude and several other young men and women. Four girls were eating and resting on the near side of the dam, their hair wet and stringy.

Maybe Gregory has already gone.

Disappointment soared inside of her, but across the water she saw movement. Gregory and a girl were sitting under a tree on the far side, hidden from the swimmers by a bush.

Cosette almost called out to him, but then she saw that the girl and Gregory were leaning towards each other, talking. The girl put her hands on the sides of his face, pulled him close, and kissed him right on the mouth.

Cosette froze and her heart died.

The pair separated; the girl laughed and poked at Gregory's chest. He pulled the girl close and kissed her again.

Lucas waved at her from the water and yelled, "Cosette! Come on in! Gregory's here!"

Claude stood on the bank, clutched his chest and once more cried "Cosette! Cosette! I will die without you!" With great drama, he fell backwards into the water.

Gregory looked up from the girl and saw Cosette. He smiled and waved.

He thinks there's nothing wrong. He knows I saw him kissing another girl, and he doesn't mind.

He's nice to everybody. Anybody. Even me.

I'll never kiss him.

I'll never have his children.

She turned away from the cool water, from the other farm youth. She grabbed her work dress and ran back towards her farm, brushing tears from her eyes.

She ran into the field she had just harvested and collapsed among the remains, sobbing. She was beyond thinking. She couldn't put into words what her pain was; all she knew was that she hurt. Her body hurt and her heart hurt worse.

When she had exhausted her self-pity, she wiped her eyes with the hem of her work dress. She stood, her mind vacant, slid back on her work dress, and pushed her blonde hair into place with her fingers. The pump provided cold water to wash her face, and she walked back to the house looking as though nothing had happened, as though her world was still intact.

Her stepfather's quadrant was only half harvested. He would make her and Claude and Lucas finish it at the first light of dawn, so that the fruit would be ready for the buyer. Out of pique, she ripped off a ripe fruit and dropped it into the pocket of her work dress.

She entered the side door, went to her room and changed, putting on her other set of clothes. After the buyer took the fruit, she would ask Auguste for money for new clothes, especially for a coat for winter. He would grumble and complain, but after the buyer came he was usually in a more generous mood.

"Is that you, Cosette?" she heard her stepfather call.

She slipped the stolen fruit into her personal bag, and then entered the kitchen calmly and quietly. A methane stove stood in the corner beside a worktable and a sturdy plastic sink. Her stepfather sat at the table under the cheap photon tiles that lit the kitchen. He wore his work clothes, with a sturdy pair of suspenders to keep his pants up on his belly. He had grown heavy, and his hair that used to be black as night had become more salt than pepper.

On the table in front of him lay several legal-looking documents, which he studied through a battered pair of reading glasses.

"Yes?" she said.

"You finish your quadrant?"

She nodded.

He raised his eyebrows without looking at her. "Really? How about Lucas and Claude?"

"They're done. They're swimming."

"You didn't go?"

"I didn't feel like it."

He grunted. He held up a piece of paper, high quality paper with official seals. "The Unionist party at the capitol is having problems with the Federalists again."

She didn't respond. The politics of Sorine didn't interest her, didn't affect her life. Tomorrow she would wash clothes and prepare food, just as always.

Gregory kissed the girl.

221

She winced, and took a deep breath.

"This here," he said, tapping the paper, "I got a couple days ago. The Unionist government is drafting. Looks like there might be more fighting."

She didn't comment. He hadn't asked her opinion.

Wouldn't it be nice if Lucas got drafted? He's older than Claude, and without Lucas, Claude couldn't tease her as cruelly.

Maybe both of them will be drafted.

"They're taking the oldest of each family that has over two children, if they're of age. I sent back that we would do our duty." He laid the paper down on the table, took off his glasses, and looked up at her for the first time. "Did you hear the van pull up a few minutes ago?"

She shook her head. "No, I was, um, washing."

What did that mean, the oldest of each family?

"There are two men sitting in the living room. Off-worlders." He looked back at the paper. "They've come to take you for training. I said you'd be available around sundown."

The second shock of the day was too much. She grabbed a chair and sat down, almost falling to the floor. "Me?"

"Yes, you. You're the oldest."

"But I'm small, even for a girl I'm small...."

A smile played on his lips as he looked at her again. "Remember, the planetary council said you can't legally discriminate between men and women. You're the one to go, you're still the oldest."

She squeezed her hands together, still trying to understand. "For how long? When do I come back? What..."

"You don't come back. At least, this paper says not until the crisis is over, not until the fighting's over, and it's been going on as long as I can remember."

"But," her voice seemed small, "what about my farm?"

"My farm," he said. The smile remained on his face. "It's my farm, and it's going to my sons when I die."

"Legally, it's mine," said Cosette, frightened that he might cane her again. "I'm the oldest."

222

"If you're a soldier, you don't own anything." He shrugged. "Maybe the fight will end. Maybe you will come back." He waved the document at her. "I wouldn't count on it."

"But why offer me up to them? You could have claimed I was unsuitable, that I'm not fit to be a soldier."

"You're not fit to be a farmer, either." The cold smile vanished. "We won't miss you. Those boys of mine can learn to do for themselves."

"But..." She felt tears trying to fight their way out through the wall. "Father Auguste, you didn't need to offer me up. Don't you have any affection for me at all?"

He waved away her question. "If you'd been my own, or if you'd been the youngest, it would be different, but don't take it so personally. It's a matter of property and business. Now go grab your things. The men are waiting."

She put her face in her hands. She had been born here. She had been raised here. She knew all the people in the small village. She had never traveled more than a day's journey in her life, had only seen the spaceport once. How could she leave?

The girl had kissed Gregory and he had kissed her back.

How could she stay?

Her legs trembled but she stood. She went to her room and threw a few items into her bag, including a couple of romance novels she had borrowed and her dirty work dress. Auguste watched, making sure that she took nothing of value, though there was nothing of value for her to take.

She still had the fruit hidden in the bottom of the bag. It was a very, very small victory, but she was taking it.

He led her into the living room.

Two men with scowling faces stood there in black shirts and gray pants, with knives and pistols at their hips. They were twins, each one with a pair of heavy gold earrings, and thick gold bracelets on their wrists. Their hair was tied in back with red twine, and they wore black boots, scuffed and worn.

Cosette's head did not even come up to their shirt pockets.

"This is her?" said one.

223

"You've got to be kidding. The Union can't be that desperate."

"She is the oldest," said Auguste, bowing respectfully as he handed over her papers. "It is a great personal sacrifice to give up my eldest daughter. Promise me you'll keep her safe?"

"She's going to war, old man, you know that."

Auguste pressed his hand against his chest and looked pained. "Her dead mother would weep in her grave if she knew it had come to this. Will you not promise to keep her safe?"

"Yeah, sure. Safe."

The other twin addressed Cosette directly. "What's in your bag?"

She startled. She had been staring at them; they were not of her race, they were from another star, human, but separated by vast amounts of time and space. The corners of their jaws were wider, their foreheads broader, and their eyebrows shaded their black eyes. Their large tough hands reminded her of the roots of the ambrosia vines. "My bag? Um, just some personal items, books, and my other dress, my work dress."

"Leave the work dress. They'll give you a uniform. You'll just have to throw it out when you get there."

They looked down at her like they expected to be obeyed, so she did obey. She pulled the dirty work dress out, embarrassed by its sweaty condition, and tossed it towards the kitchen.

Let one of my stepbrothers clean it. Or burn it.

"Hold out your arm." One of the twins drew a metal bracelet from a pouch and clicked it around her wrist. He held up a silver rod. "Now listen carefully. If you walk away from this key, you'll feel a tingle at ten meters, a shock at twenty, and at thirty you get electrocuted. You touch the key, you get electrocuted. It won't kill you, but you won't try it twice. When we deliver you to the Union, and we get paid our bounty, it gets removed and they're the only ones that can remove it. Until then, you can't run away. Got it?"

Numb, she nodded her head. The nightmare kept getting worse.

He folded her papers and tucked them into a satchel. "That's it. Say your goodbyes."

Cosette lowered her head and walked out the door. Auguste had no goodbyes for her, and she was too much of a lady to say what she wanted to say.

A worn van stood in the dirt road, more of a trail than a road. One of the twins tossed her bag in the back seat and tilted his head to indicate she should get in.

The turbine whined to life, and the van turned and headed down the trail. She glanced back, one last look. The porch was empty and the door to her childhood home was tightly closed.

She turned away. Her face was impassive, her small bag clutched in her lap. No tear ran down her cheek, no sound escaped her throat.

But behind her stone wall, a lost little girl huddled in the corner and sobbed.

Made in the USA
Charleston, SC
29 August 2012